PIRATES OF THE CRETACEOUS

PIRATES OF THE CRETACEOUS

BAD TIMES BOOK SIX

CHUCK DIXON

DISRUPTIVE IMAGINATION

Copyright © 2019 (as revised) Chuck Dixon
Cover Art by Jake @ J Caleb Design
http://jcalebdesign.com / jcalebdesign@gmail.com
Cover copyright © LMBPN Publishing

LMBPN Publishing
PMB 196, 2540 South Maryland Pkwy
Las Vegas, NV 89109

First US edition, July 2020
eBook ISBN: 978-1-64202-852-2
Print ISBN: 978-1-64202-853-9

SOMEWHERE IN CHULA VISTA

The two-lane strip of asphalt was the only sign that man had ever been in the ancient hills.

As she drove, Caroline Tauber's thoughts wandered to how she'd gotten here and what might be coming next. Green heights of acacia-covered hills rose on either side of the road that wound its snaky course eastward. The roadway sloped down to where it curved around the face of a mountain. From verdant shadow, they moved under the Mexican sun to follow the narrow band of asphalt that ran above a two-thousand-foot drop with only rusted sections of guardrail between them and oblivion.

She was piloting the soccer-mom van she and Dwayne had rented in Cabo for a kind of vacation. A kind of couples vacation shared with Rick Renzi as he recovered from injuries suffered in prehistoric Nevada. Rick was dozing in the back seat with his leg, in a hip-to-ankle cast, propped next to the car seat holding Stephen, the infant son of Caroline and Dwayne Roenbach.

The petite warrior woman sat in the passenger seat across from Caroline. Unlike the boys in the back seat, N'itha was awake and alert. She scanned the verges of the road ahead as well watching in the side mirrors for any pursuit. Raised in a world of constant threat and unexpected perils, N'itha had the senses of a natural warrior and hunter. Dwayne had sent her back from an ambush to warn Caroline and make sure they all got away. They were two days distant in the mountains of western Mexico with no sign of anyone on their tail. Next to her fierce devotion to Rick Renzi, was N'itha's loyalty to Caroline and Dwayne and their little boy. She turned her dark, wide-set eyes from the road for a moment to regard Caroline.

"Dwayne is a good man," she said in her strangely accented English. "Tough as balls. He is safe."

"He is a persistent one. Hates to lose. It's a Ranger thing," Caroline said. She loosened her grip on the wheel, fingers pained.

"Ricky is Ranger too. Very good men. Strong."

"Yes, they are. We are lucky girls."

"Lucky?" N'itha's head tilted, bright white teeth visible between parted lips to form the word.

"Fortunate. Favored by fate. Or God, maybe. Basically, we both found good men."

"Yes. Lucky. We are lucky girls."

They returned to silence. N'itha's concentration returned to scanning the way ahead and behind. And Caroline's thoughts were once again consumed with wondering where and when Dwayne Roenbach was.

SOMEWHEN IN CHULA VISTA

E ight miles north and west, and a million lifetimes away, Dwayne Roenbach wondered the same thing.

Something huffed behind him. A shift of sand.

Dwayne rolled to his back and into a crouch, the needle gun leveled in his hands.

On the crest of a slope behind him, a mounted figure sat watching, the rising morning sun at its back. It was a man with copper-colored skin, his chest bare. He wore a jaguar skin girdled at the waist. Atop his head was a wooden headdress fashioned like the snarling head of a snake with long, tattered feathers rising from it. The man's face was painted stark white with black circles drawn about his eyes, and he stared at Dwayne as though from the mouth of the fanged serpent. Across the pommel of his saddle rested a matchlock musket. In his clenched teeth, he held a smoking fuse. His mount stamped its feet and huffed through its nostrils once more.

An Aztec.

Sitting on a camel.

And, as Dwayne weighed his options, a score more of the mounted warriors topped the ridge behind the first.

Few creatures can outrun a camel at full gallop. If he was going to escape them, he'd have to use the terrain.

A snap spray of projectiles from the needle gun, and he was down the slope in a sliding trot. The riders above him made whooping noises. They could not follow him into a narrow break in the rocky ground. A boom sounded behind him. A lead ball struck the wall above him to shower him with stone shards.

The break widened to a wash that ended in some scrub pines below. He considered using the silver band on his wrist for an instantaneous escape. Too many uncertainties. He was better off in the situation he was in, as bad as it was.

He turned to look back at the hillside. Dust rose from a source out of his sight over another rib of the slope. They knew this ground. They knew right where he was heading. Dwayne picked up the pace to sprint hard for the tree line. From the shelter of the trees, he could pick enough of them off to discourage them.

That was the plan anyway.

Like most plans, it all went to shit when more half-naked men covered in paint rushed out of the trees, pounding toward him on bare feet.

Dwayne took to a knee and sighted on the man in the lead. The guy was painted red with a pattern of white dots from head to toe. A smoking musket in his hands. His face hidden by a carved wooden jaguar mask that covered his head. The whites of his eyes gleamed from the open mouth of the mask. Needles to the legs dropped the guy sprawling. His lit matchlock musket went off with an explosion of sparks and smoke. More needles dropped a second guy swinging a long wooden sword, the blade spiked along its edge with gleaming black stones. A third guy stumbled with a pair of needles driven through his neck. The others turned and ran for the shadows under the trees.

A keening cry rose off to Dwayne's flank. He turned to see first one, then another and another of the camel riders round the foot of the slope. He turned to draw a bead on them. From the tree line, musket fire erupted. Thick white smoke drifted through the hanging boughs. Lead balls raised gouts of dust and pebbles all around Dwayne's naked position.

He'd come to the "anything's better than this" place in his situation. He laid the needle gun on the ground to touch the bracelet at his wrist. His fingers touched the iridescent blue display strip.

Nothing happened.

Dwayne ran fingers along the strip again as he had done before. Again, no result except the display went dark.

"Shit. Shit. Shit," he said.

He stood and raised the needle gun at the camel riders loping straight at him. The one in the lead swung a stone cudgel, whirling over his head on a leather thong. The man whooped, eyes wide with fury in a mask of black paint, hair braided with beads flying in a wild mane.

A stream of needles drew a honking sound from the camel as it dropped, sliding. The howling man leaped airborne from the big animal's back. He loosed the cudgel as he dropped. The rounded stone head struck Dwayne with a glancing blow to the head.

Dwayne stumbled, dizzy. The world went white then black then white. He struggled to stay on his feet. He raised the needle gun at the other camels loping close to ring him in. He was surprised to find his hand empty. The needle gun was gone. The men dropped from their mounts, weapons raised, and closed in.

The ground rushed up to meet him, and Dwayne's world shrunk around him in a field of inky darkness.

———————

His tongue was thick and tasted of metal. His nose was stoppered with blood, so he breathed through his mouth. Small hands touched him gently. Opening his eyes brought a wave of nausea.

Above him, the sky was black with a spray of stars. He tried to sit up and found that his legs were bound above the knees and at the ankles. The effort brought on a jolt of blinding pain to his head.

Hands pressed him back to a reclining position. A woman with jet black hair framing a heart-shaped face. Ebon eyes that held no affection regarded him. Her breasts were small and bare, Her only clothing an animal skin held about her waist with a beaded girdle. She was young. Probably not out of her teens. The lobes of her ears were pierced with a pair of lapis stones the size of the tip of his thumb.

His hands were free. He reached for her. She slapped them away as though he were a child. He was weak with pain and exhaustion. He lay back once more as she placed a wet rag to his head.

She spoke to him in a sing-song voice in a language he did not understand. Her voice turned into Caroline's softly singing as she rocked their son to sleep. And then all was gone, and only silence remained.

He woke again with sunlight stabbing into his eyes. He rolled to his side, where he lay on bare earth. A foot kicked him onto his back once again. A rough hand grabbed him by his hair to turn his face. A man crouched by him. The man with the mask of black grease, the man who took him down with the stone club.

The hand pulled him upright. His gorge rose. He fought the urge to retch. His legs were still bound, but he could support himself in a sitting position with his hands behind him. The man with the black mask made a hooting sound at him and turned to speak to others seated around him. They regarded Dwayne with idle curiosity.

He took a chagal made from a gourd offered to him by the woman who tended him the night before. At least, he thought it was the night before. The chagal was filled with water, and he took a few sips. He kept them down and sipped more. Sick as he felt, his stomach growled with hunger.

This was some kind of camp on a shelf of land that dropped away to dense forest below. Two dozen men and a handful of women. The remnants of a cookfire smoldered and threw off the smell of cooked fat. What remained of the haunch of a large animal was on a spit over the fire. Probably all that was left of the camel he'd dropped with the needle gun.

Dwayne took stock. His clothing was still intact. They hadn't stripped him of his sleeveless BDU tunic or pants. His sneakers were still in place. His equipment belt was gone and with it the automatic and revolver. The needle gun was nowhere to be found. His wristwatch too. Whether his captors confiscated them or tossed them away, he had no idea. He didn't see them on any of the men within his sight. The guns and gear were chronal anomalies now, lost in a time and place where they did not belong. A time and place where their discovery could cause a technological disruption. He could hear Morris Tauber's lecture on temporal contamination now. Well, to hell with that. This plane of existence was already fucked beyond all recognition. Some mook finding a rusted Colt or tarnished Tag Heuer couldn't fuck it up any further.

Camels stood munching and spitting in the shade of trees, bridles tied to a hitch line. There were no children. And no tents. This was a raiding party, moving fast and light.

A man lay by the fire where women were unwrapping a poultice and wet leaves from his leg. He writhed in agony. He hissed through clenched teeth when a woman, a woman older than the one who'd tended Dwayne, touched the swollen flesh around a pair of wounds in the meat of his thigh. He was the guy in the jaguar mask that Dwayne brought down with needles.

The others ignored him now as the squeals of the jaguar man grew louder. Dwayne took stock of his situation. It was all bad.

He was in the camp of an enemy he'd brought harm to. If the jaguar guy died, they'd take it out on him. Maybe take it out on him anyway. There was one of those swords with the black stone blades lying ten feet from him. He could make a crawl for it while they were all distracted by the wounded guy. If he could free his legs, he could run for it.

That was no plan at all. He could feel that his legs were numb from being bound. This gang would probably just laugh their asses off at him trying to make a getaway on legs that were asleep.

His nose was still so stuffed that he couldn't breathe. He touched the bridge of his nose, and pain lanced from the spot. The nose was broken. Again. His nostrils were clotted with blood. He fought the urge to clear them. Dwayne had been in enough fights to know to leave his nose alone to heal. If he cleared it, he'd pass out for sure. He wanted to be conscious. If he passed out now, he might never be allowed to wake up again.

The wounded man was screaming now. Four of the men held him down, knees on his arms, seated on his shins. The older woman, some kind of shaman, was pressing hard on one of the swollen wounds. Thick black blood welled up from the jagged hole left by the needle. He threw back his head and shrieked. The man with the black mask stood over him, wearing a deep scowl. Black Mask did not approve of how his man was dealing with the pain. He judged his buddy's manhood cheap. The contempt was plain on his face.

Black Mask waved the others away with angry barks. They released the wounded man and backed off. Black Mask was the boss, top dog, of this crew.

Whimpering now, the wounded man looked up at Black Mask, sucking air in gasps. The wounded man's eyes were damp and pleading. Black Mask stood across him, straddling him, and raised the stone club high in the air. The club came down with a wet crunch. The wounded man went still and silent, his face bashed to meat.

"Fuck this," Dwayne said.

He reached for the bracelet on his wrist to take another try to go anywhere, any*when*, but here and now.

The bracelet was gone. His wrist and hand were dark with the bruises made when the bracelet had been worked off his arm. His thumb joint was painfully swollen. They'd nearly broken his hand removing it. Blood dried in patches where it had broken the skin in passing.

It was shining loose on the wrist of the man now smiling at him. The man holding a club sticky with blood and brains.

3

ANTEDILUVIAN

The *Ocean Raj* sat at anchor in the lazy current of the broad estuary. To the west, a sun the color of an egg yolk sank in a blood-red sky over the shore of what would be, tens of millions of years from now, the coast of China.

"We're almost out of the good beer," Chaz Raleigh said. The lawn chair under him creaked as he shifted to pull a dripping long neck from the tub between them.

"You look out at this, and that's what you have to say," James Smalls said from the lawn chair by his side. They both sat on the aft deck, sweating in the meager breeze coming off the jungled shore two miles distant. The stink coming off the banks of the river mouth was rank with a rot they could taste.

"You look at any scenery long enough, and it becomes same-old, same-old," Chaz said with a shrug.

"I guess," Jimbo said and fished a fresh Tsingtao from the melting ice.

"'Sides, I don't mean the beer in this tub. I mean we're down to four cases. Gonna have to start drinking Bud tomorrow."

"That's all we could ever get back on the reservation," Jimbo said. Smalls was a full blood Pima and only joined the US Army to break out of the cycle of poverty in the res. He'd volunteered for the Rangers because he was told they were the baddest of the bad.

Chaz was a former Army Ranger himself and had served in Jimbo's unit in Iraq and Afghanistan. He'd joined because his daddy was a Ranger and his granddaddy, too. In fact, his Grandpa Albert was among the first black men to pass through Ranger school back when Eisenhower integrated the military.

They both lay taking in the sights, smells, and sounds of the prehistoric wilderness drifting to them across the water from miles of distance either side of their anchorage. The sounds especially. Grunts and shrieks and the occasional deep roar rose from the dense forests that covered the highlands that marched inland. And below it all, the constant hum of insects. Flying bugs, the size of sparrows, struck bug zappers rigged up along the superstructure of the *Raj*. Showers of blue sparks and sizzling bug bits rained down on the decks all night, creating a sticky varnish that covered everything. The mostly-Ethiopian crew had the devil's own time hosing and scraping the stubborn goo away every morning.

The zappers, each around the size of a fifty-gallon drum, were the work of Parviz and Quebat, the pair of Iranian gentlemen who maintained the shielded nuclear mini-reactor deep in the *Raj's* hold. It was the reactor that had brought them here to the far past. It was the tireless atomic furnace that was allowing them to operate in a place seventy million years from anywhere they could refuel the ship.

But even the mighty nuclear generator wasn't invulnerable to the conditions they found here.

"Parviz told me we need to take on fresh water," Jimbo said.

"They should tell Boats. We're surrounded by water."

"Not that easy. The Iranians tell me this water's no good.

"It's like soup. They rigged up filters to catch all the shellfish and parasites. The sieves clogged up inside of five minutes. Boats says he can't even get enough to feed through the evaporators. This river water *teems*, man. Take forever to fill the *Raj's* tanks. And that reactor is a thirsty son-of-a-bitch."

"Shit," Chaz said. He flung his empty far out over the rail where it landed in the dark with a plunk.

Mo Tauber wouldn't like that, but the Doc could go to hell right now.

Everything about this time and place caused problems for the Rangers and the crew of their cargo container ship. Curiously, the least of their worries was the giant carnivorous saurians that seemed to be everywhere on the land and in the water and, occasionally, in the sky. More challenging was the crippling heat and humidity. The Rangers and Boats, their former Navy SEAL skipper, had been deployed in hot places before. Scorching deserts and broiling jungles. But never anything like the cloying, constant sauna heat of this era. Their clothes stuck to their skin within seconds of exposure. The Rangers and crew went about stripped to skivvies most of the time.

The only relief was the frequent rainfall. It seemed to drizzle most of the day when it wasn't an outright downpour. They thought they'd arrived here at the start of a monsoon season. But after weeks of low skies and near-constant precipitation, they realized these were the local conditions on a daily basis. *Local* meaning the entire planet, the Earth having no ice caps in this period.

Another saving grace was the lushness of the air they breathed. Sure, it stank like a dumpster behind a sushi restaurant most days. But it was also far richer in oxygen than what they were used to. Doc Tauber had explained to them all that these conditions, the heat, and atmosphere, made the giant life forms possible. But it wasn't the giants that were troubling them now. It was the little things, trilobites, clams, jellyfish, and smelt the size of a pinky nail. These were clogging the intakes the *Raj* would normally use to provide the water needed to cool the reactor.

And that precious little mini-nuke was their only hope of ever seeing the twenty-first century again.

"We're gonna need to find a source of fresh water," Jimbo said.

"What you mean 'we,' Tonto?" Chaz said.

"I mean, me and some palefaces, including you, are gonna go in-country and find ourselves some *agua*."

"Don't include me with the palefaces, bro."

"Some palefaces and a brother then."

"That's better. So, what do we do then? Just run around out there with a bucket?" Chaz pointed a fresh longneck at the shoreline. A thunderous bellow echoed across the water to further make his point for him.

"We'll scout ahead with a drone."

"Sounds like a plan."

"Then we'll go ashore with lines and pump."

"Sounds like a shitty plan." Chaz swung his arm and a second empty sailed into the night to land in the water and sink to the oozy bottom ten fathoms below.

A beer shortage wasn't the only supply problem they faced.

The *Raj* was at seventy-five percent fuel, and the nearest gas station was a long way off. More than one wit pointed out the irony that they were surrounded by critters whose essence would one day be coming out of a pump as unleaded.

Food was a lesser problem but still posed a challenge. There was plenty of protein everywhere. The water around them was populated with sea life that would make record-breaking trophy fish look like guppies. Along the beach were single animals who could feed the crew for years.

But, as Doc Tauber informed them, nothing like any kind of fruit or vegetable they would recognize had evolved on the planet yet.

A meeting was held around the big table in the chartroom. Boats made the coffee. Two creams and sugar for Doc Tauber. Black for Lee Hammond. A dollop of honey and a splash of Maker's Mark for himself. The Navy man was known by the Rangers only as "Boats." No Christian or surname. SEALs take their secrecy seriously.

Bathsheba Jaffee joined them as well. More from boredom than anything else. Bat was the sole woman aboard and keeping house with Lee in a cabin they alone shared. The other men aboard knew to look but not touch. And that wasn't just because Lee Hammond would twist their heads off and shit down their necks if they so much as thought of Bat as anything other than a team member.

No, the lady was a former Israeli Defense Force sniper and was capable of Krav Maga-ing any man on board into a body cast. She might look like a swimsuit model, but she was all badass and combat-trained. She sat at the end of the table, nursing a Bud and working on a Sudoku book.

"Then what are all those plant-eaters eating?" Lee Hammond said. He pointed at the bulkhead in the general direction of the riverbank where they'd seen long-necked saurians feeding in the muddy shallows. A herd of a hundred or more were munching away on long, ropey vines growing under the water.

"They're eating plants. Ferns and conifers, mostly. They eat leaves, twigs, bark, cones," Morris Tauber said.

"All those trees and there's not a single apple? Not one fucking banana?" Boats said.

Lee's face creased in a broad smile as he thought of the big red-headed sailor picking apples in a forest filled with king-sized man-eaters.

"No fruit. No vegetables. We're early in this period, so there aren't even flowers yet. No flowers, no fruits, and veggies," Mo said.

"No grains? Rice even?" Lee said.

"No wheat. No corn. No barley. There's not even *grass* out there. There won't be for tens of millions of years."

"What the fuck?" Boats said. "I like steak as much as the next guy. But I *need* my greens. This shithole's got nothing I want. No lime for my tequila. No donuts, and no pussy."

Lee asked, "If I had a box of Krispy Kremes and a bikini model here right now, Boats, which one would you want more?"

"I could fuck the donuts and wouldn't have to share them with some hungry bitch," Boats said.

The Rangers snorted, as did Bat. Mo blushed deep red, which set them to howling. Boats poured a generous shot of Maker's in each of their coffees.

"The challenge remains for us, guys," Mo said when the two Rangers had recovered. "We can't leave, and we can't stay here. This ship and the crew are threatened by almost every aspect of this environment."

"I figured this was a one-way trip, Doc. We jumped back here to get away from those Chinese pricks," Boats said.

"The Tube is still intact. We could open a field and escape back to our own time period. The crew could slide life craft down the tube and manifest back into friendly water near the time we came from."

"That would mean leaving the *Raj* behind. Leaving all of yours and Caroline's work behind," Bat said.

"And, believe me, I hate to even *think* of what my sister would say about leaving a cargo ship and nuclear reactor back in the Early Cretaceous."

Caroline Tauber was Mo's sister. Together, they'd created the Tauber Tube, the electromagnetic field that punched holes in time. She was the genius theoretician. He was the genius engineer. Their intellects and talents meshed like fine gears, and the end product was the complex device that rested beneath the deck plates at their feet, deep in the hold of the *Raj*.

"Maybe we don't have to leave it behind," Boats said. "The *Raj* can't make the jump on its own. We need a tungsten, carbon steel super-structure like the one they built for us in Shanghai. And we don't have anywhere near the capability to mine for ore and refine steel. Even if we did, we couldn't get it to the level of tensile strength and composition integrity needed to hold the level of field energy required to shift something the size of this ship."

"But we could if we knew where there was a cage already set up in The Now," Boats said. The Now was their reference to whatever year they'd departed from.

"And there's only one of them. It's back in Shanghai. You want us to pop right back into the arms of the assholes we just got away from?" Lee said.

"What if there was another cage? Somewhere else?" Boats said. Even his thick red Viking beard couldn't hide the grin building on his face as he spoke.

"And you know where to find something like that?" Mo said. He was starting to feel the nip of bourbon in his coffee.

"Nope. But we have someone on board who can build one for us." Teeth showed through the SEAL's ginger bush.

4

MEXICO LINDO

Moths bumped against the flickering fluorescents that hung over the pumps at the Pemex station. For some reason, it reminded Caroline Tauber of snow. That made her think of Paris. She turned her thoughts away. It was night on the desert beyond the lights of the gas station. The cool air felt good as it blew across her sweat-stiff blouse. She loved the clean, crisp smell of it. There was a hint of jacaranda on the breeze.

She leaned against the side of a battered Chevy Tahoe and held the lever pressed down on the gas nozzle. They'd traded their rental car and some cash for the Tahoe at a car yard in a little flyspeck town called La Yuta the day before. Through the dusty rear window, she could see seven-month-old Stephen, her son, asleep in his car seat. Curled by him slept N'itha, the world's most dangerous babysitter, Caroline thought. It brought a smile to her face.

"The only thing I recognized in there was Coca-Cola," Rick Renzi said. He hobbled toward her from the garishly lit market at the back of the gas station lot. He was making the best time he could with a hip-to-ankle cast on his leg, a plastic bag swinging from the same hand that gripped the crutch. A cigarette waggled in his lips as he spoke.

"I know the signs are in Spanish, but you know better, right?" Caroline nodded toward a sticker on the side of the pump. NO FUMAR.

"Shit. Can't smoke near the baby. Can't smoke near the gas pump. I might just have to go to the patch," he said. He crushed the butt out on his cast and limped closer.

"Should you be walking on that leg?"

"Look, Carrie, I know you're a mom and all, but I can look after myself." He leaned past her with a grunt and held the bag open for her. It was packed with sodas and brightly colored cellophane packages.

"Is there anything Stephen can have in there?" she said. "Beats the hell outta me." Ricky shrugged. "I can't tell if this shit's candy, cookies, or chips. I think one of these might be condoms."

"We still have the fruit we bought at that stand earlier. I can mash it up for him. But he'll need a protein."

"They had chicken inside."

"*Is* it chicken, though?"

"Good question. *Looked* like chicken."

They stood in silence for a while. Caroline watched the empty two-lane that ran by the Pemex, not certain what she was watching for. Ricky stared sullenly at the Marlboro butt he'd dropped on the gravel.

"What are we going to do, Ricky?"

"I'm sure there'll be like a Gordita's somewhere between here and Hermosillo."

"I'm not talking about Stephen now."

The fuel pump clunked shut. The Tahoe's tank was full. "Christ, I need a smoke."

She hooked the nozzle back in place and followed him away from the pumps. Ricky lit up a cigarette and blew a lungful of blue smoke at the stars.

"There should be a bank in Hermosillo. I mean, one you can make a cash transfer at," he said.

"Won't he be monitoring things like that?"

He was Sir Neal Harnesh, the multi-billionaire. Harnesh had sent the men who were hunting them across Mexico. The men who, even now, might be holding Dwayne Roenbach, Caroline's husband, prisoner. N'itha had escaped the encounter with Harnesh's mercenaries to come back and warn Caroline to flee. That's what they were doing now, trying to stay ahead of pursuit or, as Caroline feared, running straight into a trap.

"Lee Hammond's good at all that sneaky shit. He's been hiding guns, cash, and who-knows-what from the government for years. I'm sure your accounts are safe," Ricky said.

"*Our* accounts."

"Yeah, I keep forgetting I'm rich now." Ricky's laughter carried smoke across the lot.

"Will there be questions at the bank?"

"It's *Mexico*, Carrie. Hell, we're in Sinaloa. Slip the bank manager a few grand, and the transfer never happened."

"How much will we need?" Caroline said.

"Enough to charter a plane for all of us. And a pilot who doesn't ask questions."

"To where?"

"Anywhere but home." Ricky flicked the spent butt over the gravel, a tiny rocket glowing red into the dark.

The black ribbon of road ran straight east toward hills turned ghostly white in the moonlight. The traffic was light at this hour. Mostly trucks, their lights making star patterns in her eyes.

"Damn," Caroline said to herself. Her hand was fisted atop the wheel.

"You tired, Carrie? You need to pull over a while?" Ricky sat sideways in the backseat, his leg stretched over the hump.

"I'll be fine." She felt like she was choking.

"You been driving sixteen hours," Ricky said.

"Maybe you teach me to drive," N'itha said from the passenger seat.

"Hell, babe, I let you use the microwave, and you almost burned the house down," Ricky said.

"Shit. Shit. Shit," Caroline said.

She jerked the wheel and took them off over the shoulder. The Tahoe came to a shuddering halt in a cloud of dust. Caroline rested her head on an arm across the steering wheel. And the tears came.

"I miss Dwayne," she said between gasping sobs.

With a grunt, Ricky leaned to reach past the headrest and put a hand on her quivering shoulder.

"It's gonna be all right," he said.

N'itha slapped his hand away.

"When woman cry, you let woman cry," she said.

———

It was coming up on sunrise when she recovered enough to drive. The hills ahead glowed like embers, the stars vanishing in a lightening sky. Her eyes were dry now. But she felt the need to talk.

"The worst thing? You know the worst thing? I'm not sure if I'll ever see him again. That's what's so messed up. I keep thinking I'll never see Dwayne again. But he got to see *me* one more time. It was in Paris. He came to me for a while. He was older then, from some future time, I guess. So, I got to see him a century and a half ago, but that's in his future and my past. That's so screwed up. It's all so screwed up."

Stephen was waking now and made a raspberry noise from his car seat.

Caroline burst into laughter. N'itha joined her.

"He's calling 'bullshit' on me. Just like this father," Caroline said.

They rode on toward dawn, the anvil of the asphalt highway heating up under the hammer of the sun.

5

THE MARCH SOUTH

They shared some camel meat with him, along with a thick slice of cactus. He washed it down with a nasty brew with corn pulp in it. From the aftertaste, he recognized it as some kind of beer. Easily the worst he'd ever had.

It wasn't until they cut his leg bonds and helped him to stand that Dwayne realized how much taller he was than his captors. He had at least a foot of height over the tallest of them. A few, mostly the women, were well under five feet.

He was shoved from behind and stumbled forward on numbed legs. The men laughed as he fell to his knees. No one helped him regain his feet this time. Instead, they busied themselves breaking camp. The men prepared the camels to ride. Two of the women wrapped what was left of the camel meat in broad leaves tied with vines. Three other women returned to the camp laden with skins loaded with fresh water they'd found somewhere. It was all done without commands or direction beyond a few grunts and gestures. Within minutes, they were de-camped and moving down into the trees.

The man with the mask of black grease led the way, mounted on a camel. Most of the men rode behind, the big animals picking their way down the stones to where the forest began. A half-dozen of the men and all of the women followed behind on foot. The sensation had returned to Dwayne's legs and feet. But for the incessant throbbing pain in his head from the blow of the club, he was fully operational.

One man, a guy with an ugly set of teeth and a greasy mop of matted hair that nearly covered his eyes, was assigned to keep an eye on Dwayne. He was a few inches shy of five feet and armed only with a wooden club that looked like a cricket bat sanded with a fine edge all around. Dwayne could have dropped him easy and run into the woods on either side of the trail. Only how far could he get without that bracelet? If he could get it to work again, it was his only way out of this time and place. He'd go along with the caravan until he saw an opportunity to get the device off Black Mask's arm.

The trail dropped level in the trees and went on that way until the lengthening shadows told Dwayne that it was afternoon. Even though it was cooler under the trees, he broke into a sweat in the damp, unmoving air. Clouds of biting flies landed on every inch of his exposed flesh. Within an hour, his arms were smeared red with his own blood from crushing them against his skin. The blood only drew the bastards in greater numbers. He was the only one being tormented. The flies avoided his captors.

The girl from the night before touched his arm to stop him. She exchanged a few angry words with his snaggletoothed guard, who stood watching with a sullen glare. The girl removed a clay jar with a wood stopper from a woven basket she wore on a strap about her shoulder. She unplugged the jar and dipped her fingers into a gooey mess inside. She smeared a thick glaze of some kind of evil-smelling goop down Dwayne's bare arms. He stooped so she could slather some across the back of his neck. He smiled at her, showing teeth. She recoiled as though stung. She turned her eyes from him to return the jar to the basket and trotted away after the others making their way deeper into the trees.

Snaggletooth growled and gave Dwayne an ungentle push with the tip of his club to get the bigger man moving. The rest of the caravan was now out of sight in the forest gloom. The big Ranger was alone with his guard. He could beat this guy senseless and vanish. He knew how to run, and he knew how to hide. He was schooled in it.

And what then? Trapped in a world he had no place in and didn't understand a word of the language?

"I'm gonna shove that bat right up your ass," he said.

Snaggletooth couldn't understand the words but knew the tone. The little man had grit. Didn't back up a step from the bigger man looming over him. He barked a string of words and held the club back as though for a swing at Dwayne's ribs.

"But not today," Dwayne said.

He turned to follow the caravan, the smaller man grousing behind him as they walked.

The trees thinned as the ground rose throughout the afternoon. Dwayne's training on countless route marches left him with an intuitive ability to count miles. By his guesstimate, they'd covered twenty-five miles since breaking camp that morning. That was without a break except for sips of water for the entire party. No one showed signs of tiring. As the trees gave way to greasewood and rocks, the camel riders dismounted to lead their mounts by the reins.

The sun was going down over the heights to the west. Dwayne determined that they were moving on a south/south-west course deeper into what would be Mexico. Whatever their ultimate destination, they were keeping him alive for now. He could wait for his moment to get that bracelet back. The sky was turning gray when Black Mask called a halt to the march. They stopped on a broad area of rock sheltered on three sides by steep slopes, a natural defensive position that hid them from sight but offered a clear view of the approaches from below. They camped without building a fire, and their conversations were hushed so as not to echo from the walls of the natural bowl of rock. They were in enemy territory now, behind the lines.

Dwayne accepted strips of cold camel meat and some kind of mush of dried corn and berries. As he ate with the others, he wondered what sort of threat would make these guys take the precautions of a cold camp. These people wore decorations that identified them as Aztecs or Toltecs or Mayans. If there were other parallels to the world, he knew then this area of northern Mexico was probably under the control of nomadic tribes like the Yaqui or Apache. If not them, maybe the turban-topped slavers he'd seen along the coast to the North. In any case, his captors set out sentries, each man and woman taking turns to listen and watch.

He thought they might leave him unbound for the night. They barely paid attention to him, growing used to his company over the course of the long day. Even Snaggletooth turned his back to him to eat. He was already working out his options of slipping the bracelet off Black Mask's arm and winking the hell out of here. Give these little mothers a *real* story to tell when they got home. When the sky was full dark, Black Mask brought along three of his pals. They tied Dwayne's wrists and ankles with leather thongs and left him that way to return to guzzling corn beer.

The girl—he'd taken to calling her "Heather" for some reason —brought him a bowl of the beer and he drank it dry. Her eyes held more curiosity than kindness. Most of her attention was for his clothing and his sneakers. He was wearing the pants from a mesh cloth outfit he'd taken from the mystery gunman that he'd "ridden" to this place and time. It seemed like a lifetime ago, though it was a little over a month that he'd spent in this place so far. He'd walked half the length of the Baja in that time. The only alteration he'd made to his clothes was to cut away the sleeves of the tunic.

That exposed his arms and the tattoos that covered them from above the wrists to his shoulders. A skull with crossed daggers. Paratroop wings. An ace of spades pierced with bullet holes. A snarling fox for his old Ranger company. And the newest, a black silhouette of a wooly mammoth just above his left wrist. The images inked on his skin fascinated Heather. He saw others stealing glances at the tats. Heather touched them tentatively. Her hand jerked away as though they might begin to move.

She touched the laces of his sneakers. They were in sad shape after weeks of hiking, even though most of that was on sand, and he often went barefoot to conserve wear. He'd tossed his only pair of socks long before. The day's march across harder ground of flint and loose rock ripped them up even more. The soles were holding but coming loose from the uppers. He'd need to find a way to bind them before they went much farther. But to Heather, they were a marvel. Her fingers explored the seams and traced the logo embossed in the leather of the heel plate.

Heather and her people went barefoot, the bottoms of their feet as thick with callus as a boot sole. A week or more of this kind of marching and he'd be barefoot too. He wasn't looking forward to it.

"They're called shoes," he said.

She looked up, startled. He made sure not to show teeth when he smiled. She blinked and returned her attention to his sneakers. He hoped her interest wouldn't turn to theft. Her child-sized feet would be lost in his size fourteens. That didn't mean she wouldn't take them if only as a trophy. Even with a fresh layer of hardened skin from walking barefoot on the Baja beaches, his feet would be bloody tatters after only a few hours travel in this country if he was forced to hike shoeless. She moved away, taking the empty bowl with her, to join others huddled against the rock walls.

Dwayne lay back, looking up to the stars. Without the light pollution of the modern world, the stars showed bright and clear against a sky of velvet black. He recognized the constellations he could see. That brought him a degree of cold comfort. At least that was one familiar feature in this strange place.

He wondered about Caroline and his infant son. She would have no idea where he was or what had happened to him. He hoped and prayed that N'itha had reached them in time to get away. He hoped and prayed Caroline listened and ran as fast and as far as she could. The men hunting them were the same ones who had been pursuing them across the planet and the ages since the day Dwayne and his Ranger buddies helped Caroline and her brother steal the Tauber Tube from the man who'd financed it.

Sir Neal Harnesh wanted his time travel device back. He spared nothing, not cash or human lives, in his efforts to get it returned to him. And equal to his desire to have his device back was his need to see anyone connected with the theft dead. Being one of the world's richest men wasn't enough for this guy. He had a strategy cooking to take control of the fate of humanity, and for that to work, he required absolute secrecy. The last thing he needed was a gang of Army vets using his own gadget to turn his master plan to shit. And he literally had all the time in the world to hunt them down.

Dwayne was powerless to help Caroline. But he knew she was as tough and resourceful as they came. She'd stay a step ahead of Harnesh. The only trouble was that she didn't have access to the Tauber Tube. She had only The Now to hide in. She was left with only the option of putting geographical distance between her and the goons who almost captured Dwayne back on the Baja. There was no escape into the past for her, it was not an option. The Tube was currently still aboard the *Ocean Raj,* the cargo ship the guys leased to keep the device as mobile as possible. Dwayne had no clue where or when the *Raj* was. Hell, he didn't know where or when *he* was.

He missed his wife and his son, Stephen, with a pain he could feel in his chest. They'd had so little time together. An anomaly separated them when he was trapped back in Roman Judea. He'd returned to The Now to find he had a son, and the boy was already six months old.

To get his mind back to the current mission, he thought about the technological level of this place. His captors were armed with matchlock firearms. They were probably taken in a raid or picked up after a skirmish. They had prepared cartridges of greased paper in bandoliers hanging from their camel saddles. They carried a firebox of embers to light the cloth fuses that ignite the powder charges. He doubted they had a supply of gunpowder or the knowledge to manufacture more. This was borrowed technology.

The lateen-rigged ship he'd seen off the coast of California had ports for cannon. The men he saw were too far distant to see if they carried muskets. He could only assume they did and were probably the source of his captors' weapons. The men in the boat, the slavers, might even have more advanced weaponry.

And who were the slavers? Arabs? Turks? The corpses he'd found on the beach a few weeks back were Asian Indians and clearly kept as slaves. Whatever the history of this time turned out to be, it was a significant divergence from the one he knew. There was no evidence of Spaniards here, no conquistadors, and no missions. In fact, he'd seen not one permanent structure of any kind since blipping into this parallel.

In fact, he had no way of telling when he was in relation to his own era. For all he knew, this was the same year here as the one he left. No reason to believe that this world was in the centuries past. Perhaps technological development had slowed here. This could be any year from the late fifteenth century onward. In any case, it wasn't really relevant to him *when* this was. It was a gunpowder era world where slavery was still a thriving basis for the economy. And here he was a captive at the bottom of the chain, a slave.

It struck him that was the best he could hope for. To be a slave. With a cold realization, he recalled that the Aztecs were known for ritual human sacrifice. But they wouldn't walk him all this way, treat him with this much care, only to cut his heart out.

Would they?

6

THE MESSENGER

"Why should I help you?" Jason Taan said.

"Because you're stuck here just like us," Lee Hammond said.

The billionaire smirked. "Perhaps I am spiteful enough to allow you to continue to share my misery."

"You could be more comfortable. You could have free range of the ship instead of being locked in here," Lee said. His gaze ranged over the eight-by-ten-foot, windowless cabin they'd kept Taan in since the night they left twenty-first century Shanghai for the prehistoric past.

Taan's only answer was to hiss something in Mandarin at the other Chinese man standing stolidly with his back to the cabin entry. Shan Li Ti was a former hired gun in the employ of Eastern Star Security Solutions, a subsidiary of Taan Enterprises wholly owned by the man now held prisoner in the belowdecks cabin. Shan had switched sides when he objected to the cold-blooded murder of the men who escaped with him from the horrors of the Taiping Rebellion. He went so far as to kill one of his own comrades to save Lee Hammond's life. Five other

Eastern Star men, less cooperative types, were being held in a locked cargo container deeper in the bowels of the *Raj*.

Shan chose not to answer his former boss.

Lee snapped his fingers in Taan's face to bring the man's attention back to him.

"If it were up to me, I'd toss you overboard in a heartbeat. As it is, we're in the middle of an existential survival situation here. If it comes down to sharing the last can of peaches with you or putting a bullet in your head, well, that's no choice at all, is it?"

With a sullen expression, Taan looked away from the big American. He was not used to negotiating from a disadvantageous position. He searched his mind for bargaining room and could find none. They fed him and gave him water and even books to read. But he was confined to swelter day and night in a cell half the size of the largest closet in his smallest condo. Even the walls sweated in the wet, heavy, furnace heat of this hell.

"All we're asking is for a little help, and we all go home. You have my word you'll walk, Taan."

"Your word."

"I never lied to you. Not once."

"You have hijacked me. You have kidnapped me."

"Never promised I wouldn't. And it was you who kidnapped us, remember? And stole our ship. And forced us on that crazy chase over half of China looking for a treasure map. We even found the damned thing for you." The legendary original draft in Chinese of the memoirs of Genghis Khan with detailed directions to the treasure trove of the greatest of the Mongol khans.

"And in addition to my life, will you return to me the scrolls?"

"That's negotiable."

Taan repressed a smile. A bargaining chip. A thin one but it was something. Still, it rested on the goodwill of his captors. They held all the cards in this game.

"What must I do?" Taan asked with a sigh. "That's better," Lee said.

The letter turned out to be a project in itself. Jason Taan composed it with help from Morris Tauber. It took most of the afternoon and into the evening to put together. A version in English and another, supervised by Shan, in Chinese script.

The heart of it was directions from Jason Taan to several of his corporate officers to have the recent steel construction off Changxingxiang Island disassembled and transshipped to a Chinese port facility on the west coast of Panama. There, the massive steel cage was to be reassembled at a location fourteen miles offshore in the Pacific, precisely as it was before.

"Once we know the superstructure is in place, we can make plans to dock the *Raj* inside and return to the present," Mo said.

"How will you locate the cage so far in the future? I am assuming that global positioning does not work here," Taan said.

"You're right. But we'll know the location. Its coordinates are included in the instructions, remember? We'll work it out," Mo said.

"When do I leave to deliver my letter?" Taan asked.

"You're not going anywhere," Lee said.

"What if my associates do not believe the letter is from me?"

"You'd just better hope you were persuasive enough," Lee said.

"Then have whoever goes take this with him." Taan wetted a pinkie finger and pulled from it a ring of dark gold, a blood-red oval-cut ruby grasped in a dragon's claw at its center. A delicate piece of work.

Lee took the ring and dropped it in the plastic pack that included the letter from Taan and instructions from Doc Tauber.

"I'm thinking," Mo said, "Maybe a letter isn't enough."

Jason Taan asked, "Is it necessary to read this again?"

"That's the whole point, Taan. It *sounds* like you're reading it," Lee said.

"I *am* reading it," Taan said. He waved the paper in his hand with growing impatience.

"Okay. Okay. But you don't want them thinking you're being forced against your will," Jimbo said. He stood behind a video camera set up on a tripod.

"This *is* against my will and my better judgment," Taan said. He stood from his chair, slamming the sheet of paper down on the chart table.

"You want to go home? Then read it like you mean it," Lee said. He picked the sheet up and tossed it back at Taan.

"From the top," Lee said, his eye on the camera's monitor screen.

Taan took the paper and heaved a sigh before sitting down once more, squarely in the view of the camera. He spoke in Mandarin Chinese. Shan stood by, following along with his own copy of the paper to make certain his former employer did not vary from the script.

"My name is Jason Taan, and I have urgent instructions that must be followed to the last, most minute detail..."

———

They left the choice of messengers up to Shan. He knew Taan's bodyguards best. The man he picked was named Jinhai, and Jinhai was not pleased with the prospect of being put alone and unarmed in a raft and shoved into the monster-haunted waters surrounding the *Ocean Raj*. He had not seen the creatures that roamed the sea and land here, but he had heard them. The Conex container that had served as a cell for Jinhai and the other four Eastern Star mercenaries was deep in the hold against a bulkhead. Sounds of muted rumblings and the scraping of long, scaled bodies came to them through the hull night and day.

Mo explained to the terrified man, through Shan, that he would not be going into the ocean of the Cretaceous but returning to a more familiar era through a rip in time. That did nothing to calm Jinhai. Like a man condemned to death, he took a seat in a Zodiac. He was given a waterproof packet containing his boss' personal letter, DVD testimonial, pinkie ring, and detailed instructions from Morris Tauber on how to proceed if Taan Enterprises ever wanted to see their beloved founder alive. Also in the packet was a special sender-receiver that would be used to provide further instructions on a special wave frequency that would reach out from the distant past.

Jinhai sat in the raft on the angled steel roller platform that ran into the opening of the Tauber Tube. The steel rings above him dripped with frost as a chill cloud of cold air covered every surface with a white rime. A frisson of static electricity crackled in the air. He turned back to look at the pair of Americans gripping rubber handholds set in the rigid surround of the Zodiac. They were awaiting orders from someone behind an ice-covered observation station set in the rear wall of the Tube chamber.

His grasp of English was limited to obscenities and lines he recalled from American action movies. But he realized that it was a cadence he was hearing from a speaker set in the ceiling. It was a countdown.

The Americans gave a shove to the raft, sending it rolling down the platform and into the dense cloud of icy air. Jinhai felt the cold grip him, bite hard into his joints. His face burned with it. Everything around him wobbled in a cascading vibration that had his teeth gnashing against one another. He tasted copper in his mouth.

And then...

The air was warm, and the wobble was replaced with the gentle rise and fall of mild chop. The white mist about him thinned to lace and then gone, parted by a balmy sea breeze. Jinhai sensed rather than saw this as he was on hands and knees vomiting up his breakfast. When he finally recovered, he remembered to be terrified and looked around in every direction, expecting to see the heads of monsters exploding from the foam.

What he saw was nothing at all.

Even the ship he was on a few moments before was nowhere to be seen.

From the position of the sun, he determined that it was early evening. To the west, he could see a jewel-like line of lights along the horizon. A shoreline. A city. He started the motor at the rear of the raft and steered the Zodiac toward the lights.

Jinhai was happy. He had not been eaten by a monster. He was off that terrible ship. He took comfort in the idea that he would sleep in his own bed that night, in his father's apartment in a tower behind the International mall off West Nanking Road.

And that's all that it was. An idea. Jinhai Ho would not see his own bed for many days and nights. That is until he had talked to what seemed like hundreds of executives from every level of the corporate structure within the Taan organization. From there, he was placed in the rough hands of the company's security men, who treated him like a criminal complicit with the disappearance of Jason Taan.

Jinhai was surprised to learn that his boss had been missing for nearly a year. To Jinhai, only a week or so had passed while he was confined with the others on the horrible ship. The humble private guard found himself in the center of a mystery that had been debated to exhaustion in the media across the world. The vanishing act of one of the world's richest men became a ripe subject for pundits and late-night comedians. Jason Taan's whereabouts and the circumstances of his disappearance were grist for conversations for months following the night the *Ocean Raj* evaporated into the ether. Theories were bandied about, each one wilder than the next. Books were written. Even a movie was in production about the mysterious disappearance of one of China's richest men.

None of them could be as wild as the story that Jinhai insisted on telling, insisted until he was hoarse with the effort, about what actually happened to the missing billionaire. He was being held in a room in the basement of one of the many Taan office towers in Shanghai. Pleasanter accommodations than the rattling sweatbox of the Conex container. It had a nice bed and private bathroom, and he was fed three times a day off a menu from one of the fine restaurants that was in the building above. But a cell is a cell, and captivity wore on him. And what wore on him most of all, like a weight bearing down, so heavy he felt he could not breathe, was the fact that no one would believe his story.

He was taken from his cell one morning, expecting to be brought once again to the featureless interrogation room where he had spent so many of his waking hours these past weeks. Instead, the uniformed guards bundled him into an elevator that climbed and climbed up the throat of the building and finally came to rest at the penthouse.

Jinhai was led, rather than shoved, along a carpeted hallway to an expansive conference room walled on two sides by twelve-foot windowpanes that offered a breathtaking view of the city. The towers below rose from a blanket of early morning mist. A very attractive young Chinese woman in a tailored business dress sat at the end of the conference table at an open laptop. So, fascinated by the finely dressed, manicured, and coiffed young woman was Jinhai that he did not even see the man standing at the window, back to the room. The man turned to gesture Jinhai to a chair.

The tall gentlemen had white hair and beard set off in dramatic fashion by a dark teak complexion. The man wore a silk suit of deep blue with the finest stripe pattern and a brilliant white shirt with the collar open at the neck. His eyes were black and lids heavy. He moved like a man apart from the world and its troubles. There was power in his every gesture, an assurance that put Jinhai at ease for reasons that the bodyguard was unable to understand. Jinhai had a sense that this man was the one who would make sense of all this, bring order from the whirl of chaos of the last few weeks. This man would *believe* him.

Jinhai looked at the young woman, expecting her to speak, as the well-dressed gentleman was obviously not Chinese. An Indian most likely. He was surprised when the white-haired man spoke to him in flawless Mandarin.

"I want you to tell me what you told the others and leave out not one detail, no matter how insignificant you feel it to be," Sir Neal Harnesh said.

7

RENDEZVOUS

Dwayne's captors moved with great caution the following day. It was rough country, broken ground cut by dry washes gouged by violent seasonal rains and arroyos created by tectonic shifts in the past. Cacti and thorn bushes were the only vegetation, and those grew only in the shadows of deeper depressions. Dwayne surmised that whoever occupied this land had to be some tough sons of bitches. No wonder the Aztecs were being vigilant bordering on fearful.

The riders walked their mounts so as not to raise dust. They moved in a long column and kept to depressions whenever possible, never sky-lining themselves. Silhouetted against the yellow sky, a figure could be seen from miles away by anyone watching in this kind of land. They followed a definite path along the floor of shallow canyons, clearly a familiar route. They'd moved through these lands, by this route before, many times. Perhaps this hunting and raiding trail had been in use for generations, centuries, even.

Before setting off in the pre-dawn hours, Dwayne used hand gestures and mime to make the girl he named Heather understand that his sneakers needed attention. She brought him strips of tough rawhide that he used to wrap around his instep to keep the uppers bound to the soles. The step was a bit uncomfortable at first, but nothing compared to the agony he'd experience if he lost the shoes.

They moved steady and silent through the hottest part of the day. Every now and then, they would come to a halt, directed by gestures passed down the line from the point of the column. At one of these stops, Dwayne risked a turkey peek over the top of the wash that concealed their march.

The sun hammered down on the wasteland that surrounded them. All he could see was a mirror sheen off the rocks to the east and west. Whoever stopped the march was running on pure intuition. Dwayne had been downrange often enough to know to trust in that intuition, that phantom sense of dread that told you that unfriendly eyes were on you. A few of the stops had his captors ready with weapons, prepared to defend the natural trench they were following. He saw the man in the serpent helmet poised in a crouch atop the hump of his kneeling camel, match fuse smoking in his lips. His eyes were fixed from the open serpent's mouth to stare at the emptiness beyond the edge of the trough.

The sign moved down the line to move once more, and they marched south, always south.

By Dwayne's stride count, they covered close to forty miles before they came to a fault in a bluff and entered it as late afternoon shadows fell from the rocky walls. It was cooler within the narrow cleft they entered. There were trees growing along the walls, leaves stirred by wind. The rustle of leaves mimicked the sounds of a rushing brook. Dwayne's mouth went drier at the sound. They were running low on water as evidenced by the shrinking portions they allowed him as the day went on. He'd had not a drop for hours. He'd been sucking on a pebble most of the afternoon to keep spit flowing.

The troop relaxed some as they went deeper into the cleft. He sensed that the danger was passed. Whoever owned the region behind them would not pursue. Perhaps they had been seen, and the locals decided that it wasn't worth the effort to take on an armed group of men. Or they were just feeling generous and forgiving. Dwayne was willing to bet it was discretion over mercy.

Night came on fast in the confines of the canyon, but his captors marched on. He had a sense that they were coming to their destination. There was enthusiasm, a pick-up in the pace, as they moved along. The Aztecs were anticipating something welcome down the trail. They were eager enough to get to it to keep moving through the dark.

The canyon walls grew farther and farther apart as the trail rose to higher ground. They were marching across a tabletop now, the way ahead silver in the moonlight. The rocky ground gave way to sandy soil dotted with patches of razor grass. Black Mask barked an order. As one, the men brought the camels to their knees and climbed atop them. With whoops and yelps, they rode off south at a gallop.

The men and women left behind watched with smiles as they broke into a trot to follow. Dwayne followed with Snaggletooth's encouragement. He really didn't need it. His own curiosity at what lay at the end of the trail overcame him.

He loped through the cloud of dust after the others. In the distance, he could see something obscuring the stars.

Streaks of smoke rose into the sky from campfires.

A *lot* of campfires.

Hundreds came from the glow of the fires to greet the newcomers. They carried lit brands over their heads. Mostly men in the same dress as his captors. A few women and fewer children. Dwayne could see the shapes of buildings here, one-storied adobe structures. Even in the shifting light of the torches, he could see that many of them were in disrepair. Walls and roofs were collapsed.

There was a remuda for camels surrounded by a stake wall that served as a fence. Dwayne was surprised to see a few ponies mixed in with the dromedaries. Chickens leaped about to escape being trampled underfoot.

A wonderful, greasy aroma hung everywhere. Dwayne's stomach rumbled at the sight and smell of a row of goat carcasses slung on spits over a glowing cookfire.

It was a big reunion. The arrivals were greeted with calls and smiles. Women came out to speak to Heather and the others. They gabbed away easily, the silence forced on them by the dangers of the land they just passed through was over. They were safe among friends in number.

Black Mask was already off his camel and speaking to an older man with long white hair capped with a headdress fashioned to resemble an eagle's head. The older man wore a striped woolen cape fringed with feathers. He was fit, with ropes of muscle down his arms and across his chest but carried a sagging belly on spindly legs. A chief or shaman or maybe Black Mask's elder judging by the nature of the conversation. Snaggletooth shoved Dwayne into the light of the largest fire at the center of the camp. There were a lot of appreciative noises made by the crowd that gathered. A child, boy, or girl with a mop of black hair, rushed up and touched his leg before running back to the shelter of a woman's arms. Others came forward to run hands over his arms, back, and, those who could reach it, his hair and beard.

The wrinkled old guy in the eagle headdress—Dwayne dubbed him Big Bird—made clucking sounds as he came close. He poked Dwayne's ribs with the end of a curved stick. When Dwayne responded, the old man laughed, toothless mouth wide.

"So, everyone's glad to see me," Dwayne said and showed his

teeth. The gathering mob looked aghast at this. They shoved one another aside to get a better look at the interior of his mouth. One of them hooked a filthy thumb in his mouth to pull his lip up. Dwayne shook free.

In all his travels to different eras, it was the dental work that most astounded the natives of any given time. The fact that he still had all his teeth was a wonder to all. They would be even more astounded if they knew that most of his lowers in the front were implants. He'd lost his natural teeth there when he struck his face on a log obstacle at Fort Benning back in boot.

Bowls of corn beer were handed out all around and drunk down by Black Mask and his party. Heather brought Dwayne a bowl of his own, and he drained it dry in a second.

"Any chance of some chow?" he asked. She blinked at him, brows knitted. He mimed eating, crooked fingers motioning to his open mouth.

Snaggletooth stepped up to push Heather away. The girl fell hard on her ass. Either from hunger or seeing someone who'd been kind to him get shit on, Dwayne reached the end of his patience.

He struck Snaggletooth with a fist to the side of the head that sent the smaller man crashing to the ground and rolling across the dirt to lie motionless at the edge of a fire.

All sound stopped dead. Hundreds of pairs of eyes turned to Dwayne as he bent to take Heather's wrist and pull her back to her feet. Her eyes were wide, whites all around the black pupils, as she stared at him. He glanced about him to see the whole damn tribe with faces frozen in masks of astonishment. Dwayne's fists tightened at his sides. He set his feet and dropped into a crouch. He'd take as many of these fuckers with him as he could before they brought him down. Big Bird broke the moment with a high-pitched whoop that was joined by all the others. Grins and laughter all around. He was the hit of the party. The same little boy who'd touched Dwayne's leg prodded the unconscious Snaggletooth with a toe and giggled at the groan the man gave.

The white-haired old man took him by the arm in a vise grip and led him to a spot where some flat stones were piled near the fire. The crowd followed, making agreeable noises. He was urged to take a seat, and Big Bird took a perch by him and called to the gathering ring of faces. A trio of women approached with wooden bowls filled with food and more beer. These were offered to Dwayne, and he made a dent in every course. Dried corn. Peppers. Spiced yams. Strips of goat meat. And lots and lots of beer.

Other men, including Black Mask, joined them to take seats on the stones. They wore ceremonial masks of bears, hawks, and fish that they removed to share in the banquet. Drums with leather skins were produced from somewhere, and almost all the younger women joined in a ring dance, arms linked and breasts bobbing. They looked bright crimson in the firelight that rose higher as more bundled brambles were piled atop the blaze.

Dwayne relaxed. More bowls of the nasty brew than he could count took the knots out of his muscles. And some harder stuff, a kind of cactus liquor did the rest. But there was also the relief of knowing that they didn't walk him all this way and go to all this trouble to kill him. Or eat him. He was the goddamned honored guest of the party.

His worries about human sacrifice faded to the back of his mind only to come back as the sky to the east turned pink with the dawn. Just before the last cup of mescal hooch took its toll, he recalled something he read long ago or maybe saw on the History Channel.

The Aztecs always treated their captives like gods.

Right up until the dagger fell.

8

THE SPRING HEAD

The drone found a source of fresh water farther up the riverway.

A natural spring ran out of the rockface of a long escarpment that coursed along the north bank of the river for about fifty miles. The water fell a few hundred feet in a white torrent as regular as a tap. The images the drone transmitted showed a natural tank along the foot of the escarpment. From the overflow, a swift-rushing stream coursed over rocks through the dense conifer forest toward the river.

Down in the chartroom of the *Ocean Raj,* the former Rangers, the former SEAL, and the former IDF sniper watched a monitor, showing them the views from the drone being piloted by Jimmy Smalls up on the weather deck. The screen was displaying live shots of a world no human eyes had ever seen. The entirely alien world of Earth's past.

"The water's moving too fast to pick up many bugs or algae. This is as clean as we're gonna find," Boats said. He leaned over Lee's shoulder to point a finger at the monitor.

"Is that vapor coming off the water? It might mean the water's geothermic hot," Chaz added, leaning over Lee's other shoulder.

"Even better, right? Boiled water right out of the tap," Boats said.

"If you assholes would give me room, I could confirm that," Lee said. He tapped the keyboard, and the image on the screen became a shifting pattern of psychedelic colors. The rock and surrounding trees blanched to a hazy blue color while the water cascading down the rock now looked like a stream of lava. The collection tank glowed crimson.

"Thermals." Lee turned to the others and grinned.

"Does that work on life-forms?" Chaz said.

"Let's see," Lee said. He touched a tab and spoke. "Jimbo, can you do a flyover of the area? We want to look around a little."

Jimmy Smalls' voice came over the laptop's speaker. "Roger that."

Jimbo was up on the weather deck, piloting the drone through the afternoon sky. He could see what they saw through a smaller monitor mounted on the drone controller. The monitor displayed the rock-steady progress of the drone as it soared above the tops of the massive redwoods that grew up the gentle slope that led to the foot of the escarpment. The thermals picked up the movement of small critters moving on the ground. They showed up in brilliant orange and red and sparks of yellow. Smaller saurians traveled on the ground singly and in groups. Unfamiliar birds flittered through the branches, looking like sparks of light.

"Look at these motherfuckers," Boats said. He stabbed a finger as if Lee and Chaz could possibly miss the huge shapes glowing warmly on the monitor. A herd of fat ceratopsians fed off low branches and whatever lay on the ground. A crown of bone atop their skulls and long, curved horns jutted from their brows.

"They almost look pretty in those colors. Like party pinatas," Bat said.

"Those are vegetarians," Chaz said.

"So are bulls. Ever been to Pamplona?" Lee said.

"Saw it on TV." Chaz shrugged.

Jimbo's voice came over the speaker. "You see enough? My battery's heading for the red."

Lee told him to bring the drone on back. On the monitor, the view climbed high into the sky. They could see the *Ocean Raj* in the distance, anchored in the ruddy water of the river. Lee closed the laptop.

"That tank is close to a half a mile inland. That's a long hike through an ass-load of hungry fuckers," he said.

"And dragging a pump and all that hose with us," Boats said.

"We're gonna have to use the drone to pick our way around them," Chaz said.

"Gotta say, Charles, I don't know whether to admire your optimism or wonder if your mama dropped you on your head a lot," Lee said.

Jimbo heard the drone before he saw it. He shaded his eyes with a hand and searched the yellow sky and found the tiny speck dropping toward him. He directed it onto the deck a few feet from where a compact man with braided blonde hair leaned on the railing, looking out over the water. The Macedonian was normally fascinated by the mini-UMV and never missed a flight. Something had pulled Byrus' attention away from the drone's return.

Known as "Bruce" to the Rangers, the fugitive out of time was once a pit-fighter and then a slave in a quarry back in Roman Judea. He'd returned with the team to the present at the insistence of Jimbo. The pair had spent months stranded in the ancient past. Together they had defied and escaped from a cohort of Roman legionnaires. The Pima had been badly wounded in the fight. The little Macedonian nursed Jimbo back to health while hiding him from the Empire. Byrus' reward was to be brought to the modern world where, though he was a free man for the first time in his life, he took on the role of constant companion and personal bodyguard to Jimbo.

Not for the first time, Byrus was wondering if he might not have been better off left in the past.

Just off the *Raj's* port bow, a drama never before seen by human eyes was playing out.

A herd of sauropods had moved out of the marshes along the southern bank of the river to feed on a thick growth of reeds. Thick-trunked, long-necked animals with lozenge-shaped heads and dumb eyes. They ripped bundles of reeds from the muddy water to champ them in jaws lined with rows of flat, crushing teeth. A few had wandered into deeper water where the ocher water churned to cream as it coursed around their enormous bodies.

One of them, a juvenile the size of a mini-bus, lumbered too far into the swell and was caught in the slow current. Its feet lifted off the bed of the river, and it was being carried from the herd, bleating and honking in distress. The mass of giants seemed undisturbed by its piteous cries and kept right on ripping and munching.

The calf 's progress was halted with a sudden jerk, and it bobbed violently in the swirling water. Its shrieks echoed over the water as its body turned on its side. Its cries turned to gurgles as its head was dragged under the surface. As it rolled over, a second form surfaced, a forty-foot creature with a long, snake-like body and a head shaped like a spade. Fins splashed in the stream, sending sprays of foam high into the air. The jaws of the tylosaur were locked on a leg of the sauropod and not letting go. Together, the animals rolled over in the water until the sauro-pod's head emerged once more with a strangled bleat.

Now a second tylosaur, a bit smaller than the first but still a titan, burst from the water to clamp its fangs deep into the flesh of the calf 's neck. The weight of the two predators was now enough to drag the sauropod down until only a length of its long tail was visible above the roiling water. That too sank away in a flurry of crimson foam.

Byrus, witnessing this, was more convinced than ever that they had traveled to Tartarii. Hell. The land of the cursed. What else could these creatures be but demons and devils? Jimbo tried to assure him that this was only another time, that they were still in the same world as before but in a distant era long before the advent of man. Byrus could not believe even his beloved friend. He saw nothing that looked like any world he knew on the earth or in the sky. This alien landscape could only belong in the realm of the damned.

"You watching the perpetual feast, Bruce?" Jimbo said. He pulled the battery pack from the body of the drone before replacing the drone in its case.

"We must leave this place, Zim." The Macedonian could not get his tongue around a soft "J" sound. "Zim" was as close as he could get.

"That's what we're trying to do, buddy. Tomorrow we go ashore to refill the fresh
water tanks."

"Go? On land? Go there?" Byrus pointed toward the far bank.

"Has to be done. The *Raj* needs water to run."

"You will go, Zim?"

"Yeah. I'm going."

Byrus could still hear the calf 's keening shriek. He could still see the doomed creature being hauled beneath the muddy water where it was even now being torn apart by dragons. And now his friend would travel to that land where he and the others would be prey for everything that walked, crawled, and swam in this blighted world.

"Then I will go, too," Byrus said.

Back in their shared cabin, Bathsheba Jaffee was only starting to lose her temper. They both lay in bed atop the covers, stripped to their underwear. A fan played across them, drying the sweat standing on their skin in beads. The air conditioning was off. They were trying to acclimate themselves to the conditions here and now.

"Hell, yes. I'm going with you," she said.

"It's going to be rough," Lee Hammond said. "I'm going to pretend you did not just say that."

"I'll be worried about you the whole time, babe."

"And don't hand me that horseshit. You don't worry about Jimmy or Chaz or the others."

"It's not the same."

"It *has* to be same, Hammond. That's the promise you made when you brought me along on this thing. You'd treat me the same as the others in every way."

"Not every way." His fingers brushed along her naked thigh.

"We have a lot of walking to do tomorrow," she said. She turned away from him to lie on her side. He admired the curve of her hip, the twin dimples either side of her spine just above the band of her panties.

He hooked a finger in the elastic and began to draw the panties farther down over her ass.

"I mean it," Bat said. She reached back to catch his wrist in a painful pinch that made him release his grip. Lee pulled his hand back, the muscles at the base of his thumb numb.

"I guess you're going."

"I guess I am."

9

A FAMILIAR WORD

He wasn't sure where the pain of his concussion ended, and the agony of his hangover began.

Dwayne woke up where he'd fallen in the ash-covered dirt near the fire. The glare cast from an overcast sky was like a pair of drills through his eyelids. He rolled to his side, head swimming, and puked up a stinking mess of corn beer and *pulque.* The camp was quiet except for the occasional bleat of a goat from somewhere beyond a collection of tents and wigwams made of tanned skins. Women moved among the slumbering men lying where they'd dropped the night before. Dwayne was still tactical. He looked for Black Mask. If he was going to find that bracelet, he'd never get a better chance. The guy was not in sight. He'd have to look for him. Snaggletooth wasn't where Dwayne cold-cocked him the night before. He'd have to keep an eye on that guy.

It took a week or so, but he managed to get to his knees and then his feet. He stumbled from the smoldering fire, stepping over inert bodies, in search of the latrine.

That's when he remembered where he was, and when he was. He found a patch of tall weeds and emptied his bladder with a contented sigh. He was zipping up when the girl he'd named Heather materialized at his elbow. She held up a wooden bowl to him, pointing her chin at it.

"Sorry, honey. The last thing I need is a drink," he said. He made to step past her. She moved into his path and held the bowl up to him. He took the bowl and gave it a sniff. It wasn't the hair of the dog. It had an herbal scent and a hint of something else. He lifted it to his mouth, and Heather went up on her toes to tilt it upward until his mouth was full. She cooed encouraging words. No choice but to spit or swallow. He swallowed.

The brew was a viscous goo. It burned all the way down. His best guess was the base was raw eggs. Pure certainty that it was laced with habanero. There was a tang of sweet honey, too. He drained the bowl and stood a moment for it to settle. The mix opened his sinuses, and the painful pressure he woke up with melted away inside of five seconds. He actually felt better.

"Damn. That shit is the shit," he said. Dwayne handed the empty bowl back to Heather, and she beamed at him. He returned the smile, taking care not to show his teeth.

She took his hand and yanked his arm to follow her. He pulled back, but she wasn't having it. She scolded him and increased pressure on his hand.

"I guess I don't have any other plans this morning." He followed her through the camp. They walked a path between the rows of tents and the fence around the remuda. Behind the remuda, he came across a row of stakes driven into the earth. Seated on the ground around each stake were men with bound wrists and ankles and leather collars about their necks that were secured to the stakes with knotted thongs. About ten stakes with three or four men seated around each. There were brown men and some different from his captors. Or were they his hosts now? Most of the men had thick manes of black hair. A few were shaved bald. Dwayne was surprised to see two men were bearded. All were naked. Not Aztecs.

They were prisoners or slaves. They regarded Dwayne with sullen eyes.

The beefiest Aztec Dwayne had seen so far was seated on a drum with a long-handled club across his knees. Thick arms and shoulders and the start of a belly. He was sucking on a shaft of cane sugar. Dwayne guessed his height at about 5'7". The tallest man he'd seen since arriving here.

The collection of captives made this a slaver party. They spread out and raided across what would be the border area in his world. Then the parties met at the rendezvous to compare captives and, Dwayne presumed, move on to slave markets at whatever passed for civilization to these people.

The clouds cleared away, and sunlight streamed down. Heather led him on down the path, the ground falling away as they walked. They left the camp behind. Tall prairie grass grew head high around them. He sensed this place was a way station, a rendezvous. It showed all the signs of a temporary bivouac. There were no permanent structures and no signs of cultivation anywhere. They grew and brewed corn somewhere but not here.

Coming the opposite way up the path were women toting skins of water. They came to the bank of a pond, a tank where rainwater gathered. Reeds grew across most of its surface. Dragonflies thrummed over the tops of cattails. Ducks fluttered down from the sky to land out of sight somewhere behind the screen of tall growth. There were tracks in the mud, both human and animal. The freshwater source was the reason the camp was situated where it was. Women stooped in the shallows, filling water skins that they handed off to others on the shore.

Dwayne looked at the water with longing. It had been days of hard marching since he'd bathed. His skin was greasy with sweat and bug repellent, and his clothes stank of smoke. He looked at Heather, tilting his head toward the water. She wrinkled her nose and nodded with a solemn expression. Dwayne sat on the bank and removed his sneakers. The women stopped their work to stare at him in open curiosity.

"Get a good look, ladies," he said. He stripped off the rest of his clothes, the tunic, and pants. All eyes locked on him. The raised scars of skin grafts that covered the left side of his torso, the result of burns he got from an IED in Iraq. His t-shirt was a ruin, and he peeled it off and tossed it aside. The boxers stayed on until he'd waded into the water to above his waist. The water was surprisingly cool, given the heat of the day. He slid the boxers off and tossed them to the pile of clothes on the bank. The women looked away then, leaving him to his bath.

The floor of the pond was sandy. He used handfuls of it to scrub the grease from his skin. He ducked his head beneath the water and used his fingers to loosen days of grit and ash from his hair and beard. He surfaced to see Heather on the shore with his clothes spread on a rock. She was running a flat stone over them and dipping them into the water, wringing them out, and starting the process over again.

"Heather. Hey girl," he called.

She looked up from her work. He gestured and pointed until she got the idea and tossed him his boxers. He stepped from the water and laid down on the sandy bank to doze in the sun, falling into a deep sleep to the sound of the wind through the reeds and the rhythmic slap of his clothes on the rocks.

Camp was broken later that morning. The tents were folded and placed on various travois to be pulled behind the camels. The horses of the tribe were strictly pack animals and loaded up with water skins and woven baskets of other gear. Tortillas were warmed on rocks heated by the sun then stuffed with meat and wild rice spiced with jalapeños. The women did most of the work while the men nursed hangovers.

Dwayne's appetite had returned with a vengeance, and he helped himself to burritos washed down with watered-down corn beer. He was starting to like the stuff. He watched Black Mask moving among the bleary-eyed troops like a staff sergeant. He had them up and moving with kicks and growls, hustling them to get the camels bridled and saddled. Snaggletooth gave Dwayne a few evil looks as he tightened the cinch on his mount. The guy had an angry goose egg, his right eye swollen nearly closed.

They were up and on the march in no time at all. Black Mask led the scouts to ride ahead while the rest followed on foot. Big Bird, the elder, rode lounging in a travois. He was still drunk from the night before. The slaves were brought along. Their legs were free but their wrists were still bound. A thick, braided leash connected them all by their collars. None of them could make a move without dragging the rest along. The big brave with the long-handled club prodded them forward with pokes in the spine and taps to their bare asses.

Dwayne joined in the march, following the rest into the cloud of dust thrown up by the scout camels racing off over the open ground. Heather led a pair of pack horses. She glanced shyly at him a few times until chided by an older woman.

The course was due south. The face of a butte could be seen, purple in the distance. The path would take them up to the higher altitudes of the plateau that covered most of central Mexico. The royal city of the Aztec empire was located where Mexico City was in the world that he was familiar with. He recalled that much from what he learned in school. No way he could remember what that city was called. Some long-ass name with a lot of consonants. Whatever fate they were saving him for, he'd find out what it was there. And *there* was a good two/three weeks away by his estimation.

He hung back a bit until the slave train drew even with him. The big brave was on the other side of the long string of men walking single file. Dwayne named him Patrick after Sponge-Bob's big dopey pal. As he walked, he studied the men. They kept their eyes on the ground ahead, making sure of their steps. Walking with hands bound at the back isn't easy. And if a man stumbled, others fell with him. And Patrick didn't look like a guy who had a lot of patience for klutzes.

The two bearded men fascinated Dwayne the most. Their hair was dark. Their eyes, too. They had more body hair than the Indians they marched with. And their noses were long and bladed. One of them had strips of old scar tissue across his back. The sign of a lashing sometime in his past. The other had a tear to the lobe of his right ear that was still crusted with dried blood. He'd had an earring ripped from its place and not long ago. His lip was swollen where it had been split by a blow.

Dwayne walked closer to the slaves. He matched pace with the slave with the torn ear.

"Hey. Hey, buddy," Dwayne said.

The slave's brow twitched, but he did not look up.

"*Habla Espanol? Parlez vous? Verstehen?*" Dwayne tried.

No response.

"*Sabaah an-nuur?*" Dwayne said.

The slave's head turned then, fierce eyes locking on Dwayne.

"*Varangi alqurf!*" he barked and spat at Dwayne's feet. The guy had called Dwayne some kind of shit in Arabic.

It was a start.

10

BEER RUN

The sun had been down for hours. With the burning rays gone, the humidity rose in a visible mist in the air. The *Raj's* running lights were at a minimum. Even so, a cloud of insects swarmed along its decks, the millions of fluttering forms creating a constant moiré pattern against the glare.

The chartroom was crowded with guys who had lots of opinions but few answers. They stood around the broad table looking at a map that Jimbo had sketched of the riverbank and location of the geothermal spring. He based the map on watching and re-watching the video of the drone flyover.

"I can't just pull a mile of hose outta my ass," Boats said. He topped off his Maker's and Coke and set the glass on the chart table.

"And we cannot anchor any closer to shore. The soundings show a grade too shallow," Geteye said. The first mate on the *Raj.* First among the half dozen Ethiopians who served as the crew of the ship.

"How much hose *can* you scrounge up?" Lee said.

"I can strip lines all over the *Raj* and add them to coils we have. Still not near enough." Boats wagged his head over the map as he traced a line with his finger from the *Raj's* position to the location of the tank at the base of the escarpment.

"Do you have enough to run to here?" Jimbo pointed at a feature on the map.

"What the hell is that? It's a squiggle. What the fuck?" Boats leaned forward to squint hard.

"It's the edge of the marsh. We can get the Zodiacs in that far."

"Still just over one hundred yards to the tank, right?" Boats said.

"Can you get that much hose together?" Jimbo said.

"Sure. It won't all be 300 psi. I have a container full of cheap polyurethane line. Bangladeshi shit. It'll hold to 200 psi, but we'll have to make some custom fittings to tie the sections together." Boats took a long pull from his tumbler.

"What're you thinking, Jimmy?" Lee said.

"We have tanks on board. We float one in, fill it here at the edge of the marsh then ferry it to the *Raj*. What's the weight capacity of our largest Zodiac?" Jimbo said.

"The Mark Six can carry three kay pounds. That's...let's see..." Boats rubbed his beard, brows twitching.

"Three hundred and sixty gallons." All turned to Morris Tauber, who had spoken up for the first time. Morris had been hitting the Maker's too, lacing a mug of coffee with it. He regarded the Rangers with an owlish expression.

"How'd you happen to know that, Doc?" Chaz said.

"Worked it out in my head."

"How many trips would we need to top off the tanks?" Jimbo said.

"Like twenty trips to capacity." Boats shrugged.

"Twenty trips. Fuck me." Lee said.

"Fuck *us*," Chaz said.

"Anyone have a better idea?" Jimbo said.

"Can we go back in time to before you assholes showed up to recruit me?" Boats said.

They assembled on the aft deck before dawn and lowered the Zodiacs in the water. The large Mark Six was strapped down with a four-thousand-gallon tank the crew worked all night to unship and haul up from below. It was a tubular vessel of heavy plastic.

The smaller Mark Three would tow the larger raft which would also be loaded to capacity with the three Rangers, Boats, Bathsheba, and Byrus. Shan insisted on coming along as well. In addition, they'd be hauling large coils of heavy hose, an immersion pump, generator, and gas can. Adding to the weight was weaponry and ammunition. The largest of these was a Savage rifle in .338 Lapua Magnum that Jimbo insisted would make even the largest monster with the smallest pea brain think twice. The smallest was Lee's Alaskan Guide Gun, a massive handful of a revolver in heavy .500 mag.

Morris stood, watching Geteye and another crewman help the men get loaded into the raft. Moths the size of his open hand fluttered around the lantern over his head, throwing crazed shadows across the superstructure. He was joined at the rail by Jason Taan, who, true to Lee's word, had been given parole to wander the ship without a guard.

"A dangerous undertaking," Taan said. "Perhaps even foolish."

"Maybe you'd like to go along. Stretch your legs a little," Morris said. He felt no affection for Taan after the way he'd been abducted and abused while the billionaire's captive.

"I'm content to be an observer."

"Yeah. Why get your shoes muddy?" Mo nodded down at Taan's custom Italian loafers now showing wear after his time aboard the *Raj.*

"Believe me, I wish them success. I'm anxious to get back to my affairs. As fascinating as this trip has been."

Morris said nothing in reply.

"I'm curious, though. About your device, doctor."

"What about it?"

"Just how fine can you tune it? I mean, how accurately can you fix the time in which we will return?"

"I can usually manifest an opening within three weeks of the target. Sometimes closer. There are variables."

Taan nodded. "More than I can imagine, I'm sure."

"Why the sudden interest?"

"I only wanted a rough estimate of how much business I was missing out on."

"I think the SSE can get along without you for a while." The Shanghai Stock Exchange.

"You're probably right." Taan allowed himself a smile before wandering away.

Morris returned his attention to the men below. The engines started with a whine that fell away to a rumble. With a jerk, the lead raft towed the tank raft toward the shoreline invisible in the swallowing dark.

The drone sailed above the trees with an angry hornet buzz, following the course of the marshes toward the riverbank.

Jimbo leaned over a pad at the prow of the Zodiac, watching a bird's-eye view of the way ahead. The screen crawled with gnats that landed on the glowing surface. Next to him crouched Chaz, staring ahead through night vision goggles, M4 rifle ready and charged.

Despite the heat, they wore long sleeve shirts and long pants to discourage biting insects. All but Byrus, who went shirtless and barefoot as always. His one concession to modesty was a ragged pair of cargo shorts and, of course, a belt from which he could hang his sheathed gladius. Every inch of exposed flesh was slathered with greasy bug repellent. Clouds of gnats and nits and thumb-sized flies still followed them in an eddying fog. They hoped conditions would be better on land but suspected the misery quotient would remain much the same.

"A little to port, Boats. There's a course through the reeds we can follow. Open water to target."

"Fuck the reeds. What about any of those toothy motherfuckers?" Boats growled where he stood at the tiller. He slapped at a bottle fly that clung to his sleeve and wiped a handful of green guts on his pant leg.

"Switching to thermal," Jimbo said.

The screen on the pad showed a few signatures off to their west. Large beasts glowed pumpkin colored against an indigo background. They were unmoving, down for the night. They looked like herbivores from their shape, the same variety they'd seen grazing in the shallows throughout most of the previous day. Smaller flashes of warm colors flitted here and there. Birds hunting flying bugs in the night. The marsh ahead showed blue-black on the screen. No heat signatures were visible across the entire surface of open water between the reed islands.

"We're good. No contact," Jimbo said.

He glanced back to see the others seated behind him, guns at the ready. All wore NODs arrays, giving them bug eyes except Byrus whose eyes were bugging all on their own, the whites showing as he swiveled his head from side to side in search of krakens.

Jimbo guided Boats between obstacles of sandbars and vegetation to bring them to the edge of the marsh. They clambered out onto drier land and began offloading gear. Jimbo brought the drone down to save batteries but did not stow it away in its case. They'd be needing their eye in the sky again before this long day was over.

Byrus humped a heavy ammo box of magazines for the Savage. He followed Jimbo up to a raised spot on the bank where the Pima set up his overwatch post in a copse of barrel-shaped palms. Bat joined him as spotter and back-up gun. They left the big Savage in place and returned to the edge of the water to help get the remaining gear off the raft.

Boats dragged the tank raft closer to shore and secured it in place with lines and pegs. He then hooked the end of a heavy firehose line to the intake at the top.

"Now we hump this shit inland," Boats said.

"Eyes open. Ears open. Check your sight lines." Lee led the way, his M4 slung and a spool of heavy hose in each hand. Chaz and Shan followed with the same loads. Boats had the pump in a sack on his back and pulled a two-stroke generator and two-gallon gas can on a dolly behind him. The dolly's wheels were switched out for bicycle tires to make the pull easier over the rough ground. The big SEAL was packing seventy pounds of gear and hauling a hundred more. He resisted offers to help share the load, gesturing with his head for the rest to get their asses up the trail pronto.

They moved off, single file, up the muddy slope. Boats cursed the whole way as the dolly's wheels clotted with mud and slid rather than turned. Above them, redwoods towered against the sky, blocking out the stars. They marched into the deep shadows of the monster trees. Jimbo watched their progress through the scope on the Savage, eyes on the massive tree boles and deep darkness between.

Bat watched as well through a spotter scope. Lee turned back to give her a thumbs up. Soon the men were out of sight. "We're gonna need a gallon of this shit," Chaz said. He stopped on the trail to pull off his NODs. The night was giving way to pre-dawn gloom. He slapped more Deet gel on the back of his neck. Stinging gnats swarmed around him.

"They love that brown sugar, huh." Boats humped toward him out of a waist-high cover of broad-leafed ferns.

"Man, I'd *drink* this shit if I thought it'd work." Chaz replaced the squirt bottle in a pocket of his Molle vest and picked up the twin hoops of hose once more.

"Hold up." Boats had come to the end of one of his spools. He took the end of one of Chaz' and joined them together using a clamp wrench to make sure the connection was secure. He took the new spool from Chaz and gestured for the Ranger to march on.

"The farther we go, the lighter the load," Boats said.

"The farther we go, the more things that can eat us," Chaz said.

"I hear something," Byrus said.

Jimbo took his eye from the scope and canted his head. "I hear a lot of somethings." Jimbo shrugged.

"I'm trying not to imagine what I'm hearing," Bat said.

The water behind them and woods above them were filled with a cacophony of tweets, honks, grunts, and caws. Beneath them, the constant thrum of insects provided a wavering leitmotif. The level of sound rose in direct relation to the rise of the sun over the water. The world of monsters waking up to a new day. Jimmy Smalls had lived on a Pima reservation until the day he joined the army. Most of his life was spent outdoors in forest, desert, and lake country. In all that time, he'd never been in an environment as *alive* as this one. Or one so damned noisy.

"Down in the water. I heard a splash." Byrus rose to his knees, parting some fronds to look down at the marsh.

"Could be anything. A turtle maybe." Jimbo realized that this was no comfort. They'd seen turtles the size of pickup trucks since they'd arrived here.

"There's something in the water. Under the water."

"I'll take a lookie-loo." Jimbo turned from the Savage to pick up the drone controller.

The drone came to life with a chirp and leaped into the air over them. Jimbo piloted it over the marsh. The lens was set to thermal. The water showed up indigo with flashes of pale gold here and there. Fish. Not even monster fish.

"Got some trout or bass in there. Flintstone size but nothing we need to worry about."

"Yabba dabba doo," Byrus said under his breath. He was an avid TV watcher and knew all about Bedrock and its denizens. In fact, in their current situation, he was missing Netflix more than any other modern comfort. The video library on the *Raj* ran to porn and Bollywood, favorites of the crew. There were a few Charles Bronson movies, but Byrus had practically memorized them by now.

Jimbo recalled the drone. It hovered over them. From below, they heard a churn of water followed by the slap of chop that made the reeds brush against one another.

"That was something big," Bat said.

"Okay. I heard that too." Jimbo sent the drone back over the water. Still no readings. No heat signatures on the shore or in the water. Even the fish were gone now. Just dead water. Byrus stood and looked down at the glassy surface. Ripples spanned all the way to the shore where they raised a muddy foam. Nothing broke the surface. It was a momentary shift in the mirror plane of water.

"Could be anything. All kinds of tectonic activity going on. What it's *not* is an animal." Jimbo brought the drone back to land by them atop its carry case. Byrus took a seat, cross-legged, by him.

"Where are the men of this world? We have seen no one," Byrus said after a moment.

"There are no men here. There won't be for a very long time."

"Not in the entire world?"

"Nowhere. No men. No women. No cities. Just what you're looking at here from one end of the world to the other."

Byrus thought on this as he watched his shadow lengthen in the dawn light. So much of the new world he'd adopted took his attention from the larger questions. There was television and automobiles and airplanes and telephones and all the magic of technology and science that were everyday events to his new friends but a constant wonder to the Macedonian. The microwave oven was as much a revelation to him as learning that the Earth was actually round and that men had walked on the Moon. This world of amazements and conveniences was seductive. He was aware that he could lose himself, become soft over time in a place where even the humblest man had all the comforts of a Caesar. Among Byrus' many blessings was that he was brought to this place by hard men, warriors, who could indulge in pleasures without surrendering their spirit. They lived in civilization and were of civilization but as wolves rather than dogs.

"There was the time of the titans, then the time of the gods, and then the time of man," he said after a bit. "This is none of those times. A time before any other time."

"Yeah, bro. That's why we call it prehistory. This is all before history began," Jimbo said.

"Right, bro." The Macedonian nodded, satisfied.

Out on the black water, the first pair of eyes breached the still surface, glowing copper in the reflected sunlight.

11

TENOCHTITLÁN

They crossed rivers and followed trails through deserts, forests, and grasslands. As they traveled, they were joined by more raiding parties. The force of warriors reached close to fifty. The slaves numbered over two hundred. Weeks of walking brought the slave train to the center of Aztec power at the southern foot of the central plateau.

As they hiked south, Dwayne coaxed Heather to teach him some of her language. She pointed out things as they walked and named each in her consonant heavy tongue. Sky. Bird. Grass. Dwayne memorized them all and asked for more. At camp each night, he listened to the men speaking around the fire. Cups of mezcal encouraged them to tell stories. Grand gestures and exaggerated voices drew laughter or derision from the others. Guys bullshitting around a fire. Some things never change. Dwayne sat close, listening for inflection and phrase construction. It wasn't easy. The way they spoke bore no relation to any other language he knew.

Over the long days of walking and nights about the fire, Dwayne picked up a rudimentary command of the simpler aspects of Nahuatl. He tried a few sentences on Heather. She was startled to hear him speaking to her in familiar words. After her initial surprise, she grinned at his child-like fumbles and corrected some of his gaffes.

Listening to conversations of others, he was able to understand the basics of his place here with these raiders. He was a prized possession, a kind of living oddity like an albino tiger. Black Mask was anxious to get him home. Finding a white giant covered with skin pictures would make Black Mask a big man in Aztecland. Dwayne wasn't sure what that meant for him.

He knew he wasn't anxious for this long march to end. The game trail of packed earth gave way to a broad roadway paved with stones. It was an ancient engineering marvel and ran straight as a string between cultivated fields of amaranth and corn. A half day's march on the stone surface and the peaks of pyramids rose into sight at the end of the road.

Dwayne noticed that weeds grew between the paving blocks. In other places, rain had washed the ballast away, leaving the roadway to collapse. There were also signs that paving blocks had been removed by thieves. Once an object of pride, this road of kings had fallen into disrepair and neglect.

Collapsed adobe huts and fallow fields dense with brush gave further evidence of a society whose best days were in the past. What he thought were neat rows of grain and maize were revealed to be haphazard plantings as they marched closer. Probably more the result of natural reseeding than planned agriculture. Filthy children came to the roadside to watch the parade of animals and men pass by. Many had swollen bellies below ribs visible through skin like paper. There was famine here, and disease Dwayne had seen it before. Many of the children had running sores and rheumy eyes. Rather than showing compassion, the warriors walking escort swung weapons at them and shouted to chase them away from the roadway.

The city must have been a thriving community at one time in its past. Paved roads ran out from the center like spokes of a wheel. What once were probably neighborhoods of neat homes of white-washed adobe were now collections of sagging shacks surrounded by acres of rubble. The walls of the brick homes now provided shelter for skin tents and shacks of woven reeds. Smoke spread from community dome ovens to create a fog between the buildings. The stink of the smog covered the smell of feces and corruption that rose from the densely packed hovels.

Desperate-looking peons came out of the shadows of the huts to line the road and watched the procession pass with hollow eyes. Dwayne noticed an astonishing number of missing limbs and eyes. These were sights he'd seen before in Third World countries in the throes of civil war. Whatever strides the Aztecs had made in the past had been erased by dissolution, conflict, and some brand of societal rot.

They reached the foot of the long causeway that crossed Lake Texcoco and led to the sacred city itself. The pyramids and multi-story buildings were impressive as seen from a distance across the water. But, as the slave train drew closer, Dwayne saw that the paint on the structures was faded and peeling. The steps of the largest pyramid were choked with vines. Much of the city was overgrown. The canals that cut across the island stronghold were green with algae and choked with reeds. Skiffs and canoes lay half sunk in the unmoving brackish soup. Mosquitoes moved in clouds across the still surface.

A gaggle of aged men stepped from the foot of the largest pyramid to meet Black Mask and his entourage. They were bent nearly double under the weight of their ornate headdresses of bone, wood, and feathers. The slave train was formed into a ragged line for the old priests to inspect. They poked and prodded the slaves, inspecting hands and teeth, pinching muscles. Heavily muscled goons shouldering war clubs walked with the old men to make sure the slaves behaved. The priests stopped before a man who was bent double, wracked with a painful wet cough. A priest took a brush from a pot in his hand and marked the man with a daub of yellow paint on the chest.

He did the same for other men down the line. A slave with running sores on his leg. Another with a twisted knee. These men were cut away from the others and dragged clear of the line by the goons before having their brains dashed out with blows from the stone-headed clubs. The rank of slaves stood and watched. They were broken men with no loyalty left for those in their company. They watched placidly as their comrades were executed, content that they were not chosen.

Black Mask clapped hands and called orders to some of his crew. They brought leather bags of cargo from the pack horses. Black Mask spilled the contents of the bags to the dust. It was junk they'd picked up along the way south. Other raiders did the same. Soon there were heaps of loot waiting for the priests' inspection.

Dwayne could see some metal pots, a comb, something that looked like chain mail. There was a dagger or two and a painted earthenware jug. And Dwayne's equipment belt with the revolver, automatic, and needle gun that he hadn't seen since being taken prisoner.

The priests examined the goodies piled up for them. They poked through the mass, picking up objects, commenting on some. A great deal of attention was paid to Dwayne's weapons. One of the old guys held the revolver in palsied hands and put an eye to the end of the barrel. Dwayne made a silent prayer that the ancient fucker would blow his own brains out. A priest made a gesture to one of the goons, who roared a command back toward the pyramid.

A line of young women, naked except for sashes of white cloth, came from the shadows of a low entrance. Each had a basket of woven reeds atop their heads. With the priests fussing over them, the girls loaded the baskets with the loot.

Black Mask took Dwayne by the arm and pulled him forward.

The priests gathered to look the tall stranger over, making cooing and clucking noises. Just as Heather had done, they touched his tattoos with hesitation. Powerful medicine. They stood open-mouthed in amazement when Black Mask pulled Dwayne's head lower and pulled his lips up to reveal even white teeth. The priests' own teeth, what was left of them, were worn black nubs in swollen gums.

One of the priests, a wizened little bastard with skin like parchment and a headdress in the shape of a crow, noticed the silver bracelet dangling from Black Mask's wrist. He touched it with spindly fingers and began tugging on it. Black Mask resisted at first until one of the priests' goons stepped forward with a grunt. He surrendered the bracelet with barely hidden regret. The old priest slid the bracelet onto his skinny arm where it swung easily on his spindly wrist.

The other priests continued their interest in Dwayne. Their hands explored him in a frank, sometimes rude, way. One of them reached into a pouch at his side and blew a handful of dust into the Ranger's face. It stuck to his sweaty skin in a fine yellow powder. Dwayne realized at once that it was gold dust. The priests were weighted down with the stuff. Necklaces, amulets, bracelets, earrings, and nose rings of soft yellow metal.

Black Mask was getting over his disappointment at losing the bracelet. His chest puffed up at the attention his gift was receiving. He bowed his head to the priests. They showered him with praise. They tossed handfuls of gold dust at him that stuck to his skin and hair.

At the priest's direction, the goons came forward to take Dwayne by the arms. Their grip was firm, guiding him rather than pulling him, to join the procession of priests following the column of naked girls along a lane that ran before the pyramid. Dwayne looked back at prideful Black Mask and the beaming Heather, standing with the other raiders watching the parade move away. The slaves were being prodded with clubs to shuffle back toward the causeway. A short life of hard labor in the fields awaited them.

Dwayne broke from the grip of his guides. They stepped back, eyes wide. They glanced at one another then at the priests. The old men had stopped to regard the tall stranger with wary expressions.

"I will not go alone!" Dwayne said.

His Nahuatl was certainly wretched. He knew he probably sounded like a backward child to them. They blinked as he pointed back at the line of the slaves. He held up two fingers and pointed again.

"Two men! Two of these men I want!"

One of the priests stepped forward, head tilted toward Dwayne. He had a wooden eagle's head atop his skull and a long cape of white feathers. He tapped a carved stick on the ground. The goons stepped forward to renew their grip. Dwayne took a step from them.

"Two men! Two men are mine! My slaves! They go with me!"

Eagle Head's eyes drew down to slits. His chin bobbed. He waved a feeble hand and chirped an order at the goons. They stood, frozen with indecision until the old man pounded the stick on the dust again.

Dwayne took that as permission, and he trotted toward the retreating slave column with the two goons on his heels.

Patrick, his barrel-chested buddy from the march, stepped forward shouting questions. Dwayne ignored him to move along the row of slaves until he found the two Arabs. In broken Aztec, he pointed at the two men and ordered them freed to come with him. The goons cut short the leads from their collars and used them as leashes to jerk them free of the line. Dwayne stepped up and pulled the rope ends from the goons' fists.

"Come with me or die out there. Your choice," Dwayne said in Arabic.

The pair of Arabs regarded him with suspicion bordering on hostility.

"Your promises mean nothing," an Arab said. The one without lash marks on his back. Even half-naked and filthy, he had a bearing about him. A man used to finer things. And having his own way.

"I have influence for now. In the fields, you won't last a month. As my slaves, I can protect you."

"Why?"

"Does it matter?"

The Arab shrugged. Both men stepped forward to follow the goons back to where the priests stood waiting. The parade moved on past the foot of the great pyramid. Dwayne could see the long gutters that ran up either side of the stone block steps that led to the altar on the summit. The gutters were crusted black with dried blood. At the bottom of each side of the steps lay sticky pools of the stuff with clouds of black flies swarming above. The smell was sickening.

The words of the aristocratic Arab came back to Dwayne.

"Your promises mean nothing."

SWAMPED

The Rangers and the SEAL reached the water tank at the foot of the narrow falls without event and with eighteen feet of hose to spare. The tank was narrow, no more than ten feet across. It ran deep for fifty feet or more following the base of the escarpment. It was clear, the scree of white rocks at the bottom visible even at a depth of twenty feet or more. No sign of life. Nothing with fins, eyes, or teeth. Not even a sign of plant life. The insects were maddening, and the heat draining. Their clothes were sodden with sweat and chafing their skin with every step and every movement. Ranger training and years spent down-range allowed them to compartmentalize, put the discomfort aside, and prioritize the operation.

Chaz set his rifle aside and jumped into the still water. He was out in an instant, gasping and spitting.

"Shit! That water's hot!"

"You knew that already, you dumb fuck," Boats said.

"I thought it'd cool off some!" Chaz snapped back.

"Least you got wet," Lee said.

Boats hooked the butt of the hose to the immersible pump and the pump's power line to the generator. Two pulls, and the generator kicked into life with a chugging noise. He tabbed the waterproof switch on the pump. It started with a whirling purr. He tossed it into the water. The hose bucked and plumped as it filled under pressure. The length of it became engorged with water, making popping noises as the sheath expanded down the line.

Shan climbed on top of a shelf of rock above the water and sat with his rifle across his knees, eyes on the trees below. A flock of bottle-blue birds with hooked bills flitted among the spiky boughs of the cycads. He watched a centipede as thick around as his forearm lazily slither away between rocks.

"Sixty gallons a minute. The tank'll be almost full when I get back down there. I'll ferry it back to the *Raj*," Boats said. "Gonna be a long fucking day," Lee said. He dipped a hand in the water and slapped some on his face. "So, what do we do?" Chaz said.

"Play with yourselves for all I care. But shut the pump down when I tell you to. I'll radio when I get back so you can start it up again." The SEAL held up his handheld radio. Lee and Chaz each had one. Jimbo, too.

"Sure you want to go back alone?" Lee said.

"Fewer of us moving around the less attention we draw. I'll be quiet as a little mouse." And Boats was gone in the forest gloom.

Less than two minutes after, he departed a boom of thunder rose toward them to echo off the rocks above.

A wet snort and persistent gurgle came from the marsh behind them. Byrus barked something, and Jimbo was moving to swing the big rifle around toward the noise. Bat joined him, a modified M4 rifle to her shoulder.

At first, it looked like a massive log broaching the surface of the black water, some impossibly huge redwood remnant broken free of the ooze below, dredging tangles of vines up with it. Clear of the muddy depths, its movement became more purposeful. A head took shape, an elongated wedge covered in thick scales. On powerful legs, it climbed up the muddy bank. A long tail with a double ridge of spiny protrusions trailed behind it. It stood, all forty feet of it, fully out of the water. Rows of wicked yellow teeth lined the gate-like jaws. Atop its head, a pair of eyes gleamed, reflecting the sun like burnished bronze.

A crocodile. Or a crocodile's great-granddaddy. Jimbo had seen crocs before but nothing close to this size. Still, he could see no difference other than scale. The croc came to rest in the reeds along the bank in a band of sunlight that streamed down through the conifer tops.

"That's why the drone didn't see it. It's cold-blooded," Jimbo said.

"That's forty feet at least," Bat said in a whisper.

"A dragon," Byrus said, staring.

Might as well be, Jimbo thought.

A thumping sound made Jimbo turn his head. A second croc had surfaced near the smaller of the Zodiacs. It glided along to bump the raft holding the tank, causing it to bob in the water. The tank was now filling with water from the hose strung through the forest. The tank rose and fell, rose and fell, swinging side to side as the big animal nudged it again and again. If the tank became capsized, they'd have to drain it to right it. A bitch of a job in the best of conditions. Here it would be sheer hell. If the crocodilians sank both rafts, they were fucked totally.

The Pima threw himself on his belly and sighted the Savage in on the croc nosing at the rafts.

"Cover your ears," he said. Byrus and Bat clapped hands over their ears.

The boom of the big rifle sent birds flying skyward from the reeds all across the marsh. The spear of lead, the length of an index finger, punched a hole through the big reptile's head with a meaty slap audible even over the after-roar of the Savage. The croc was dead but didn't know it yet. It tossed in the water, making the rafts sway violently on their mooring lines atop the brown foam.

"Son bitch," Jimbo said.

"Too dumb to die," Bat said. She sent a long spray of fat Beowulf rounds into the monster's head.

Jimbo sent a second round through the spine just behind the base of the skull. A spray of blood and matter gushed from the fist-sized hole. The enormous animal kicked once or twice before settling in the shallows where it slowly turned on its side to expose its yellow-white belly.

The croc on the shore raised up on its legs and moved with astonishing speed back into the marsh. It slithered to its dead brother, prodding the fresh corpse with its snout. A film of greasy blood was spreading atop the water. The croc hinged open its jaws to bring them closed with a powerful bite on an exposed leg of the carcass. It worried at the limb, tearing it free of the body. Its entire body, tip to tail, convulsed with the fury of feeding. The water churned violently around it, causing the two rafts to collide with one another over and over. The raft holding the tank sank lower in the water as the weight of its contents increased. It was rocking back and forth, threatening to capsize with each swing.

Jimbo sighted and sent two more rounds into the torso of the hungry croc. Chunks of meat and bone exploded from the exit wounds. Bat joined him with controlled bursts. The monster seemed not to notice and continued gnawing at the limb of the carcass, blood gleaming in its teeth. A third round created enough catastrophic damage to cause the croc to release its hold. It slid back in the water away from its meal. Jimbo placed a fresh magazine in the Savage and re-sighted on the water below them.

"Where's the brain? I'm loading the skull up, but it's still moving," Bat said. She traversed the rippling water, looking for a target.

"It's just a nub the size of your fist at the top of the spine," the Pima said, his eye to the cup of the scope.

Some bubbles rose where the second croc had submerged. The first target floated on its back alongside the pair of rafts. Fat flies were already gathering over the water to land on the croc's pale belly.

"It is dead?" Byrus said. It was a whisper. Jimbo noticed that the Macedonian gripped the gladius, blade naked, in his fist.

"Maybe. But those aren't," Jimbo said.

He nodded at the marshlands, where more snouts were surfacing to push themselves through the reeds to the feast.

"Jimbo! Jimmy! Bat? What the fuck?" Lee was shouting into his handheld. His only answer was the rolling thunder from the Savage. The Pima was firing that big gun as fast as he could chamber rounds.

"What do we do?" Chaz said. He was standing now, eyes on the treetops.

"Nothing till we know what's happening," Lee said. "Where's Boats?" Chaz said.

"Boats? You hear me? What can you see?" Lee said.

The SEAL's voice came from the speaker. They could hear the echoes of the Savage over the transmission.

"That crazy Indian's shooting at something I can't see. I'm above the landing site, but there's still trees in the way."

"He's not responding to our calls," Lee said.

"No fucking way he can hear you over that noise. Jesus, that piece is loud."

"Recommend you stay put till we have a sit-rep. Jimmy's in a good position. We'll all stay as we are till we hear from him."

"Roger that. If Jimbo's in trouble that cannon can't get him out of, then there's shit-all I can do to help anyway," Boats said and signed off.

"I don't like just sitting here like this," Chaz said.

"And I do?" Lee said. "But we stick right here. He knows what he's doing. If Jimbo needs us, he'll holler."

And Jimmy Smalls was hollering. He was hollering insults at the backs of crocs clambering out of the water and splashing around the pair of rafts. He was calling to Byrus for fresh magazines. He was cursing at the weight and heat of the enormous rifle in his fists. Bat was cursing as well but at her own rifle. A powerful man-stopper on the battlefield, the M4 was just not enough gun for killing dinosaurs.

Jimbo had to stand now, firing the heavy rifle from the hip in a way it was never meant to be used. But the angle from his hide was all wrong. The big animals were too close for him to fire from the recommended prone position. With each explosion of light and sound and fury, the weapon threatened to tear itself from his grasp. The punishing recoil made him feel like he'd gone six rounds in a boxing ring with a heavyweight.

At the base of the hummock of ground they held, the water was crowded with giant crocs dead, dying, and very much alive. The dumb brutes had no clue who was punishing them, punching pie-plate holes in their skulls and torsos. Their tiny brains fixated on the only new things in their environment, the pair of Zodiacs swaying and bobbing in the churning chop. They were attacking the rafts with tooth and claw, buffeting them with the full force of their bodies.

Jimbo worked the Savage hard to discourage the crocs while taking care not to put a hole in either of the rafts. He was down to two mags for the rifle, and there were still a good half-dozen monsters thrashing and gliding below. A few were feeding on the unexpected buffet of the dead while others continued to be curious about the rafts. Jimbo planted a shot between the eyes of a crocodilian nearing the smaller Zodiac with jaws open. Brain matter and blood sprayed back from the ragged hole before the beast sank out of sight. Jimbo stopped to wipe sweat from his eyes with his sleeve and raised the Savage again to sweep the marsh below.

A great mound of water rose beneath the raft holding the water tank. The spiny hide of a croc, muddy water running off its back, rose up under the Zodiac, sending it tumbling onto its side. Filled to near capacity, the top-heavy craft lurched and then turned over. The flat bottom of the raft turned skyward, the zero-buoyant tank partly submerged beneath it. Under the dark water, the croc's legs became entangled in the heavy canvas hose. The animal spun about, succeeding only in wrapping the hose about its body. The line went taut and then began to slide along the muddy bank. The dumb beast was drawing their pump line into the water with it. The other Zodiac, secured to the first with a mooring line, was drawing toward the tank. If the line became ensnared as the pump line was, they'd lose their only way back to the *Raj*.

Jimbo turned at a movement by his side. It was Byrus running past him to leap out over the water, the naked blade of the gladius in his fist. Bat called out a wordless warning. With a walloping splash, the Macedonian plunged into the water ass-first. He surfaced to kick for the second Zodiac, the water around him alive with writhing leviathan.

"Fuck!" Jimbo stood and fired the Savage down at an oblique angle to provide his maniac friend cover. Bat could only stand staring in horrified fascination.

The immersible pump came out of the pool with a rush, missing Lee Hammond by inches.

The pump, still whining as it sucked air, vanished into the ferns below. It went banging and clanking against the tree boles as it was drawn back to the marsh. The generator was flipped on its side and dragged fifty feet before the cord came free. The pump went silent but for the thrashing sound it made as it was tugged along the forest floor. The booms of the Savage came up through the trees. The Pima was still functioning.

"We're going, right?" Chaz said, leaping to his feet. "Damn right we're going," Lee said.

Shan dropped down from his position to follow the Rangers running back to support their comrades.

They found the pump wedged in the roots of a redwood a hundred paces down the trail. The hose had been ripped from it.

Lee lifted the handheld to his mouth. He felt an iron grip on his arm. Chaz was by him, eyes wide. The three men stood listening to the woods around them. A sound was coming from above them. Branches were snapping somewhere in the forest. Something big was approaching on a direct course for the marsh. On an immediate course for the three men in its path.

The two Rangers and Shan ran full out down the slope.

13

THE SCORE

I t was the morning after their first night on the sacred ground in the shadow of the grand temple. They were housed in a one-room hut with stone walls and stone floor. A thatched roof covered it, raised above the top of the walls to allow air to circulate. It was clean and dry with a brazier to keep it warm at night. Bowls of fresh fruit and sweet cornbread along with clay jars of mezcal sat in a niche of the wall. There was a stout wooden bed with a down-filled mat over stretched ropes. This was Dwayne's place of honor. The Arabs slept on the floor the first night. In the morning, the same women who hefted baskets the day before brought food and scented water and reams of fresh-cut flowers. The aristocratic Arab didn't show up for breakfast, and Dwayne went looking for him.

The Arab was dead.

He appeared to have been strangled. Dwayne found him lying in high weeds behind the lime-washed hut that was their new home. Eyes crimson with burst vessels, black tongue swollen in blood-crusted lips. The ants were already at him, black trails traced over cold flesh.

He searched for the other Arab. Dwayne found him kneeling by a pool, washing his hands.

"Why did you kill him?" Dwayne said.

"He is the one who gave me these," he said. He jerked a thumb at the raised lash scars that crossed one another on his back.

"You were his slave?"

"I was his soldier. This is how he inspired loyalty. By fear. With pain."

"My name is Dwayne. What are you called?"

"Wahid."

"Why did you kill him?"

"What matter is it? We will both be dead soon. They will carve your heart from your ribs. I will die right after."

"Yes. I read enough history to know that. I am a god now, to be pampered. The fatted calf."

"You read this? You do not look a scholar. You look a warrior, Verangi."

"Verangi. You called me that before. What does it mean?"

"Your tribe. The Verangi. How can you not know this?"

Wahid's eyes narrowed.

"Maybe I have another name for my people."

"I only know Verangi. The Rus. Men from the north. Men of the hammer."

"You mean Vikings?"

"That word is not known to me." Wahid shrugged.

A wail went up from one of the women. They gathered at the back of the hut, whispering at the sight of the corpse lying in the weeds. This attracted the attention of one of the guards, who trotted over with his club in his fist. Dwayne joined them to take the rap.

"I killed him. He displeased me." Dwayne hoped that he had that kind of discretion. Were there lines a god couldn't cross? Chances were good that they would forgive him but they'd punish the other Arab.

The guard bowed his head to Dwayne before turning to bark commands at the girls. They took the corpse by the ankles and hauled it away out of sight. The guard returned to his post in the shade of an acacia tree. The ants scattered to seek other food. Just another morning in Aztectown.

Dwayne wondered what his god name was. He knew better than to ask.

He was allowed free run of the grounds on the island. Guards discouraged him from approaching any of the causeways that crossed Lake Texcoco to the shore. They didn't go so far as to threaten him, just stepped in his way with heads bowed and eyes lowered. Dwayne decided not to test them. Killing a servant was one thing. Wandering off the reservation another. His first days were spent exploring his new home. There were three pyramids standing side by side. The priests stayed mostly within their chambers in the base of the largest structure during the daylight hours. In the evenings, they would emerge to perform various ceremonies that remained obscure to Dwayne. He watched for Eagle Head, the priest who wore his bracelet. He glimpsed the man a few times, seated in a circle of chanting men. The heavily muscled goons were always nearby, those wicked clubs ready over their shoulders. There was a zoo of caged animals that looked mostly neglected. Tapirs and javelinas, jaguars and pumas in pits covered over with cages of latticed wood. The women who did most of the menial work attended to them, but most of the animals looked poorly fed, and the pits stank of dung and piss.

Flies swarmed everywhere.

Every few days, there was a procession that crossed the main causeway from the hovels that covered the hills all around the lake. They brought baskets of corn, peppers, fruit, dried fish, and yams. There were also clay jars of corn beer and jams. Dwayne saw sacks of feathers and bales of straw. Live pigs were herded along into pens. Sleds piled with cut firewood were dragged through the sand by slaves. These were offerings for the hundred or so inhabitants of the sacred island. From the number of empty huts on the island, Dwayne guessed that the city had suffered a population drop over time. There was room for three times the number of priests, servants, and guards that currently called the place home. He thought maybe the same was true across Tenochtitlán. There were a few hundred souls showing up to bring goods to the elite class. Even if they paid this tax on a rotating basis, there should have been a lot more people crossing the causeway on offerings day. He wondered how many of the white-washed homes in the heights that ringed the lake were abandoned.

He could see a number of them were unroofed.

The smoke from cookfires was concentrated in the houses closest to the causeway on the other side. That led Dwayne to believe that most of the buildings he could see were unoccupied. Further proof that this was a society in steep decline. Either disease or war or some kind of diaspora had trimmed down the population to a severe degree.

Dwayne spent afternoons swimming in the water and sunning himself on the long embarcadero that ran along the western shore of the island behind the row of pyramids. At the center of the long granite-block pier was an ornate stone carving set in the ground. Thirty feet across, it was divided into equal pie slices that ran from the center image of a snarling cat. Each slice was dense with relief sculptures of animals, plants, and what he assumed were celestial bodies. Three hundred and sixty pie slices in all.

A calendar.

At the widest point of each slice, running about the circumference of the circle, was a dimple of an impression. In one of the dimples rested a smooth river stone. It fit perfectly into the impression. It marked that day's date on the Aztec almanac. Dwayne wondered when it was changed each day. He guessed it was done by the priests. Probably at dawn.

He also guessed that it marked off the remaining days of his life.

14

FEAST

"Swim, you stupid son of a bitch! Swim!" Jimbo shouted as he worked the action to charge the Savage with a fresh round. Bat added her own fire, more out of frustration than any hope of doing real damage.

Below their position, the little Macedonian was stroking hard for the Zodiac. The sun cut through the blood-slick atop the water. In the gloom below, a dark shape glided under Byrus. It rose into view ahead of him, water streaming from its scales. The same monster that tipped over the water tank. The raft was between them.

Jimbo rested the forestock of the big rifle in the notch of a stubby pine and sighted on the croc. He held the rifle braced to his shoulder. The target was too close to use the 20X lenses. He sighted instead over the scope to send out a triple tap.

The slugs raised gouts of blood and tissue along the beast's spine. The damage was unforgiving but did nothing to slow the croc's headway. A bow wave of muddy foam spread from its snout, aimed at the tiny figure splashing toward the raft. The distance between them narrowed. Jimbo went for a headshot and missed, only making a hole in the water near the croc's jawline.

Byrus stopped himself to grab onto the line that was stretched tight toward the overturned tank raft. He severed the nylon line with a swipe of the razor-sharp gladius. The monster crocodilian brushed the capsized Zodiac aside like a pool toy. It came on in an arrow-straight line for the Macedonian treading water. Byrus vanished in the dark water a half-second before those horrible jaws opened to take him. The raft was set adrift to bump against a wall of reeds growing along the shore.

Jimbo was up, running along the edge of the raised ground. Bat stood where she was, sighting her rifle. The Pima took snap shots at the croc, but it had submerged. Its tail rose into view as it turned about. The tail raised a splash of froth with one mighty swipe before vanishing beneath the surface once more. Jimbo sighted and pumped one then two rounds toward the rising skein of bubbles before the bolt locked back on an empty mag. The croc was hurt for certain. The cloud of fresh blood was proof of that. But it was a long time dying.

He hunted for a fresh magazine. There were none. He'd shot through forty or more rounds and could feel the recoil of every one of them in his joints. The Pima snatched up his own M4 and trotted along the ledge, looking over the sights for sign of his friend or the croc. The croc surfaced near the Zodiac snagged in the reeds. Jimbo let fly with controlled three-round bursts that struck along the length of reptile's body. He wanted to go full auto on the son of a bitch but was unsure where Byrus was.

The little guy burst from the water and scrambled into the raft on the far side. Jimbo opened up on the croc then, sending the rest of the magazine into the body before switching out for a fresh one. He trained again on the croc and saw it lay twitching feebly in a pool of its own guts. The last burst had opened its belly up like an undone seam. Byrus waved from inside the raft. Jimbo gave him a fist pump in reply and turned to the shoreline where a number of the crocs were actively tearing the tank raft to pieces. Their cousin was still hopelessly tangled in the hose and mooring lines. It turned its body over and over, jaws snapping, in a mad effort to free itself. It only managed to snare itself further.

Bat realized for the first time that voices on his radio were calling for someone, anyone. They sounded urgent. Her ears still rang painfully from the Savage's roar. She had to turn the gain all the way up and hold the speaker near her ear to hear anything.

"Yeah. Go for Bat."

"Babe! Motherfuck!" Lee's voice. He was out of breath, running.

"Where are you?"

"Heading to you! We're out of here! Get the boats ready now!"

"Negative. Problem with the Zodiac. Problem with the boats."

"Say again!"

"The boats are a no go! They're fucked, Lee!"

"Then *un*-fuck them! We're sixty seconds out your position!" The transmission died.

Bat tossed the radio aside. Down in the water, the crocs were crawling over their dead cousins to slide into the water for the floating island of steaming gore from the last monster Jimbo took out. Twenty yards beyond it, Byrus clung to the raft, bobbing in the chop created by all the fresh movement in the water. All the little guy had was a sword and a pair of balls the size of grapefruits.

And a case of grenades.

"There's a case of grenades in the raft, right?" Bat said.

With his hands cupped to his mouth, Jimbo called down to the raft.

"Bruce! Grenades! By your feet!"

As the Macedonian searched the deck of the raft, Jimbo and Bat sent down a stream of rounds into the crocs that had reached the gutted carcass. They were feeding on ropey lengths of innards and organs. Even the custom Beowulf rounds were only tickling them.

In the raft, Byrus found the hardened plastic case of M-67 frags. He pulled a pair from their padded sleeves and held them up for Jimbo to see.

"Throw them!" Jimbo mimed tossing the grenades.

One following the other, Byrus overhand tossed the baseball-shaped grenades. One landed with a plunk on the bloody water. The other caromed along the back of a croc. Good throws. On the money. In the ten ring.

"He didn't pull the pins," Bat shouted.

"Shit! Bruce! The rings! You have to pull the rings!" He made an exaggerated charade of yanking the pull from an imaginary grenade.

One of the crocs broke from the feeding frenzy, noticing for the first time the shiny black shape wobbling on the water in the reeds, a tiny figure dancing inside and shrieking.

The Pima's mime act sparked Byrus' memory. He'd seen the Rangers deploy grenades before but had never done so himself. He plucked a new grenade from the case and yanked the ring and cotter wire loose. The spoon went flying as he flung the ball toward the croc closing on him, water rushing down its flanks in a gurgling wake.

The frag sank in the water next to the croc. It went off with a muffled whump. A dome of spray flecked with red flew upward. The croc convulsed, snapping madly at the rent in its side that had appeared with such suddenness. Byrus threw a second grenade which bounced off its scales and detonated in the air, nearly cutting the animal in half in a scything arc of wire shrapnel.

Finally getting the hang of it, the Macedonian pitched frag after frag into the mass of thrashing crocs still feeding. Rushes of mud, blood, and gore rose into the air as the five remaining frags turned the last of the sarcosuchuses into stew meat. A sustained shower of white-hot shrapnel whistled into the air. Bat and Jimbo hugged the ground.

The last ambulatory croc was the one still snarled in the hose line and lashings of the larger Zodiac. The raft was a dead loss. The struggles of the giant animal had smashed the hull and flattened the ridged flotation nacelles. Though fatally wounded and enmeshed to near immobility, it still presented a danger to their exfiltration. Jimbo climbed down through the cycads from the hummock, firing at the jerking form as he moved. Bat slid in the mud, catching her boot sole against a palm trunk to stop herself from dropping into the water. She sat in the muck, adding to Jimbo's fire, blasting at the still-stirring monster through a veil of fronds.

Their fire was joined by a second source. Boats ran at a trot from the shelter of some ferns, firing controlled bursts as he moved. The croc twisted and swung its tail in deadly arcs under the storm of lead. To Jimbo's astonishment, the crazy SEAL actually waded into the bloody water to get closer. Boats fired a long burst from near point-blank range into the softer flesh under the croc's jaw. With a shower of blood from between its teeth, the animal settled back into the water as though falling asleep. Its webbed claws kept flexing as the signals from its brain finally died away.

"Yeah! Fuck you, gator! Fuck yo mama too!" The SEAL spat on the monster as he slapped a new magazine in place.

"Where are the others?" Jimbo called down to him. "The hell should I know?" Boats shrugged.

Just then, Lee burst from the tree line with Chaz and Shan on his heels. All three were running full-out.

"Get to the boat! Now!" Bat called to them.

Behind them, something moved in the trees. A massive form took shape in the shadows between the redwoods.

15

NIGHT TRIPS

Dwayne might have been a god, but he was still an outsider. After their initial curiosity, the inhabitants of the sacred island lost interest in him. Food, water, and flowers were left for him each day. Other than that, he had almost no interaction with any of the locals. He was glad for the total absence of children on the island. Kids were always more attentive to change and actually had longer attention spans than adults. He was always wary of juveniles when he was in-country. You had to keep an eye on kids because they damned sure kept an eye on you, acting as watchdogs and alarms.

He took to sleeping through most of the day. The days were hot, and the hut provided shade. The cooler nights allowed him free range to explore the island. Most of the guards dozed off in the small hours.

The lake provided access to the section of the stone embarcadero that ran behind the grand pyramid. He took evening swims in the tepid water, strokes taking him far from the shore. Few of the Aztecs ever entered the water. Those that did only waded. He suspected that few, if any, of them could actually swim. The first time he swam away from the shore, a crowd gathered along the pier to watch him. At first, he thought they might be waiting to watch him get eaten by an alligator. But he thought he recalled that gators were only found in the lower, tropical regions of Mexico. In any case, nothing came out to take a bite.

On his third night of nocturnal wandering, Dwayne swam across the lake all the way to the far shore. He waded through reeds to where the land rose into wooded hills. He could run into the trees and be twenty miles away by morning. As he slept in most days, they might not miss him until late in the afternoon. He knew how to escape and evade. He'd done SERE school as part of his Ranger training. He was a goddamned expert.

He fought down the temptation. He could run. But run to what? Without the bracelet, he'd be trapped in a world where he would never have a place. More than that, he'd have to resign himself to never seeing Caroline and his son ever again. He'd have no way to return, and they would have no way to find him.

Wherever that bracelet took him would remove him from the situation he was in now. Even if it didn't return him to a place he should be. Even that was problematic. With his limited grasp of how the bracelet functioned, he might return to his own reality but a million years in the past or future. He'd be just as lost as he was now.

More disturbing would be to return to a time close to when he left but not close enough. He might show up thirty years after he left to find Caroline a senior citizen and his son a stranger to him. Or come out when Caroline was a child or before she was born.

Deeper questions troubled him. He could very well manifest into a world and time that seemed like his own but was different in significant ways. If his long talks on the subject with Caroline and her brother taught him anything, it was of the endless variables in question with time travel. If the theory of an infinite number of parallel universes, existing side-by-side with the one he knew, was true, then the odds against getting back to the "right" one were insurmountable. Fellow Ranger James Smalls was no scientist but had a view of the whole idea of mirror worlds that Dwayne took some comfort in.

"I think this whole clusterfuck was created by Harnesh fooling with the plan," the Pima told him shortly after their last trip back to prehistoric Nevada. They'd been sitting in deck chairs on the stern deck of the *Ocean Raj,* watching the creamy wake churn behind. They shared a bottle of Jim Beam as they shot the shit.

"What plan?" Dwayne said.

"God's plan. Harnesh screwed with the way things are supposed to be. The results are a cosmic fuck-up. There's consequences when you mess with God's plan."

"You have to believe in parallel universes. We've seen them."

"Man-made anomalies."

"But science believes that there's always been multiple universes, an endless series of realities. Sir Neal only added a few more wrinkles."

"Bullshit."

"You're a soldier, Jimmy."

"And I know bullshit. I know what feels right."

"What makes string theory bullshit?"

"This universe is unique. I mean down to the smallest, smallest detail. You change the distance between the nucleus and satellites of an atom, and life couldn't exist anywhere. I mean, *nowhere, anywhere.* And those teeny, almost immeasurable distances are the same right here in front of us as they are a trillion miles from here. A hydrogen atom is exactly the same no matter where you go."

"There's a point there?" Dwayne said.

"Damn sure is a point. This didn't happen by accident. It had to be a plan. Right down to the finest specks. And someone did all that work."

"What about all those parallels where life didn't happen?"

"Where's the proof of that?"

"It's a theory."

"A fucking theory with no proof. That means it takes faith to believe in it."

"Takes faith to believe in God, Jimmy."

"Doesn't it take that much more to believe in a world you'll never see than it does to believe in the one you're looking at right now?" The bottle sloshed as Jimmy used it to point at the amazing sunset turning the sky from peach to vermilion and the water a sea of gold behind the ship.

"Kind of hard to argue with that," Dwayne said.

Those thoughts occupied Dwayne on his long, leisurely swim back to where the squat pyramids stood black against the stars. He drifted silently to the edge of the pier behind the grand pyramid. Hands gripping the stone edge, he raised himself up until his eyes were above the ledge.

A pair of guards sat either side of a broad entrance that led to the inner chambers of the pyramid. They were still, heads resting on arms propped on their knees. Their clubs lay in the dust by their feet. The night air had chilled. They were draped with sewn skins.

Somewhere inside the pyramid, the priests slept. Eagle Head was in there somewhere with Dwayne's bracelet on his skinny wrist. He'd never been allowed inside and had no idea what the interior looked like. He could take down the sleeping guards easily. Only then to get lost inside the pyramid and never find the priest he was looking for.

As he watched the entrance, he could see the shadows inside pale. A glow came from within, and a priest emerged, carrying a burning taper on the end of a stick. Pre-Columbian flashlight. From his hidden vantage, Dwayne watched the old guy shuffle away from the pyramid to a lean-to set in some escobilla trees. It was too dark to see which of the priests it was. His head was bare. Without the headdresses, the priests all looked the same.

Dwayne levered himself out of the water to move along the pier. He crept to the shadows cast from some shrubs closer to the lean-to. From the sounds within, grunts and splashing, the old man was on the shitter. Everyone else on this island pissed and crapped wherever they happened to be. Turned out the priests had their own privy.

Peering through the stalks of brush, Dwayne watched the old man leave the lean-to and wobble back to the pyramid a few pounds lighter. He waited until the priest was out of sight inside the structure before breaking cover to return to his hut. The priests were elderly, he thought, they were probably up a few times a night to go to the latrine. That meant he could take Eagle Head in the open if he timed it right.

As a plan, it had its own problems.

One lesson always stuck with Dwayne from Ranger training. A good plan today is better than a perfect plan tomorrow.

16

THE KING AND HIS COURT

A mallet head emerged from the tree line followed by ten tons of gristle and sinew. Pig eyes the color of dull amber glowed with malice and hunger. A double wicket of gleaming daggers lined its long jaws. It didn't roar. It gurgled and hissed, thick flecks of foam spraying between champing teeth and from flaring nostrils.

It was a biped saurian of some variety, moving bent forward on sturdy legs. A head the size of a compact car lowered, clawed forelegs scrabbling to help it forward. Its rough hide scraped sections of bark from the thick growth of redwoods as it passed. The impact shook pinecones free from the treetops to fall to the forest floor like hail.

It was in direct pursuit of the three men now sliding down the muddy slope for the anchorage. It was only slowed by its need to find a course between the close-set mammoth evergreens. The last of the crocodilians scattered from the path of the charging newcomer. They leaped into the water with staggering speed to vanish in the depths about the reeds.

Shan and the two Rangers waded into the bloody chum along the bank. Boats was already making a torpedo path for the raft dancing atop a swell offshore. Unable to start the twin Evinrudes mounted in the stern, the Macedonian was paddling madly to bring the Zodiac closer to his friends.

The big saurian broke from the trees and raced headlong over the open clearing of ferns that led down to the banks. Atop the raised ground, Jimbo and Bat Jaffe emptied two magazines each at the big fucker lumbering down the slope. It didn't slow. It didn't notice. The heavy Beowulf rounds were pinpricks, penetrating the pebbled hide to a depth insufficient to cause mortal damage. Jimbo shifted his aim to the head. In spite of its size, it presented a difficult target as it swayed back and forth on the gimbal of a long neck with each stride. The angles of the skull planes deflected most of the rounds. Jimbo doubted he was even annoying it.

"Bat, you got to go while I cover you," Jimbo said. "Who's going to cover you?" she said.

"Maybe Jesus. Go." His smile was fierce. His eyes were hard. To help her along, he gave her a shove. Bat moved down the trail they used to reach their perch. Behind her, the M4 barked again and again.

The beast waded to its haunches into the bloody water lapping the banks. Ignoring the tiny figures wallowing away from it, the saurian dipped its head to sink chisel-edged teeth deep into the flesh of a dead croc. It took the entire carcass in its jaws and lifted it from the water with a meaty crunch.

Boats was the first to reach the raft and rolled over the nacelle onto the deck. He had the twin engines belching then purring. He and Shan helped pull Chaz on board, choking and spitting. Lee hung back to wait for Bat entering the shallows along the shore. The water was covered over in a swirling haze of insects drawn by the stink of fresh blood. Lee ignored Boats' shouts to come back. He reached out a hand for Bat, who was swimming to him. He took her wrist and pulled her close, half-carrying her onto the raft. She didn't resist even as he shoved her over the hump of the gunwale and into the Zodiac. He climbed in after and stood on the deck, searching the fringe of palms above.

"Get down here, Cochise!" Lee called up to Jimbo, standing on the ledge above, rifle in his fists.

"There's still crocs in the water!" the Pima shouted back.

"There's always gonna be! You gonna make them extinct?"

"I'm gonna cover your exfil!"

"Get your red ass down here, or I'm coming up there and drag you down!" Lee's face was flushed with anger.

"Fuck it, then," Jimbo said. He tossed the rifles down to the raft and, with a running start, leaped clear of the ledge to hit the water feet first. He was submerged long enough to catch a fleeting glimpse of dark reptilian shapes resting on the floor of the marsh at the base of the reeds. He kicked for the surface, accepting the grips of his friends who hauled him on board the Zodiac. Once out of the water, Boats hit the throttle, and the raft headed for open water, bow lifted high.

"Sure got cornholed on that one! Total clusterfuck!" Boats shouted from the helm.

"We still need the water." Lee was shouting to be heard over the roaring engines. Bat sat silent and shivering close against him despite the tropical heat.

"I have other pumps and generators, but we're fucked for more hose! It's all back there!" Boats nodded toward shore where they could see two more biped saurians, smaller than the first, stepping out of the forest. They would be joined by others and feeding for days.

"They T-rexes, you think?" Chaz said.

"Who gives a flying fuck?" Boats' face was as red as his beard.

"Jesus!" was all Jimbo could say for the longest time. Over and over again.

"We're all going to get very thirsty," Morris Tauber said. "And the reactor most of all," Parviz said.

It was a rare general meeting that was attended by the Iranians, but they crowded into the chartroom with Mo, the Rangers, Boats, Geteye, and Shan. The bulkhead door was propped open, and the fans stirred the muggy air. With everything now being rationed, they were conserving electricity by not running the AC.

The shore team had showered as best they could with buckets of seawater. The adrenaline rush was wearing off now, and the exertions of the day settled into their joints and muscles. A growing surprise at still being alive was the only comfort they could enjoy from what turned out to be a disastrous day.

"That's why we're here. We need everybody's ideas on how to work this out," Lee said.

"The sea water is for shit. The filters can't handle it. Even if they could, the evaporators can't keep up with what we need," Boats said. He was drinking right from a bottle of Maker's.

"And the evaporators require power we cannot spare," Quebat said.

"What did I just say?" The SEAL glared at the little Iranian who recoiled.

"Back off, sailor. We're all just trying to help. It's a simple logistics problem," Jimbo said.

"It's a science problem, and it's far from simple," Morris said.

"Isn't there better water somewhere, Mo? Near the poles maybe?" Lee said.

"That's a good theory but, no. The whole planet is at tropical temperatures. There are no ice caps at either pole. No ice anywhere. Ironically, there's more open water on the planet in this period than any of us have ever experienced. And all of it is unsuitable for our purposes."

"We could build larger sieve filters and fill them by hand. Bucket brigade it, right?" Chaz said.

"Shit. That sounds like work." Boats took a pull of bourbon.

"There is still the presence of salt in the water," Parviz said. "We cannot cool the reactor with such water. The intakes would corrode quickly. The reactor would shut down and overheat. We do not want this."

"No one wants to say it, but we might be looking at abandoning the *Raj* as our only option," Lee said. "We head out through the Tube into friendly waters and scatter like roaches."

"When and where?" Jimbo said.

"Pick a place. Pick a time. Maybe you and Bruce could play Lone Ranger and Tonto somewhere," Chaz said.

"A modern cargo container ship left derelict in the Cretaceous with an active nuclear reactor on board," Morris said. "That's the kind of temporal anomaly we've been trying to avoid all this time. Not to mention leaving a time travel device to be found."

"You told us we didn't need to worry about that shit here, doc," Lee said. "You said we were on the right side of the extinction event. No butterfly effect this far back."

"Sure. Sure. An asteroid's heading this way right now. Due to arrive in a few million years. It'll take out the dominant species and clean the slate. Any animals you killed today have no descendants. No harm done. No ripple effect. But even tens of millions of years might not be enough to hide evidence of a ship this large even if it winds up as a stratum of rust somewhere where there should only be fossilized remains."

"This shit makes my head hurt," Boats said.

"It might be our only out, Mo. I'm not willing to die here just so some geeks never make a Reddit page about the million-year-old mystery boat," Jimbo said.

"It is more urgent than this, gentlemen," Quebat said. "We are days from meltdown if we cannot cool the reactor."

"So, shut it down," Lee said.

"We have explained this until you are blue in your face," Parviz said. "Even were we to shut it down, the core will not cool without many, many thousands of liters of water. Clean water without salt."

"And your little engine that could melts right through my hull," Boats said.

"Precisely," Quebat said with a nod.

The men sat about the table without speaking. Lee gestured to Boats, and the SEAL handed over the open bottle for Lee to take a swallow. From there, it made its way around until Morris poured the dregs into his coffee mug.

"You're thinking too conventionally."

All turned to Jason Taan, leaning in the open hatchway, wearing a crooked smile.

"You have something useful to add, Taan?" Lee said.

"You have a time travel device on board, do you not?" Taan said.

"Yes. Yes, we do," Morris said. A grin opened up on his face that only further confused the others around the table.

AN ANTI-HISTORY

W ahid wasn't a learned man. He was limited to what he saw and heard in his own experience. Trying to put together a larger picture of this world was frustrating with the illiterate Arab as a source. Wahid shared what he could recall of his life with Dwayne.

He had been conscripted at a young age into the army of the Mughans. From his description, Dwayne surmised that these might be the Mughals, the descendants of the Mongol khans who ruled India all the way into the eighteenth century. In this version of history, the Mughal lords were not brought down by a combined army of British and native Indian troops. Dwayne recalled from some novels he read that the army that defeated the last of the despots was led by the Irish general Arthur Wellesley, later the Duke of Wellington. None of that occurred here, and the Mughals expanded their realm to most of Asia and eventually the new world which they called *Altaghazar,* the Golden Land.

Their supreme raja, the Nahja Khan, sent an armada of warships to create a military presence on this new continent. They subjugated the native population, mostly using the tactic of annihilation. The natives who weren't killed fled east and south.

Wahid had no idea how long ago any of this occurred. "Before the time of my grandfathers" was the best he could do.

Boats loaded with slaves were brought as well to lay roads and build settlements. Wahid described walled cities to the north. There were port and river towns with roads connecting them all. That took centuries. The Mughals were firmly established on the western continent with some settlements east of the *Gazhra Nuhru,* the Rockies.

Farther expansion east was halted by the Verangi. These people looked a lot more like Dwayne, according to Wahid. Tall and fair-haired and wearing pictures on their skin like his tattoos. These men maintained a series of forts running north to south. In some sections, there was even a high ramparted wall that ran for hundreds of miles uninterrupted. War was near constant along this divide. It ebbed and flowed over the years in a stalemate that sounded like it had been in place for hundreds of years.

Dwayne remembered that the Norsemen who came down out of Scandinavia during the medieval warming period found their way south through Russia to Constantinople. There, many of them enlisted as mercenaries to the last Caesars of the eastern Roman empire. They took the name Varangians. Probably the source of Verangi, the name for the men who would become the Normans and the Rus. With his beard filled in over the past months and hair almost to his shoulders, Dwayne had no doubt he looked akin to these invaders.

Dwayne had so many questions, but Wahid was a reluctant storyteller. Unimaginative and inarticulate, the guy couldn't fill in a lot of blanks for the Ranger. It was making Dwayne crazy. These long days with nothing to do but swim and tour the same hundred acres was making him antsy. Nothing to read and no one to talk to but a sullen slave soldier.

He did learn that Wahid worshipped Ba'al and had never heard of Islam or Allah. There was no worship of Christ or

Buddha. The gods of the Mughals were roughly the same as the Hindu pantheon. Wahid knew little about that.

The absence of any monotheistic religions confirmed for Dwayne that this was another world with a history corrupted by Sir Neal Harnesh. He had his own experience on a world like that and with Harnesh's army of ruthless hunter/killers. His wife, Caroline, had theorized that Harnesh's grand scheme was to invade the past and create a continuity in which the leaders of the world's great monotheistic religions were either never born or died young. That was the reason that Sir Neal sought out two theoretical physicists like Caroline and her brother Morris Tauber to create the device that allowed for travel into the past.

The motivation for Harnesh's actions was to ultimately create a parallel world where he would replace God himself as a figure of worship. That was the working scenario, anyway. Maybe the guy was just a really angry atheist. In any case, he had influence over who knew how many worlds that were almost like his own but not quite. And, to support this totalitarian utopia, Harnesh raped the natural resources and wealth of the past.

Of course, the Rangers were guilty of some of that themselves. They'd financed their getaway by using their time-travel advantage to uncover prehistoric gold in Nevada and pirate treasure in the Aegean Sea. But they'd done their share of good as well.

On one of their rogue missions into history, the Rangers prevented the death of a teenaged Jesus Christ. That event would have forever altered the course of their own history to make the kind of existence that Sir Neal was working toward.

The theft of the Tauber Tube and their many efforts to thwart his plans had made them enemies of the man. He was on a constant hunt for them across space and time. His killers got close in Mexico until Dwayne led them away and, ultimately, wound up in this alternate timeline.

It made sense. The bracelet device that brought him here

probably had presets. That was encouraging in a way. It meant that there was probably a setting that would take him back to his own version of reality. He only had to get the bracelet back from the priest who took it. And hope it was still working. And hope that activating it would take him home.

And Harnesh's men could be hunting him here. Though they knew approximately *where* he left The Now, they had all of time to search in for him. Then again, they *had* all the time in the world to look for him. Literally. He had to get away from this place and put more geographical distance between himself and where he left the grid on the Baja.

And there was that calendar. Each new day, the stone moved closer to the day they'd sacrifice their god, Dwayne Roenbach Almighty. And he had no idea when that date with death was circled in their daybook.

The susurrating symphony of toad calls from the lake was giving way to the caws of birds as the sky to the east turned red along the horizon. A rooster's crow joined the din.

Ranger training left Dwayne with an internal alarm clock that woke him as the night ended. He slipped from the bed to creep past Wahid asleep on the floor. The cook fires were smoldering, a wind off the lake blowing the smoke between the huts. Nothing moved in the gray light. He made his way toward the embarcadero, following a path that led around the foundation of one of the pyramids. Some guards dozed against the wall of a drinking pool. Dwayne's bare feet padded silently past them.

He found a place in a tangle of low sabino trees that grew at the base of some steps. It gave him a clear vantage point from which to watch the area around the calendar. He took a seat to start his vigil through the feathery fronds of the trees. The clouds were limned with gold, and the pink hem of the sky was turning blue when he heard a tapping sound. Figures were coming through the early morning gloom from the foot of the grand pyramid. A column of priests in full feathers. Marching before them a young boy, naked as a jay, tapped sticks together as he led the priests into the light. The old men were chanting along with the rhythm the boy provided.

The ancients had a hard time dropping to their knees around the calendar. Eagle Head remained standing where he took up a place at the embrasure where the rounded stone now rested. He stooped to pick up the stone and held it, hand outstretched toward the rising sun. He spoke a high keening prayer in a sing-song voice before stooping once again to place the stone in the next embrasure.

The boy went around the ring, helping the old guys back up onto their feet. Once they were all upright, he skipped away, leaving them to wander back to their other clerical duties. Dwayne remained hidden in the shadows of the sabinos until all were out of sight.

All that to move the calendar forward. "What the fuck," Dwayne said to himself.

He hopped out of cover and moved low to the calendar. A look around to make sure he was alone. He picked the stone out where it rested in the newly-assigned dimple and moved it back five spaces. What would the fuckers make of that?

In addition to all the fresh fruit, meat, and cheese he could eat and all the corn beer and mezcal he could drink, the priests offered him his choice of any of their female attendants that he might want to enjoy. They were willing and curious. The signs were all there. They'd hang around, giving him the eye. Some openly touched themselves and ran wet tongues across their lips.

There were a few pretty ones in the mix, too. Until they

opened their mouths. It reminded him of the *before* pictures in an orthodontic textbook he'd seen at the library. And there was no way to know what kind of parasites and viruses were crawling over their bodies. No penicillin anywhere in this reality, he imagined.

Besides, he was a married man, and his vows meant something to him. Back in the days when he was "young and dumb and full of cum," he might have been tempted. Early days with the Rangers was a continuous pussy party, and he did indulge. Red-blooded American killing machine and all that. "Party today because tomorrow we die" kind of life.

Caroline changed that. The birth of his son Stephen sealed it. What they had was something he treasured and wouldn't risk even if offered an opportunity that no one would ever know of other than him. Even if he never got home, Dwayne was determined to remain true.

Nothing like that held back Wahid who worked his way through the willing women. The Arab was a horny one and was more than willing to give Dwayne's cast-offs a workout.

Wahid brought it up during a late afternoon swim.

"Why do you not fuck them? You have a *quadib*. I have seen it," Wahid said.

"I made a promise. To my wife."

"She is not here."

"She is here." Dwayne touched a hand to his heart.

"You know what Wahid thinks?"

"What does Wahid think?

"Wahid thinks you like boys."

Dwayne didn't take it as an insult. The statement was made without judgment.

Apparently, the *muchachas* of Azteca shared this opinion. Dwayne came back to his hut after the swim to find the same naked boy who'd led the priest parade lying in his bed. The boy grinned broadly at him, eyes swimming in his head in a peyote-fueled delirium. He threw the boy from the hut and sent him stumbling off with a few tossed stones. The women stood in a clutch and gabbled at each other about the mysteries of the gods.

"A eunuch. You are without balls, Verangi," Wahid said.

He shook his head.

"More for you," Dwayne said.

"Too many for me," he said. He waggled a drooping finger.

The man had worn out his unit.

"Tell me about when you were a soldier." Dwayne wanted to change the subject.

Wahid snorted and spat.

"Come on, Wahid. Tell me your bullshit war stories."

"What is 'boo shit?'"

"Your *legend*, my friend."

Wahid told him a rambling story about an attack on a Verangi fort out on the eastern frontier. They marched for days across deserts and forests. The sky was on fire during the day and killing cold at night. Their progress was slow because they brought along huge guns on carts pulled by teams of oxen a hundred strong.

"Cannons? *Mudafie?* How big are they?" Dwayne said. "Big enough for a man to hide in the barrel. Big enough to throw a stone ball this big." Wahid spread his arms four feet across.

Dwayne imagined huge guns with bronze barrels decorated with bas-relief dragons and tigers. Hundred-oxen teams to drag them over the Sierra Nevada to lay siege to a Viking fortress.

It was snowing when they came upon the Verangi who were not fortified within a simple log enclosure as they'd been told. Instead, they found a massive stronghold of stone built upon the high ground where a river bent around the base of an escarpment.

They set up tents and hacked earthworks in the frozen ground while the Verangi within the fort bombarded them with lead balls and rockets. The Mughal gunners set their big guns and fired day and night and barely made a dent in the thick, angled walls of the Northmen's walled settlement. It went on like this for months with one foray on the ramparts after another turned away until the glacis before the walls were choked with the dead of the Mughal army.

Disease raged through the siege camp, and men died in their own filth by the hundreds. Starvation took more of them. Soon they were feeding on their own dead. Retreat was impossible. The passes which they came through on their approach were sealed shut with drifts three times the height of the tallest man. Still, men deserted, stole what food they could, and vanished into the trees along the river.

"Is that how you got those scars?" Dwayne said.

"Yes," Wahid said. His eyes burned with a dangerous light. "And that man you killed gave them to you?"

"Yes. Even though, by running, I saved both our lives."

"How, Wahid?"

He told Dwayne how, when the river thawed and the snow ceased, an army of Verangi showed up to raise the siege. They came down the river in shallow-draft boats, hundreds of them, that disgorged thousands of fresh troops to attack the Mughal's northern flank. In the chaos of the rout, as the Mughal forces were turned, Wahid threw down his musket and sword and fled the field. He was followed by Tormuq, the man who was in command of his company of musketeers. "He said he pursued me to punish me as a coward. I know he ran as well, ran from the fighting to save his life." Wahid's voice was a hiss. His rage as fresh as when he choked the life from Tormuq.

Wahid made his way south along the river, keeping to the densest parts of the wood. He was on foot. His commander and three others were on horseback. Even so, Wahid eluded them for many days by moving across the roughest ground he could find. His run took him into high country that flattened onto a broad open prairie with no cover.

It was there that Tormuq and his men caught up with Wahid. It was there he was staked out and beaten with a long leather whip. It was there he was left for dead, his blood soaking into the earth to draw ants to bite at his wounds. He credited the ants with saving his life.

"There is medicine in their bite. They ate only the corrupted flesh. My bleeding stopped. The pain melted away."

He was found after many days by men on foot, red men with their skin painted in many colors. They cut his bonds. They took him to a stream where they treated the ripped flesh of his back with packs of mud mixed with herbs. When he was able to stand on his own, they asked him about the strange tracks they found on the ground near where they came across his body. The shod hooves of horses.

With pantomime and gesture and crude drawings made in the dirt, Wahid conveyed to them the concept of a horse. He described in charades that men rode these horses, men like himself. And that was how Wahid, a slave conscript of the khans, led a war party of Comanche after his tormentor.

It was weeks of travel, with Wahid's wounds still agonizing despite the administration of peyote and mushrooms to dull the pain. But hate drove him on, trotting along with the braves, following the clear trail of the mounted men riding west.

They fell upon Tormuq and his party fording a river swollen with snowmelt. The Moghul men were exhausted from almost a month of privation and fell easily to the braves' attack. Tormuq and the others were taken prisoner and their horses eaten.

There was no gratitude for Wahid's help in stalking down the foreign soldiers. He was bound like the others and marched south. His only satisfaction was that Tormuq would share his fate. All the other soldiers died on the march. One was bitten by a snake. Another fell down a ravine to bust his skull open on a rock. Another was speared through the guts while trying to escape. The braves mocked his suffering. He took an entire day to die.

The two survivors were finally taken across a wide river to a camp where they were sold to the same Aztec party who brought them south. And the only way Wahid endured that entire, arduous trek was through his determination to murder Tormuq at the first opportunity.

"You spared my life so that I might take his," Wahid said. "For that, you have my gratitude and my word."

"If you don't fuck yourself to death," Dwayne said.

Wahid's laugh was a hyena bark.

18

AN EMPTY PLACE

The *Ocean Raj* was making its way east into the deeper ranges of the Pacific.

A double watch was put in place to scan the ocean ahead for any obstructions. Without charts, the crew relied heavily on the ship's sonar to alert them to changes in the subsurface topography. There were forests of volcanic cones of lava stone rising from the ocean floor. They needed to steer around any that rose close to the surface, since running afoul of one of them could easily tear a hole in the hull below the waterline.

Equally troubling were floating islands of phytoplankton, miles of green scum suspended in a slimy soup rich in nitrogen and phosphorus freed from the ocean floor by volcanic activity. These needed to be watched for with the naked eyes of crewmen stationed along the weather decks. The colonies were fathoms deep and presented a real danger to the *Raj's* engines. The single-cell plants and the oily solution they lived in would play hell with the ship's propellers should they drift through one of the masses. The ship was already dragging long green streamers of vegetation that had taken up residence along the hull.

The weight of the plants and parasitic arthropods were

enough to overwork the engines. In the normal course of a ship's life, the *Raj* would need to go into drydock for a serious scraping. But an added benefit of taking the entire container craft through the Tesla field was the scouring effect of the electromagnetic shock. The last passage through the Tauber Tube stripped paint from large sections of railings and exterior bulkheads. The higher amperage charge running along the surface and under the waterline blasted the hull clean. A result much-desired by Morris Tauber who didn't want them bringing back any alien, time-lost species of fauna or flora to The Now.

Mo had more immediate concerns than their eventual return to the present. First among them was the urgent need of the nuclear reactor, its thirst for fresh water to cool its core. He met with the Iranians down in the control room of the Tauber Tube. Parviz and Quebat were anxious to avert a potential meltdown that would strand them all in the past. The pair of nuclear technicians put up with the same deprivations as the rest of the crew on this nightmare cruise. And they suffered inconveniences all their own being the only ones qualified to maintain the baby reactor of their own design. They shared the twenty-four-hour demands of their brainchild in overlapping eight-hour shifts that kept them belowdecks for days at a time.

The uncertainties of a fugitive life attached to the Taubers and the Rangers were acceptable to the Iranians. They were, after all, outlaws prior to being hired by Sir Neal Harnesh. Parviz and Quebat were gay and, while the rest of the world was mostly tolerant or indifferent to their lifestyle, that was a big no-no to the mullahs of their homeland. Probably an even bigger offense to Tehran than their theft of the components needed to construct the DIY reactor they built. They appreciated that they had been taken in without question by their present company. But enough was enough. They wanted, *needed*, time away from the close quarters they shared in the hidden compartment down in the hold of the *Raj*. Two weeks in Cabo or Vegas or Wildwood, New Jersey even. Allah make it so.

All in all, the two men were an attentive audience for Morris Tauber's proposal.

"We open the field and run a hose line back into the past. I mean *way* back in the past. Precambrian period. We'll need to go to deeper water to do this to increase the chances that we manifest where there's water. But most of the planet was covered with it in that period, so we should be good."

"And that water is pure?" Parviz said.

"Purer than pure. It's long before any life appeared on the planet. Zero organic matter. It might contain mineral sediment, depending on where we pump from. But most of that matter will settle in the tank in short order," Mo said.

"There's still the problem with salt." Quebat this time.

"Actually, no. The Earth's oceans were initially free of salt. It's not until life appears and starts putting carbon dioxide in the air. The CO_2 combined with rainfall to make the rainwater slightly acidic. The acids freed salt from the rocks which ran off into the oceans. Still does."

"So, this water from the far past will supply all we need?" Parviz again.

"A literally *endless* supply. We only need to fire up the Tube anytime we want to top off."

"Then let us please get to work," Quebat said.

"Can you open the thingy to reach that far back, Doc?" Boats asked.

"What do you mean?" Morris Tauber said.

He was in the control room watching monitors. The necessary algorithms had been worked out in advance and plugged into the program. All that was needed now was to manage the tremendous surge of static electricity that would come coursing back into the Tube's power grid.

"It's a long way. You never went that deep before, right?"

"The physics don't work that way. Punching a hole to a particular era isn't a point 'A' to point 'B' proposition."

"Not a straight course?" Boats said.

"Unh-uh. Time is not linear. That's our perspective as we live through it. We experience each second, hour, and day in the order they come at us. We live *through* time. The Tube opens a field *in* time. There's a difference. Do you see?"

"Not even a little bit. I haven't had a lot of sleep."

"I'll think of a better way to explain it. But not today."

"I don't know how you keep all that crazy shit in your head, Doc."

"It's not easy. A possible complication just occurred to me," Mo said.

"Does it directly affect us filling the potable water tanks?" Boats said.

"Not directly."

"Then fuck it."

Boats exited the control room and slid down the ladder rails to the floor of the Tube chamber. Geteye and two crewmen were busy with the final connections to the lines they would use to draw water from the Precambrian sea into the *Raj's* near-empty tanks. Shan was helping by tightening hose connections. They'd lost almost all their hose during the recent clusterfuck ashore. Boats and Geteye spent the previous night robbing Peter to pay Paul. They stripped PVC piping from non-vital areas to build a makeshift line. The crew and passengers would be sharing the same head and showers until they could put it back in place.

The plan was to load the tanks to their fullest capacity. They were also going to fill a ten thousand-gallon bladder in the keel and as many fifty-gallon drums as they could while the field was open. This wasn't an operation they wanted to repeat with any kind of frequency.

The end of the line was fashioned from hoses taken from the eight fire stations positioned around the ship. The hose was secured to another immersion pump with a long, water-proof power line running from it. Boats went up the ramp to the Tube platform carrying the pump. Geteye followed, hauling hose behind him.

The Tube was already rimed with ice. A chilling cloud of frozen air built around it, a side-effect of the Tauber process. When the field was opened, a corresponding mist of cold air would form on the other end, billions of years in the past.

Up on the aft deck, Lee Hammond was working with the Rangers and other crewmembers to raise the huge aluminum-magnesium alloy balloon. The orb would rise to a height of one hundred feet above the *Raj*. There it would double for the orb that would normally rest atop a Tesla tower. The creation of the famed Serbian genius was the source of the gigawatt charge the Tube required to open a gate in time. Bat Jaffee leaned on the rail of the weather deck behind the bridge. She watched the process with the same feeling of disbelief as the very first time she'd seen the field deployed. It all seemed so jury-rigged and impossible. That a shiny balloon could gather, from thin air, the force necessary to punch a hole in time itself. What a ridiculous idea. And yet she'd seen the effect. She had traveled back to the past with these mental cases on two suicide missions and was now trapped with them in this ugly era of carnivorous monsters.

It was wearing on her, and she felt it in body and mind. Bat knew the others were affected by the horrors they'd seen in 1800s China and in their current situation. But they were men and made a show of hiding their concern under a mask of jokes, insults, and plenty of alcohol consumption. They lost themselves in the tasks ahead, the job of survival. The challenge of getting all of them out of this place and time consumed them. As much as the men extended their camaraderie to her, Bat could only find so much comfort in that.

The balloon jerked skyward, trailing across a following sea, borne by a strong headwind. Heavy steel cable looped out behind it from a winch bolted to the deck. The cloud cover was low with a massive black thunderhead to the north. Anvil lightning was illuminating the front all along the horizon. The rainfall was building from a drizzle to a downpour. The deck was slick with fresh rain. Even with the wind rising, it was still stifling hot with no relief from the humidity.

"When this is over, I'm going to go somewhere with a desert," Jimbo said.

"Or someplace with snow," Chaz said.

"I'll be happy when we can start using the AC again," Lee said.

The radio on Lee's belt squawked. He plucked it off its clip. "Can anyone up on deck hear me?" It was Morris.

"Go for Hammond, Mo," Lee said. "I have a concern."

No one liked hearing that. Doc Tauber's concerns usually turned into ballbusters.

"Go ahead. We're all listening," Lee said. And they were. Jimbo and Chaz crossed the deck to listen. Byrus followed, but without knowing why.

"We're opening a field to a time where there is no life. Not a single life form to be found on the entire planet."

"That's a good thing, right?" Lee said.

"For our immediate concerns, yes. But we're opening a field that might extend to the area behind or below the Tube chamber. I really haven't had time to work out the full ramifications of operating the field in an aquatic environment."

"That hasn't been a problem so far, Doc."

"No. But we didn't have to think about it before. And I wasn't concerned about accidentally introducing species from our period into this one. They simply couldn't survive, or more precisely, compete in an environment as hostile as the Cretaceous."

"And we'll be sucking water from a sterile environment."

"Then you follow my reasoning, Lee. We're looking at a possible catastrophe if a species of plant or animal life were to enter the field and contaminate our target era."

"Could a critter from here survive there?"

"Not a larger species. The Precambrian's seas are without salt."

"Or anything to eat," Lee said.

"Yes. But if a plant, a single-celled organism..."

"It's a chance we have to take. Personally, as much as I like you guys, I want to get back to a time where there's cheeseburgers."

"I suppose."

"Tell the Iranians the balloon is deployed. Hammond out," Lee said and replaced the radio on his belt.

The big orb bobbed and wobbled way over the *Raj's* wake, awaiting the initial charge which would begin the chain reaction that would draw electro-magnetic energy from the surrounding air for a seconds-long surge of power.

"We better get under cover," Lee said.

The Rangers, Bat, Byrus, and crewmen made for the compartments that had been shielded as a Faraday cage with aluminum sheeting. It would protect them from the web of static electricity that would engulf the ship when the reactor loosed its burst of wattage up the line to the balloon.

"I've been thinking," Jimbo said. He was struggling to pull off a wringing wet t-shirt.

"Bad habit," Chaz said.

"What if some bug or plant or germ or something does go back to the past through the field? You know, backwash," Jimbo said. He accepted a mug of coffee offered by one the crewmen.

"Okay, what if ?" Lee said.

"Well, what if that's how life was introduced on the Earth? By some assholes fucking around where nobody should be fucking."

"And we're the assholes?" Chaz said.

Jimbo nodded.

The other Rangers looked at him blankly.

"You make me want to get drunk," Lee said after a beat.

They laced their coffee with tots of rum and waited for the storms, both man-made and nature's fury, to hit.

19

BREAK POINT

The sun rose on all hell breaking loose in Aztecland.

The priests caught on that someone was messing with their calendar.

Screeching voices echoed off the walls of the pyramids. The break in the usual morning silence drew everyone to the source. Dwayne joined the women and guards to watch the priests shouting and shoving around the bas-relief calendar. Things were getting hot.

Eagle Head stamped his feet and pointed from the sun to the counting stone. Another old guy wearing a terrapin headdress spat words at him. This only stoked Eagle Head's rage higher. He broke a feathered staff over Turtle Head's back. Other priests jumped in, and spindly arms and legs were soon flying. Feeble punches and kicks landed. Two of the priests rolled on the cobbles with grips in each other's hair. Feathers and beads flew everywhere. The beefy guards glanced at one another. They weren't certain how to break up a scuffle among such holy personages. They decided to just watch.

The gist of the argument was, from what Dwayne could understand of the rapid exchange, not over whether or not the counting stone was in the wrong place but over how it came to *be* in the wrong place. One faction's opinion was that the gods themselves moved the stone back five days. Perhaps some changes in the firmament created a glitch in the system that could only be corrected by divine intervention. Eagle Head and his supporters suspected an evil spirit in the form of a human trickster.

The theological debate wheezed to a stop as the old guys ran out of energy. They came to an agreement that, no matter which side was right, a guard needed to be placed on the calendar to watch it day and night. Calculations were made, prayers were offered, and the stone was moved to its proper place.

Dwayne needed a new plan. Any plan. He figured a few more weeks wouldn't hurt. Time enough to convince his captors that he was a god who knew his place, knew how to behave. Hell, he'd act eager to play a part in his own bloody demise.

Five slaves were brought over from the city just before noon. As the sun rose to its zenith above the grand pyramid, the slaves were hauled up to the altar at the crest of the structure. The goons dragged them, kicking and terrified, up the steps to the top. The priests waited for them in full feathered splendor. They were dressed in what looked like wrinkly jumpsuits. Other guards came for Dwayne, bowing and gesturing. They made it plain that he was expected to bear witness.

Halfway up the steep set of narrow steps, Dwayne wondered how these old fuckers managed the climb without heart attacks. The sun broiled down. The stones under his bare feet were like the floor of an oven. He was bathed in sweat before he reached the top.

The priests mumbled chants and waved staffs and loops of beads. The goons held the terrified slaves firm. All the victims were men. Four Indians and a man who had East Asian features. If an Arab could be here, why not a Chinese? They stared at the bloody altar in terrified fascination. Flies gathered in clouds as if they knew they'd be feasting soon.

The wrinkly jumpsuits turned out to be made from full human hides. They were flayed from larger men than the spindly priests and hung from them like clown suits. Eagle Head wore the palest skin of them all. Dwayne saw a kind of hood hanging behind the priest's shoulders. It bore the features of a blond-bearded face and a long mane of yellow hair. The empty eye sockets stared lifelessly from the mask of the face. A Verangi. Dwayne's stomach turned at the idea that he might be the next wardrobe change for this pious bunch.

Eagle Head howled at the sky before bending to fetch a broad wooden bowl from a niche under the altar. The curved bowl had a spout at one end. He held the bowl braced on his forearms and whispered prayers, head bowed. A second priest poured the bowl full to the brim from a clay jar. A nasty stew sloshed in the bowl. It was deep green with bits of something floating atop an oily surface.

The goons yanked a slave forward and, squeezing hard on the side of his jaws, forced his mouth open. They tilted his head back. Eagle Head released a long pour into the open jaws. The slave sputtered and gagged but got most of it down. The goons released him to drop on his knees. The slave hawked and spat and shook his body like a dog does after a bath. The fear faded from the slave's eyes and his chin went slack. A dreamy expression stole over his face. He tried to stand and failed, dropping to his knees again.

One by one, each slave was dosed and left to kneel, sit, or lie catatonic on the altar floor. The priests brought their prayers to a close, and the first slave was lifted into place to lie atop the altar. A goon stepped forward with a stone ax at the end of a long, curved handle. He stood behind the head of the supine slave and raised the ax high over his head. The slave gibbered and mewled, eyes glassy, mind a million miles away from what was going on around him.

With a grunt, the goon brought the ax head down to crush the sternum of the slave with a single expert blow. Eagle Head approached the slave with a blade curved like a skinning knife. The slave was convulsing, his body aware of the punishment it was suffering if not his mind. With the skill of a surgeon or a tanner, Eagle Head cut an expert pair of incisions and peeled the flesh away from the broken ribs. Two other priests stepped up to help him part the ribs and expose the organs underneath. The slave's legs moved in a final involuntary dance. Piss rushed from him and ran into drains that carried it away from the altar. The steaming yellow fluid joined the blood that ran along runnels gouged from the rock at their feet. Dwayne watched the stream find its way to the gutters that ran down either side of the steps.

Within seconds, arms up to the elbows in the man's open chest, Eagle Head severed the vessels to free the heart. He held it high above his head. Blood was everywhere. It sprayed in a fine mist from the chest wound. The slave vomited up a shower of it as his body jerked under the brutal attentions of the priests. The old men were painted in blood, their feather finery matted and dripping. The whites of their eyes blazed at the sky from crimson masks.

The whole time the remaining slaves watched with unconcern. Somewhere in their minds, the idea that they were next for the chop was repressed under a psychedelic haze created by the priests' cocktail of 'shrooms and God knew what else.

Dwayne watched with revulsion, willing himself not to look away. He forced himself to maintain a bland, indifferent expression. The countenance of a living god. His roleplay as a willing zealot was being tested. He'd seen his share of atrocities and carnage. More than his share. Hell, *way* more than his share. But nothing like a systematic, ritualized murder like this. Even the cannibal proto-humans he'd run into back in prehistoric Nevada didn't make a party out of killing to this degree. At least they were preparing dinner. These assholes just loved killing, pure and simple.

The heart was tossed into a waiting basket crusted black with old blood. A pair of goons took the limp corpse by the ankles and wrists and tossed it tumbling down the steps where it came to rest shy of the bottom. Each slave was brought forward for the same procedure until the flagstones of the altar floor were greasy with blood. The sluices ran full, and the retaining pools below swelled. The flies arrived by the millions in a storm of swirling black, drawn by the rich smell of blood and sharp stink of loosened bowels.

The ceremony ended with a shrieked incantation chanted in unison to the sky from the throat of every priest. They inspected the basket piled with hearts, looking for portents and signs. They appeared to be satisfied. Eagle Head, sticky from his bath in blood and crawling with flies, proclaimed that all was well, and the gods were pleased. The days of man would continue until the end of days. It was time to eat, drink, and fuck like there was no tomorrow.

At least, that's what Dwayne gathered from the words he could understand. He was just glad it was over. His vision swam a bit, from the unforgiving heat or from the horror show or both. He made sure to place his feet carefully on the blood-slick steps as he climbed down behind the goons. They walked ahead, kicking the gutted corpses to flop away before them. One of the dead struck a step with the full weight of its inert form on its head. The skull cracked with a wet pop. That was the final insult, and Dwayne turned to bend double and spew up a breakfast of boiled eggs and ham.

The goons looked from him to the priests still gathered at the top of the steps. Was this an omen? The gods vomit, and it means... what to mortal men? The old guys didn't notice

Dwayne's hurling, so the goons shared a shrug and continued on to the bottom.

Dwayne went immediately to the embarcadero and leaped into the still water. He used handfuls of sand to scrub the blood from every pore. He swam the length of the stone pier to where some flat-bottomed boats were tied up. They were punts, dugouts, fashioned from single pieces of timber. Most were in sad shape from neglect and half sunk in the brown water. He dove beneath the surface again and again to test the hulls. He chose an eight-foot boat with the least amount of rot. It was still afloat and showed signs of recent use. A punting pole and pair of broad-bladed oars lay inside. The interior was musty but dry.

Back at the hut, Wahid was napping in the shade, a woman lying with her head in the crook of his arm. Dwayne prodded him with a toe. Wahid shoved the woman away and looked up, blinking.

"What is it?" the Arab said.

"Fuck this place," Dwayne said. In English.

Wahid squinted at him.

"We are leaving here. Tonight," Dwayne said. In Arabic this time.

THE THIRSTY BLAZE

The drone soared, straight and true, through the billows of frigid mist and into the barrel of the Tauber Tube. Every surface had been sprayed with a dilution of chlorine bleach just prior to launch. No stowaway bugs or bacteria to pollute the pristine past.

Up in the control cabin, Jimbo sat at a monitor and guided the drone with a joystick. The others crowded behind him to get a glimpse of the world before life arrived. They even let Jason Taan watch the launch. All were there but Boats, Byrus, and three of the crewmen who stood below on the entry platform readying the lines and pump. And, of course, Quebat and Parviz monitoring the reactor in their shielded section of the hold.

The image on the monitor showed nothing but clouds of icy mist, the lens rimed with crystals. The image brightened then cleared, and the drone was sending back images of a virgin planet. A low sun turned the ocean bronze under a cloudless sky of gunmetal grey. There was little chop, and the view was clear to the horizon in every direction.

"Is there any land at all?" Lee said.

"There's only one continent at this point. It would be a long way to the west of us. Maybe a few volcanic islands here and there. But most of the surface is water at this point, covered in shallow seas," Morris Tauber said.

"We're all clear. Tell Boats to run out the pump," Jimbo said.

"And you're sure this water is good?" Lee said.

"Sterile and salt-free," Morris said.

Jimbo piloted the drone home through the field. Boats ducked his head as it buzzed past to hover near the ceiling of the Tube chamber. Boats fired up the pump. It chugged as it sucked air, creating eddies in the cold mist. Boats rolled the pump down the entry ramp and gave it a mighty shove that sent it out of sight. The pump's weight took the slack from the line as it sank into a lifeless sea, billions of years in the past. The others began shoving hose into the field to feed the pump more line. The line bucked and straightened as it swelled with water under pressure.

Down on the engine deck, Geteye heard the big reservoir tanks gurgle then roar as water surged into them. He checked a glass bulb at the end of a connection near the bottom of a tank. The water inside swirled clear as crystal. He radioed to the control cabin that the water purity looked one hundred percent.

Outside, the superstructure and railings of the *Ocean Raj* still bristled with the static electricity cast by the surge from the metallic balloon bobbing high above the water in the teeth of a monsoon storm. The blanket of electromagnetic energy that enveloped the ship was a reaction to a gigawatt kick from the mini-nuke. This jumpstarted the Tesla effect that drew the massive clap of energy from the surrounding air that was needed to drive a rift in the time continuum. It was the combination of nineteenth-century electrical technology married to advanced quantum physics that made the Taubers' theory a working reality.

The field could only be held stable and open for thirty minutes maximum. Not enough time to fill the ship's tanks and auxiliaries to capacity. Boats and the crew ran out two more pumps. The SEAL kept his eye on the dive watch on his wrist and ordered the lines and pumps drawn back in at the twenty-five-minute mark. He gave a thumbs up to the observation port that fronted the control cabin.

The *Raj* had taken on over twenty thousand gallons of potable, saltless water, more than enough for the journey ahead. To be doubly certain, Tauber put samples of the Precambrian water through a battery of tests and found it to be Ph neutral and free of all sediments or pollutants either mineral or organic.

Their next meal featured a rarity, a non-alcoholic toast. They filled their glasses with water from the dawn of Earth's existence.

"Not bad," Bat said after a tentative sip.

"But it needs a little something," Boats said. He poured a generous dollop of Maker's to top off his glass.

21

EXFIL

The holy city was asleep. Sated with food, beer, peyote, and sex, the privileged citizens who lived in the shadow of the great pyramid were down for the night. Even the fire tenders had forgotten their duty, and the place was murky dark under a moonless sky. The lanes between the huts were draped in pitch black shadows.

A single guard stood watch over the sacred calendar. He was the only waking sentry near the entrance to the priest's quarters. He might have been the only waking person on the entire islet of partied-out fanatics. A single guttering torch threw a nimbus of golden light up the wall of the pyramid. Carved faces leered down, eyes and mouths alive in the shifting shadows from the flaming pitch.

Dwayne and Wahid crouched in a patch of rushes watching the guard leaning on his spear by the calendar. Every now and then the man, one of the beefier of the goons, glanced at the sky as if wondering if the gods were watching. After a while, it appeared as though he decided the gods had better things to do. The goon left his post and walked to the base of the pyramid, stopping at a pile of broken pottery heaped there. He reached into the pile and pulled out a gourd capped with a wooden plug. Uncapping the gourd, he raised it to his lips and took three long swallows.

The guard was getting his drink on. Dwayne turned to Wahid who shrugged. They could wait for the man to get good and hammered or rush him while his back was turned.

The goon recapped the gourd and placed it back in its hiding place. He stole another look at the stars before starting back to his post. Dwayne rushed up behind him and clapped a chokehold on him. The goon was smaller than Dwayne but muscular. He struggled and clawed, feet kicking for purchase in the dust. Finally, he went limp. Dwayne maintained his hold, crushing the vessels in the man's neck flat, starving the brain of blood. Eight-ball hemorrhages in the man's eyes turned them crimson. He was dead.

Together, Dwayne and Wahid dragged the goon's body to the rushes and hid it there.

"We go now," Wahid said.

"No. I need my bracelet," Dwayne said.

"You can get another."

"Not like this one. Get that boat ready. I'll be right behind you."

Wahid's face creased in a deep frown. But he nodded and trotted off toward the piers.

It was darker inside the entrance at the base of the pyramid. Dwayne paused outside to remove the torch from where it rested in a stone niche. Holding it before him, he felt along a stone wall, following a corridor into the heart of the temple. The smell of rotten food, sweat, and smoke was rich in the air. Under his fingers, he could feel the unfinished stone turned to bas-relief sculptures polished smooth over the years. The floor beneath his feet shifted from stone flags to mosaic clay tiles. He came to an opening in the wall, the scent of human habitation even stronger here.

He held the torch low to his side and bent to look into the chamber. Two old men lay inside, one on the tiled floor where he'd passed out in a puddle of beer. A shattered clay jar lay beside him. The other was insensate on a bunk, mouth open and snoring like an open drain. There were stone idols and more jars against one wall. Dwayne couldn't see any of his belongings here.

Moving on, he checked more of the rooms set either side of the corridor. He found much the same thing, passed out old guys lying singly or in groups wherever the party had ended for them. He saw some faces he recognized but not Eagle Head. It figured that the high priest would have hogged any goodies for himself. Dwayne knew that he'd find the bracelet and his other stuff in the old guy's chamber.

He came to a set of steps that led down to a lower level and a broad chamber with only one exit. The curved walls were stacked floor to ceiling with human skulls secured in place with mortar. Thousands of empty eye sockets stared at him in the wavering glare of the torch. The exit was an arched doorway guarded either side by a pair of sculpted jaguars in human form. A source of light danced within. Dwayne laid the sputtering torch on the tiles before creeping in under the arch.

Dwayne's goodies weren't the only thing Eagle Head was keeping to himself. The old goat lay sprawled back on a sheepskin mat under a blanket of a half dozen of those temple slaves, the girls who wore the white loincloths. Only the loincloths were gone now. All were unmoving and soundly sleeping. In addition to the psychedelics, Dwayne thought, these guys must have come up with a pre-Columbian Viagra concoction.

The room was dimly lit by a pair of stone braziers in which some kind of oil fed a wick. The glow cast a bronze-colored light over all the exposed asses heaped on the bed. Dwayne crept past them toward a shrine set between the braziers. The shrine was piled with statuettes, strings of beads, a gold-plated skull, and coins that bore the profile of a European looking guy. And, prominent amongst this collection of junk, the needle gun, his revolver, and the 1911 automatic. The pistols went into his waistband. He found one of the ladies' discarded loincloths and tied it into a kind of sack into which he scooped a healthy share of the gold coins. He tied it off with a thong he used to secure it to his belt.

One thing was missing, the key to Dwayne's escape from this place and time, the silver bracelet. He turned to the bed where he could see the bracelet gleaming on the old man's wrist. With as much stealth as he could manage, Dwayne placed a knee on the bed between two of the sleeping girls and reached for Eagle Head's spindly arm. He was just slipping the bracelet over the wrinkled hand when he heard a gasp.

A girl had awakened next to him and stared at him with widening eyes. Her pupils were enormous black dots, made wide by ingesting the kind of drugs needed to do the nasty with the ancient bag of bones lying under her. Her lips parted to take in a lungful of air. It would come out as a scream.

"Sorry, honey," Dwayne whispered.

He struck her hard with the heel of his hand just between her rising brows.

The girl dropped back to the bed, limbs limp.

He freed the bracelet from Eagle Head's hand and snapped it in place over his own arm. He considered planting a needle in the old bastard's skull, weighed the risks, and passed. Armed, wealthy, and potentially time-travel capable, he ran back the way he came and out into the star-lit night.

Down at the piers, Wahid had already cast off in the punt Dwayne had chosen. He was poling away toward deeper water.

"You son of a bitch." Dwayne secured the sling of the needle gun over one shoulder and dove from the pier.

Wahid was all apologies and reassurances once Dwayne had reached the narrow punt and rolled aboard.

"I thought you had been captured. Had a misadventure. You were inside an awfully long time."

"I am sure that was it, you lying motherfucker," Dwayne said. The last was in English.

"You have the things that were taken from you." Wahid was trying to change the subject.

"And I mean to keep them." Dwayne took a seat at the stern of the punt, the needle gun trained on Wahid.

"As you wish."

"You know how to row, Wahid? To use an oar?"

"I do."

"Then get to work."

Wahid set the pole aside and sat down to take up an oar. He turned his head toward Dwayne with a sullen expression.

"You do not row as well?" Wahid said.

"Gods don't work. They only mete out justice."

"Remember, I was a god too, my friend." The Arab wore a brittle smile as he shifted the oar to the opposite side.

Dwayne pressed the trigger on the needle gun. With a hiss, a shining silver shaft appeared in the wood of the gunwale near Wahid's hand.

"Well, you just got a demotion. Now row," Dwayne said.

22

GRACELAND

They were looking at a week or more of sea travel. Even the frequent sightings of prehistoric monsters broaching along the hull became tedious. The Rangers turned to a favored game of theirs.

If you could go back in time, and they *could*, who would you kill?

They'd been all through the obvious ones. Hitler. Bin Laden. Manson. Mao. Jimbo's favorite target was Sigmund Freud. Lee wondered what that said about the Pima.

"Colonel Tom Parker," Chaz said.

"Who's that? You mean that dickhead at Bragg? The one who canceled our Christmas leave?" Lee said.

"Naw, man. This guy wasn't Army. He was a bullshit colonel. Like Colonel Sanders," Chaz said.

"Hold on. You'd kill Elvis Presley's manager?" Bat said.

"Bet your ass. What that man did was a damn crime against humanity," Chaz said.

"He kill someone?" Jimbo said.

"Only the King's *career*. That fucker *ran* Elvis' life. Most famous man in the world and the dude treated him like a slave," Chaz said.

"Come on, Raleigh. Elvis had *half* the money and *all* the pussy. You feel sorry for him?" Lee was laughing.

"The colonel made him make all those dumbass movies. Elvis hated that shit. Except for the gospel albums, he never let him into a recording studio for ten years. Ten fucking years!" Chaz was only getting started. "And while he's making all those shit movies the whole sixties are passing him by. The Beatles. The Stones. Marvin Gaye. Aretha. All that's happening, and Elvis is MIA singing about Hawaii on some goddamn phony beach in Burbank. That's all the colonel's doing. My boy did whatever that man told him to do."

"It is what it is," Boats said.

"Asshole was the one put Elvis on diet pills. Man killed my boy. No question."

"You've done some thinking about this," Bat said.

"Damn straight. I'd catch up with that cracker before he ever met Elvis. Back when the King was still at Sun Records. Slit his throat and watch him bleed out."

"Well, if we ever get out of here maybe we can make a side trip to Memphis sometime," Lee said.

"Naw. Can't start playing that game. Where's it end?" Chaz said.

"Yeah. Where's it end?" Bat said. She turned to lean on the rail and watch rows of scaled spines creaming the water along the hull.

23

SURVIVAL MATHEMATICS

"Here! We'll go in here," Dwayne said.

They were both working an oar to maneuver the punt around the edge of a forest of tall reeds. The sun was over the horizon by the time they found a stretch of open shoreline. They rowed for a section of muddy bank.

Dwayne got out to guide the punt forward through the shallows. He turned to look back the way they'd come. The city on the opposite side of the lake was invisible in the dense haze rising off the water.

His feet anchored in mud, Dwayne held the boat in place. "Get out. And bring those canteens with you," he said to the Arab.

Wahid clambered out with a bundle of gourds in his fist. He waded to shore. Dwayne shoved the punt away to drift into the lake. No sense letting pursuers know where they made landfall. He waded from the water to where the Arab waited. The mud along the shore was dimpled with the prints of all the animals that had come here to drink since the last rains. The split prints of deer and the paws of big cats. No sign of men.

"Fill the gourds," Dwayne said as he reached the beach.

"I am not your slave," Wahid said. But he stooped to hold the gourds down to raise bubbles in the water.

"I prefer it when your hands are busy."

"You fear betrayal."

"I am just remembering that you killed a brother Arab." Wahid spat into the water.

"He was no brother to me. I hated him. I have no cause to hate you."

"Not yet." Dwayne gestured toward the trees above the shore with the end of the needle gun.

Wahid capped the gourds and slung them from his shoulder. He walked ahead up the gentle slope of a game trail. Dwayne followed at ten paces distance.

———

The land sloped upward to level out once more. Ahead lay miles of cholla, spiny maguey, and jacaranda trees. Trails worn into the sandy soil wound between the wickets of spiny cacti. As Dwayne and Wahid walked farther from Tenochtitlán, they could hear movement all around them. Deer and big jackrabbits fled from the unaccustomed scent of man. Or *tigres* on the hunt, circling for a kill. Dwayne kept his head on a swivel, eyes on the vegetation to look for flashes of spotted fur. Their arms and legs were crusted with blood from encounters with the long spines of cacti that grew either side of the path. That smell of fresh blood would lure predators into having a peek at the newcomers.

"Have we walked far enough?" Wahid said, out of sight around a curve in the trail.

Dwayne turned his attention and the barrel of the needle gun to the sound of the Arab's voice.

"No. We'll go until the sun is more past its high point."

"They can never find us now. They will be ill from last night's revels. And they have no cause to believe we have escaped."

"Except the stuff I stole back from the high priest's room." Dwayne regretted not putting a needle in the old bastard's head.

"You must be thirsty." The Arab was still invisible around the turn.

Dwayne stooped low to creep into the shade of a jacaranda that grew close to the right-hand side of the trail. He dropped to hands and knees to crawl past the spiky bowers of the cholla, following the Arab's voice where it came from the other side of the wicket of thorns.

"Verangi? Are you still there? I have the water if you wish to have a drink."

The Ranger was belly crawling now, the needle gun resting in the crooks of his arms. His eyes scanned the sand ahead. All he needed now was to run into a rattler sunning itself on a rock.

"We will need each other's help in the days ahead. I will need you, and you will need me. We must regain the trust between us." Wahid was close, just the other side of a clump of maguey, bladed leaves reaching up to the sun.

Dwayne crept out behind the Arab and rose to one knee. Wahid crouched in the trail, head craned to where he expected the Verangi to approach. The water gourds lay in the sand by his side. The Arab held a rock the size of a softball in his fist. He blinked through sweat running from his brows, a feral grin of anticipation fixed on his face.

Two needles to the back of the skull dropped Wahid to the sand. He lay twitching for a second or two, his legs moving in a parody of walking, before going still. The rock was still clutched in his fist.

Dwayne took up the thong holding the gourds. He uncapped one and took a long swallow before slipping them back over his shoulder. He considered burying the Arab. Buzzards would swarm soon and might draw pursuers his way. He chose distance over caution. He broke into a trot, keeping the sun at his back, wending his way eastward. He could move faster now without the burden of caution, of having to watch his former partner. And he doubled his water supply in the bargain. Probably the same calculation Wahid had come to when he made his unfortunate decision.

Behind, carried on a zephyr of wind off the lake, came the sound of hunting horns.

The Ranger doubled his speed, chasing his own shadow through the forest of blades.

24

FISH STORY

The *Ocean Raj* crossed the Pacific at a steady twelve knots in order to conserve fuel. They cut back to essential power only across all decks.

Parviz and Quebat suggested rigging the air conditioning so that the nuclear reactor could power it. They stressed the health benefits of providing relief from the crushing heat. The reactor was creating super-heated water and live steam that was only going into the sea to no purpose. Wadji, the ship's engineer, did better than that. With the Iranians' help, he put together a makeshift steam turbine. It was the size of a compact car. The shell was taken from a rusting industrial heating unit discarded from some past voyage of the *Raj*. The rest was built from parts cannibalized from all over the ship.

Working in the furnace heat of the aft hold, Wadji and some crewmen installed the crude but functional turbine. They ran steam lines from the reactor room under the Tube chamber to the turbine feed. The live steam lines were opened, and the unit hummed to life, powered by the cast-off heat of the reactor. It generated a steady flow of wattage. Enough to run the AC and the ship's cold storage.

Jason Taan's remaining bodyguards were given parole during the weeks they'd be at sea on the open ocean. The four men were given free run of the *Raj* with the understanding that there was no upside to a mutiny or escape. They were every bit as stranded in the past as their captors. Taan spoke to them, ordering them to stand down and behave. He promised them a huge bonus when they returned to Shanghai and the twenty-first century. They gave their word. But the Rangers still kept a wary eye on them at all times.

———

To pass the time and add to their food stores, Boats and Chaz rigged up a fishing line on the aft deck. Instead of a rod and reel, they used a boat crane and winch wrapped with three hundred yards of three-quarter-inch swaged steel cable.

"What are you using as bait?" Shan asked.

"Some chickens went bad when the freezer drawer in the galley thawed," Chaz said.

"They stink to high heaven." Boats was grinning as he crouched to impale chicken carcasses onto barbed hooks connected to the cable with chains.

"And some streamers to catch their eye." Chaz held up some strips of orange cloth torn from a cargo tarp.

"What do you hope to catch?" Shan said.

"Something huge." Boats' grin broadened. All his teeth showed through the forest of his red beard.

"May I help?" Shan said. "My family have been fishermen for many years back."

"Sure. We might need another hand," Chaz said.

"Only this might be a whole new fishing experience for you, brother." Boats racked a rifled slug into a shotgun.

The winch lifted the stinking tangle of rotten poultry and tackle out over the water. With the long orange streamers fluttering in the wind, it looked like the world's ugliest kite. Boats released the winch to allow the lure to plunge deep into the wake of the ship. It vanished into the churning water.

Boats put the brake on the winch, and they attached an empty aluminum beer keg to the cable with heavy-duty carabiners. The keg was painted bright yellow. They hooked a keg or oil drum every fifty feet of cable until a long row of kegs and drums bobbed in the water behind the *Raj*. At two hundred yards, Boats braked the winch. The three men went to the aft rail to watch for signs of interest.

Chaz eyed the following sea through a pair of binoculars. He focused on the water beyond the last lemon-colored float, rising and falling far out in the wake. The morning sun dappled the wave caps with silver light. Nothing cut the surface. Not a fin or tail or snout.

"Won't be long. The water here is loaded with predator fish," Boats said.

He was right. They'd seen their share of shiny monsters breaking the surface around the *Raj*. Long-necked beasts with heads like snakes, sea turtles the size of yachts, nasty scaled monsters leaping into wave fronts in pods like dolphins.

The yellow keg jerked, once, twice. The impact was transmitted back up the line. The cable hummed above their heads, throbbing with tension as something out there pulled it taut. "We got a strike!" Boats jumped back to the winch controls to let out more line.

"Can you see it?" Shan said.

"No. Yes!" Chaz shouted.

A torpedo-shaped fish leaped clear of the chop, gar-mouthed and flashing pewter scales in the sunlight before crashing back down into the foam.

"He take the bait?" Boats called.

"Hold on!" Chaz scanned the water. The first float was yanked out of sight only to explode out of the water again.

Behind it, the big fish flung itself into the air, the line looping from its jaws. The hooks were stuck fast.

"He took all of it!" Chaz hollered.

"I'm reeling him in," Boats said. The winch motor torqued up, and the cable reeled back toward the crane head.

"May I?" Shan held a hand out for the binoculars, and Chaz gave them up.

"How big?" Boats called.

"Biggest fish I have ever seen," Shan said. "Four meters or more."

"That's like fifteen feet! What *kind* is it?" Boats sounded like a kid, shading his eyes to peer at the open water.

"I'm looking! I'm looking!" Chaz was flipping through a large children's picture book titled *My First Book of Dinosaurs.* The Rangers, along with everyone else on the *Raj,* had all become weekend paleontologists. The collection of books gathered before their second trip back to prehistoric Nevada could be found scattered all across the ship in the break room, galley, and cabin rooms.

"It's a zip-uh-fact-anus."

"Anus?" Boats said.

"I'm doin' my best here," Chaz said.

The three fishermen turned to see Jimmy Smalls joining them. Up on the ship's superstructure, other crewmen stood, leaning on railings and pointing sternward. The Pima's reading went beyond the picture books to more serious studies of life in the past. His interest had been piqued further by their recent experiences ashore.

"More like twenty feet," Jimbo said after a glance through the binoculars.

"Whoopee shit!" Boats shouted, followed by a wolf howl.

The big fish fought like a demon, though it was stuck hard on the barbed hooks. It rose clear of the water in high arcs, body twisting to free itself from the barbs holding it fast to the line.

More crewmen came down to the stern to join the fishing party. They helped unhook drums and kegs as the line came in. Even Taan's bodyguards lent a hand, anxious to see the creature that was making the steel cable sing like a harp string.

"It's still fighting!" Chaz shouted to Boats.

The SEAL handed off the winch controls to a crewman named Eskinder. He snatched up the pump shotgun and stepped to the rear rail.

"Slow it down!" Boats called back to Eskinder.

The winch slowed. The lemon-colored keg, battered with dents now, rose out of the water. Below, they could see the water swirling with the fury of the fish invisible in the tumbling foam of the wake. With a sudden force, the fish broke the surface, leaping high up the stern hull. As one, the men retreated from the aft rail at the sight of bloody teeth champing in a gate mouth and rushing toward them.

"We need to cap that son of a bitch," Chaz said. He returned to the rail to take a peek at the roiling water below.

"You damned sure don't want to pull that in alive," Jimbo said.

Boats leaned out, the Remington pump to his shoulder, and the bead trained along the steel line to where the big fish vanished into the water.

The winch groaned. The yellow keg banged hard against the hull. The line thrummed under the weight as the winch motor screamed.

"Shit. Is it hung up on something?" Boats said.

"Maybe your line is tangled in the screws," Shan said. "Naw. The lines still angled away. It's holding the hook down somehow. One last hurrah," the SEAL said. He shifted the business end of the shotgun, looking for a sign of the fish to come leaping out of the spray.

The line strained in the roller atop the crane. It went slack and jerked taut again. A second jerk pulled the line hard enough to pop paint flakes off the crane arm. Rangers and crewmen looked from the crane to the water, wondering what would give first, the catch or the crane or the cable?

"Punch that winch! The line will hold. We're bringing this fucker up!" Boats waved a hand back to Eskinder who pushed the throttle lever forward.

The winch motor whined higher. The line made a whip crack noise, and the vibrations from it rose an octave. Foot by foot, the line came back to the winch. A second crewman used a mallet to hammer the hot cable in place on the drum reel. The water below humped and creamed from the force of the animal struggling just out of sight below the surface. They unhooked the yellow keg as it rose above the rail. It dropped to the deck with a hollow bang, crushed like a beer can at a jock picnic.

Only fifty feet of line remained. Foot by foot the line rose toward them. The rhythmic hum of the motor, the wavering note off the cable and the tap-tap of the steel mallet cranked up the anticipation. Almost the entire crew was either at the rails or seated atop the stacks of containers, enjoying the party feel of the shared experience. Morris Tauber, Lee Hammond, and Byrus stood on the deck above. Even Taan came to see what all the noise was about.

"Where the fuck's my zippycactus?" Boats said.

Jimbo didn't correct him. The SEAL could call this fish anything he liked.

Eyes dead above its horrible mouth, the xiphactinus' head broached the foam. It was followed by the massive jaws and very much alive eyes of a larger animal. The twenty-foot length of their catch was well down the gullet of a tylosaurus. No one on board needed to check a book for the name of this mosasaur. It was the unquestioned king of the sea, and they'd spotted plenty of them in the days since they'd arrived in the era.

But never this close.

The line jerked and hummed as new strain came on the cable. The new arrival had fifteen tons of weight on it in combination with the six tons of the fish it was trying without success to swallow. The winch and line were tested to well above that tolerance. But the cargo they were trying to haul in was live weight. Big, angry, powerful live weight. And it was halfway out of the water.

The huge saurian flippers beat at the water. Its tail hammered against the hull. Sprays of blood flew from its nostrils and between its teeth clamped firmly in the scales of the fish trapped between its jaws.

"It's going to break the line!" Jimbo called.

"Or tear the crane free," Shan said.

"Why won't it just let go?" Chaz said.

"Because it's hooked!" Boats shouted over the din of the combat between animal and machine. He motioned back to Eskinder to cut the winch motor. It died with a stuttering wheeze.

The SEAL was right. The blood turning the foam crimson was from the larger beast. Barbs from the tackle swallowed by the xiphactinus were now lodged in the throat of the saurian. The hooks had pierced the fish's flesh when its carcass was crushed in the muscles of the tylosaurus' bull neck.

Boats fired a slug into the saurian's skull. The beast reacted by increasing the ferocity of its effort to free itself. The sharply pointed serpent's head thrashed side to side. A gurgling roar bubbled out around the dead fish now slowly strangling it.

"Fuck this." Boats worked the pump on the Remmy, emptying the extended tube magazine into the broad skull rising and falling below. Five more heavy rifled slugs the size of a thumb. The *Raj* was leaving a red wake now as the long body of the saurian reacted to the damage done to its fist-sized brain. The mad rage burning in the monster's eyes died away while its tail slashed free of the water with feebler and feebler exertions.

"It's as dead as it's ever gonna be," Boats said after a bit.

"Better haul it in before something bigger takes a bite," Chaz said.

The winch barked to life again. Predator and prey rose free of the water. The crew wasn't so certain of Chaz's declaration. They retreated forward as the crane was slung to lay the full sixty-foot length of the combined beasts onto the deck.

"Surf and Turf," Jimbo said.

The others looked at him.

"The fish is a fish. But the bigger one's warm-blooded. Red meat." The Pima smiled.

COLD PURSUIT

D wayne had a choice, and he waited too late to make it.
He could keep moving and create some distance between him and the men hunting him. Or he could hole up and let them pass by. He was on rocky ground now, following a dry wash that sloped down off the plateau. No tracks led to his current position.

Twin booms, like a double clap of distant thunder, echoed through the rocks. He looked back to see drifts of yellow smoke whipped skyward on the wind. He couldn't see the shooters, but they'd seen him. Where the lead balls went, he could not guess.

The shooters would be atop camels. A small force sent out ahead of the hunting force in a broad screen to search for sign. If he could drop a couple of them, he might slow down their pursuit long enough for him to slip away into the rocks at the base of the slope. Beyond the rocks, it was all table-flat open country. On camelback or foot, they'd run him down. If not today then tomorrow.

Dwayne settled down in a cleft between two rocks. He stretched prone to sight up the slope with the needle gun. This was the only practical way down from the top of the escarpment.

If they wanted to flank him, they'd have to move along the edge of the plateau to another slope to the north or south. That could take them the best part of the rest of the day. They'd come right for him, he was sure. He'd stolen from the temple, and they'd be worked up about that. Never mind that it was his own stuff he took.

Two riders sky-lined themselves for a moment. He watched them pick their way down the slope with care. The camels were more sure-footed than a horse would be on a decline this steep. Still, the riders moved cautiously, their heads raised to search the foot of the wash for any signs of movement.

Uncertain of the effective range of the needle gun, Dwayne allowed them to reach within fifty feet. He settled on the one to the rear through the rectangular front sight. The man cradled a bulky matchlock in his arms. He had the smoking fuse clamped in his teeth. His head turned left and right to sweep the rocks below him. The reins hung slack on the camel's neck, allowing the animal to find its own way down.

A long squeeze sent three steel darts into the rider's torso. Though lethal, the needles lacked a bullet's blunt force impact. The man simply slumped forward to spill to the ground off the camel's hump, hands to his abdomen. He let out a keening cry all the way to where his tumble down the slope caught him up against a rock.

His partner turned, touching the fuse from his mouth to the fuse on the matchlock. Dwayne stood to send a stream of needles that climbed the man's spine. The last one drilled into the back of the man's skull. He dropped, unmoving to the rocks. The camel, spooked, took a few gangly strides away before coming to a stop, blinking in the sun. The other camel stepped past, continuing its progress downhill.

Dwayne ducked when the second rider's matchlock went off where it lay on the ground. A lead ball struck a rock behind him and whined off into the infinite. He rose and moved past the rider lying face down next to his smoking matchlock.

A nasty line of keyhole punctures was visible on his naked back.

He found the other rider lying among some rocks. The man was clutching his belly to cover a wound bubbling blood between his fingers. It was Snaggletooth. The man glared up at Dwayne with the purest venom in his eyes. He hissed curses or insults or something vile.

Dwayne shot him through the face, and the slaver lay still. The Ranger spent a few futile moments trying to catch the camels. They didn't break into a run at his approach as a horse might. Instead, even more frustrating, they gamboled off just out of reach each time he neared close enough to grab for the rein lines. It was maddening. He wasn't as interested in hitching a ride as he was in the water chagals hanging from the saddle rigs. He was in for a long, long desert crossing and he'd need every ounce of liquid he could scrounge. "Fuck both y'all," Dwayne said.

He walked back to where Snaggletooth lay and pulled a flint knife from the girdle of the man's loincloth. Dwayne stuck the broad flat blade under his belt. He hoisted the water gourds on his shoulder and set out for the empty expanse that stretched to the east.

A walk-trot carried him into the desert, a mile-eating pace. The shadows grew longer before him, the sun settling down over the escarpment behind him. He looked forward to the evening when the sun would be gone. But he knew that comfort would be short-lived as the biting arid chill would take over. He'd need to find some kind of shelter to conserve warmth as best he could. A few hours' sleep and he'd move on again while it was still dark. He could steal another ten or more miles or so that way.

The Aztecs didn't seem to like moving around after dark. But they'd make up the miles by moving on camelback. It was going to be a near thing in any case. Dwayne had days of close pursuit ahead of him. He was certain they wouldn't give up the hunt for him. He turned now and then to look for dust rising behind him against the cloudless sky. The horizon remained clear.

The land had looked flat as he came down off the plateau but, as Dwayne crossed it, he found it was cut by shallow rifts that were often choked with cholla. It took time to either maneuver around them or find his way through the stabbing spines. His arms and legs were crisscrossed with fresh cuts that drew biting flies to him. He rubbed sand on the wounds to dry them and mask the scent of blood.

The sky went from pink to gray overhead. The sweat dried on his face and neck. The wind was kicking up, air drawn through the cacti toward the higher ground he left behind.

He found a place under a tilted slab of rock where the sand was still warm from the sun. After making sure it was free of snakes and scorpions, the Ranger curled up as far under the granite shelf as he could manage. He would be invisible to anyone walking even within a few feet of his hiding place.

While there was still enough light to see by, Dwayne examined the silver bracelet on his wrist. The strip that served as a read-out, or so he guessed, was still dead. No red symbols appeared there as before. No iridescent blue field to let him know it was still powered. He touched the nearly invisible control tabs in various combinations, and nothing happened. He had no idea how the fucking thing worked. He remembered his grandfather's confusion when the old man got a cellphone for Christmas one year. What Dwayne needed was a smartass ten-year-old to show him how the bracelet worked.

And what if he got it to work? His position under this slab of rock was not optimal. Wherever or whenever he manifested to, he might find himself under twenty feet of sand and rock or in the middle of a six-lane Mexican highway at rush hour.

He took a drink from a gourd, swishing it around before swallowing to clear the dust from his teeth. His stomach clenched. He wished he *had* found a snake in his hidey-hole. He'd eaten raw snake before. Setting the gourds aside, he nestled into the sand. He soaked up its remaining warmth even as his exposed flesh began to feel the evening chill. Dwayne set his internal clock for three hours of sleep and closed his eyes. When he opened them again, he was being dragged from his bolt hole by both ankles. Two buck-naked guys with wild manes of hair hauled him clear. Two more dropped on him to pull his arms wide. They placed knees either side of his elbows. The first two knelt on his legs above the thighs, pinning him firmly.

More men came into view out of the cholla. Flint axes in their fists and a couple of wooden clubs studded with shards of obsidian. They were all naked, and all wore the same crazy bush-cut. One other similarity among the men made Dwayne wonder if it were all a vivid dream.

Their skin shone a deep, unnatural crimson in the moonlight, like devils.

26

THE PESTS

"I'm surprised Boats knows how to use that thing," Jimbo said.

"I'm surprised he *has* one," Chaz said.

The SEAL stood on the weather deck, sighting a brass sextant on the horizon and the North Star. He ignored the remarks of the two ignorant grunts speaking about him from lawn chairs. Stripped to boxers, the pair of Rangers were on the open deck enjoying a relatively cool westerly breeze. Without taking his eye from the lens, Boats wrote down longitude and latitude figures on a piece of duct tape stuck to the rail.

"How exact is that thing, sailor? Aren't the stars aligned differently now?" Jimbo said.

"They're close enough. Astronomical time moves slower than geologic time. Though there are variables." Boats kept his eye to the scope, making micro-adjustments to the mirrors on the device.

"Like what?"

"Like Mo says that the tilt of the earth's axis would be different now. The asteroid that fucked up all the dinosaurs knocked the whole damn planet into a different angle."

"Yeah?"

"Sure. I have to make changes to account for index error. And refraction is a factor. The air is a whole lot denser here. That's why I'm sighting on a star high above the horizon."

"You know your shit," Chaz said.

"You think SEALs is just about how long they can hold their breath and clench their assholes?" Boats wiped the instrument down with an oiled cloth. He set the sextant back into its padded case with all the reverence of a priest handling a communion vessel.

"So, how close are we?" Jimbo said.

"At this speed, we'll be off the coast of Panama by morning, give or take a hundred miles."

That was good news after two weeks on the Pacific, rolling along at half speed. Even in a world where the sea was filled with monsters, the view grew boring in a hurry. The only memorable moment was when they skirted the edge of a storm that raised the seas to forty feet. Everyone held onto something solid as well as their breakfast as Boats and Geteye guided them bow-first down one wave and up another. Twenty straight hours of the worst roller coaster ride in the world. While it was a break in the monotony, no one wished for another day and night like that one.

"What are the odds that Taan's people followed his orders?" Chaz said.

"Better than even odds we're heading into an ambush," the SEAL said, taking the sextant case with him onto the bridge.

The balloon was run up, the surge from the reactor let loose, and down in the Tube chamber, the field charged up to part the curtain of time.

The full complement of armed men was on hand to watch the field open. The Rangers, Boats, Byrus, and Shan stood with weapons ready and trained into the dense cloud of mist that billowed over the array of carbon steel rings. All but Jimbo, who was busy operating a drone that lifted off from the deck to fly straight into the icy mist for the twenty-first century. Morris Tauber watched through the observation port above. Bathsheba Jaffe was with him in the control room. The crew was confined to the engine room and the bridge. The Iranians manned the reactor. For the sake of strict security measures, Taan and his bodyguards were locked in the converted cargo container deeper in the hold.

"What can you see?" Lee said.

"It's night there. I can see lights along the coast," Jimbo said. He was wearing a VR array. It gave him a live three-sixty view sent back through the Tauber Transmitter across seventy million years.

"Coast of Panama or New Jersey?" Chaz said.

"Fuck you, smartass," Boats growled.

"We're just over ten miles off Isla Jicarita according to the GPS. You did good, sailor," Jimbo said.

"You in range of where the cage is supposed to be?" Lee said.

"It's ten minutes flying time to that position. Battery life to spare," Jimbo said. He pushed the throttle forward. The dark water rushed by his eyes in high-def, so real he expected to smell the salt air.

The drone climbed to a thousand feet. From that vantage, the massive floating dock came into view. An enormous cage constructed of the same tungsten and carbon steel alloy as the Tube, in effect an industrial-sized version of the Tauber's creation. This was the same cage that Morris Tauber got Taan's engineering firm to build for him off the estuary of the Huangpu in China. It had been disassembled and shipped to the Taan's privately owned port facility on the western end of the Canal Zone. The cage had been reconstructed as per Morris' specifications and sent forward in time along with the video of Jason Taan.

Whether or not Taan's people had gotten the job done inside, the six-month deadline was moot. The field was currently open to a day, month, and year, ten years after the date mentioned in the list of conditions related by Taan on the video. A decade of inactivity would create a great degree of complacency. Any security still assigned to watch the cage would be minimally staffed and lulled to idleness by now. Jimbo could move in close, virtually, and take a full recon to make sure all was in place.

If everything looked good, they could bring the *Raj* back to The Now closer to the time they left. They'd manifest back as close to a year after their departure as Morris could manage. He assured them all that he could get them within proximity of that anniversary, within a few weeks either side.

"Only if we pop out back then, wouldn't Taan's soldiers remember we'd been there?" Boats asked at the briefing in the chartroom.

"What?" Morris was flummoxed by the SEAL's question.

"We're gonna visit the twenty-first ten years after we left. But if we were already *there* nine years earlier won't they be *expecting* us on this recon?"

"We haven't gone back to a year out yet. That's in our future."

"But it's in *their* past." Boats looked around the room at blank stares.

"Not yet it isn't," Morris said.

"Shit," the SEAL said.

Jimbo dropped the drone down level with the roof of the cage. There were lights in the windows of a crew shack. He switched to thermal imagery. Images in the vague shape of people shimmered copper-colored inside the shack. The air-conditioning was on. The unit atop the shack glowed bright orange in the tropical air. Three figures stood out in high-contrast against the cool interior. There were no living heat signatures visible anywhere on the super-structure of the cage. No active patrols. Total tactical unawareness ruled here. From the position of one of the figures in the shack, Jimbo guessed the man was asleep on a sofa.

"How we looking?" Chaz said.

"It's all in place just like we wanted. Taan's people made good," Jimbo said.

"Security?" Lee said.

"Minimal and bored off their asses."

"Won't be like that the day we show. A year out, they'll still be frosty," Boats said.

"We deal with that when we come to it," Lee said.

"Hold on," Jimbo said. He raised his hand.

"What?"

"Hold on."

Three thermal signatures, glowing red like rubies, rose off a deck atop the cage. They climbed in the air out of sight of the drone's cameras. Jimbo adjusted the attitude in time to see the three objects, brilliant as stars now, race across the night sky.

"We need to close the field. Now. Shut it down!" Jimbo called.

Morris had tried to explain again and again that, while he could open the manifestation field at will, he had little control over when it closed. All he could do was monitor the levels to see if the field remained open. It collapsed whenever it collapsed. Anywhere from just under thirty to almost forty-five minutes.

Jimbo chose the return option to bring the drone home on auto-pilot. He kept his eye on the three unidentified objects now on a direct course for the *Raj*. The drone flew back to him at maximum speed but still lost sight of the objects as they accelerated to Mach speed.

"Rig for impact!" Boats shouted when Jimbo told him about the projectiles homing on them.

"How the fuck do we do that?" Lee shouted back.

"Prepare to evac through the Tube!" The SEAL charged up

167

onto the rampway and stood poised at the edge of the icy mist. The others gathered at the foot of the ramp, ready to follow. Morris was hammering on the glass of the observation port, mouth working to call mutely through the glass.

A high scream of turbines caused Boats to flatten on his belly on the Tube platform. Three drones, identical to one another and the size of starlings, flew from the clouds of condensation and separated over the Ranger's heads.

"What the living fuck?" Chaz said.

The drones were a dull black and propelled by four tiny jet engines that moved independently of one another to steer and adjust the miniature crafts' attitude. The surface of each segmented with a carapace that mimicked an insect. They rose to the highest part of the hold, scuttling across the surface like moths bumping across a porch ceiling.

"They're looking for a way out!" Lee raised his M4 and sent a stream of fire at the whirling drones. Rounds punched through the ceiling, striking sparks.

Morris pounded on the glass and shouted over the PA to tell them there was no gunfire allowed in the Tube room. Bat had already left the room to add her gun to the others.

The Rangers and SEAL ignored him, firing up at the flitting objects. Jimbo tore off the VR headset and blasted upward with a .45 pistol. Chaz managed to catch a mini-drone in a spread of double-ought from his shotgun. One of its jets popped off to fly away on its own. The crippled drone spun, banging against the walls of the chamber before coming to rest at Byrus' feet. The Macedonian stomped on it repeatedly until it was still.

The other two mini-drones, moving like bats, vanished up into the forest of conduits and venting in the shadows above the Tube. Morris was out of the control room now and coming down the steps. The usually sedate theoretical engineer was bristling.

"Stop it! Stop it now! Do you assholes have *any* idea what you're doing? I said no shooting guns around the Tube!"

A buzzing sound rose from inside the white cloud of the field. Chaz turned to aim down the platform until Lee pulled the barrel of his pump gun down. Jimbo's drone returned to hover over them, awaiting further directions.

The Pima replaced the VR rig on his head and sent the drone up into the shadows to search for the two remaining invaders. The image that came back to him showed only the labyrinth of intersecting vents, piping and hoses, now peppered in places by shot and bullets.

The two remaining intruders were gone.

27

WIE GEHTS?

Pinned under the weight of the four men, Dwayne tried to free himself. The devil-red men were much shorter and lighter than him. But they were expert at keeping a man immobile. The pair on his legs kept him from bending a knee to get a foot flat on the ground. The pair on his arms kept him from rolling his shoulders.

They owned him.

A fifth man, older than the others, with flecks of grey in his bushy hair, leaned close to study Dwayne. He grabbed at Dwayne's beard. With dirty fingers, he pulled Dwayne's lips apart to touch the Ranger's teeth. The man cooed, eyes wide with interest.

The teeth. It was always the teeth.

"I brush and floss. You should try it. And mouthwash, too," Dwayne said when his beard was released.

The man's eyebrows shot up. He rose from his crouch, speaking to the others in a language that sounded like a series of groans punctuated with barks. The others turned to him and listened without taking their weight off Dwayne's limbs. Dwayne could only turn his head. One of the wild, naked men sorted through Dwayne's few belongings and rejected them. The needle gun and both pistols were tossed away into the dark. He tasted the water in one of the gourds. He examined Snaggletooth's flint knife and decided it was worth keeping.

The old guy knelt by Dwayne again to examine the silver bracelet. He ran fingers over it, trying to find a catch or release to open it. Dwayne watched, head turned. Maybe the old guy would hit the controls in the right order, and the Ranger would vanish right out from under these assholes. The old guy lost interest in the bracelet and leaned close to speak to Dwayne. He spoke a stream of words in a peculiar sing-song, the words more pronounced than when he spoke to the others. A different language, Dwayne realized. The old bastard was trying to talk to him, tell him something.

The old guy stood again and snapped fingers. The weight of the four men holding Dwayne down was released. The men, seven that he could see, stood around regarding him. They didn't raise weapons or challenge him as he rose to his feet. The old guy spoke a bit more in the strange language, speaking to Dwayne. The words were unfamiliar, but there was something in the meter and pronunciation. It was a European language of some kind.

The speech was over. The old guy stood blinking at Dwayne. He was waiting for a response.

"Okay. What now?" he said.

The old guy shrugged then pointed away into the dark. The men around him trotted away. The old guy took a step and turned back to Dwayne. He made a motion with his hand.

"You want me to go with you?"

The old guy tilted his head.

"Why not?" Dwayne followed the red devils out onto the silver sands. He'd considered looking for the needle gun and his pistols but decided it was best not to test these guys' patience.

Whatever he was to these guys, Dwayne thought, he wasn't a prisoner. They expected him to come along of his own free will.

These guys liked to move at a run. Even the old guy was a marathon runner. He jogged along, bare feet kicking up sand. Dwayne, a Ranger for life, could still double-time for hour upon hour, but these guys meant to test him. They might be looking to run fifty miles. He was already near exhaustion from being on the move for eighteen straight hours.

He studied them as they ran together. They weren't entirely naked. Each had a small leather bag fixed around their necks on a strip of rawhide. Some of the bags were decorated with stone beads. Dwayne knew from Jimmy Smalls that these were spirit bags, reliquaries for objects precious or sacred to the wearer. Feathers, stones, snake scales, the teeth of ancestors, or whatever might be of significance.

About their waists, they wore belts of twisted leather thongs. They used these to hold their knives or axes when they needed their hands free. Other than that, they were swinging dick naked.

They stopped at dawn at a water tank concealed in some rocks. Each man laid flat on his belly to sip from a shallow pool of water still present from a rainfall maybe months before. The water looked rank and smelled worse, but these guys drank it anyway. Their lives weren't about comfort. There was no room for anything but bare survival in a place as unforgiving as this.

Dwayne drank from one of his remaining gourds. Not one man asked for a sip from him.

They ran on a bit more until the sun was clear over the flat horizon. Then they found shelter in the shade of a broad arroyo, settling against a wall of the depression out of the morning sun. There the old man distributed strips of dried meat from a bag on his thong belt. They offered Dwayne some, and he took it. It was salted, whatever it was, and tough as leather. But it brought saliva to his mouth and stilled the clenching of his belly.

The men took up places in the shade to lie down. One man was left to crouch, awake, to keep watch. Dwayne lay down himself in the cool sand and was asleep in seconds.

They were up again in the afternoon. Dwayne estimated that he slept five hours or less. He suspected that his companions slept less than that. He had a sneaking suspicion that they waited, allowing him more sleep time than they would ever allow themselves.

In the full daylight, he could see that the red of the men's skin was from clay or dye rubbed into the flesh. Some kind of war paint or a signal to their enemies. Maybe it was of religious significance. It might even have been practical protection against the sun. It certainly wasn't for camouflage. Their brick-red hides stood out against the drab hues of the desert.

A sip of water and strip of jerky and they were off again. It went this way for three more days and nights. The desert gave way to grasslands and, at times, cultivated fields. Dwayne's new friends avoided the fields, staying to the trees and tall grass. A few times he could see figures far off, hoeing at the dirt or moving along pathways. They were always too far away, he could never make out their race or type. They were clothed, he could see that much.

They came to a forest of palms and acacia trees and followed a trail that brought them to an area where the trees were cleared by ax and saw. High deadfalls of trimmed branches lay in heaps. The trail widened to what had to be a timber road. There were long gouges in the dirt where logs had been dragged, and tracks of the hoofed animals used to pull them could be seen.

There were ruts from where wagon wheels recently passed on the road. That struck Dwayne, reminding him that he'd not seen one wheeled conveyance since arriving in this time and place. The wheel was an unknown development in the Mesoamerica he'd read about. Apparently, that held true here. So, whose carts were these?

Maybe slavers, Dwayne realized. Maybe his new pals were going to sell him into bondage to Mughals like the ones he saw up in San Diego. They'd brought him out of the desert only to sell his ass to the highest bidder. Well, he might not have made it this far without them.

The logging road exited the brush into a broad clearing in the trees. In the center of the clearing was a stockade type structure built from the trees felled locally. It had high walls of logs with watchtowers at each corner. There were some roofed structures inside, and wood smoke rose from chimneys constructed of stacked logs.

A ditch was dug all around and festooned with stakes set facing outward from its inner face. The outer lip of the ditch was a gently sloping glacis meant to expose any attacker to direct fire from the parapets above. The party of Dwayne and his seven escorts approached the end of a wooden bridge that crossed the ditch to a gatehouse. The old man led the way, hands in the air and calling out in the strange sing-song of an adopted language. Men gathered on the ramparts behind the top of the wooden defenses to watch. It was early morning, and the sun was behind them. Dwayne couldn't make out anything but the occasional gleam off a helmet above the spiked top of the wall.

A group of men walked from the gate to meet them at the foot of the bridge. They were armed but weren't holding their weapons as if they expected a fight. They wore armored cuirasses on their chests similar to what a conquistador might have worn, leather pants and boots and tunics of woven material, wool, probably. A few wore helmets, conical style steel with cheek guards and a curved flange at the back to protect the wearer's neck. On their belts were swords and daggers, big flat-bladed swords with long handles. Along with the bladed weapons, they each wore one or more flintlock pistols either hanging from lanyards or stuffed into cloth sashes. One of them cradled a long flintlock musket with an octagon barrel, the wood stock inlaid with ivory or pearl. And each wore either powder horns or brass gunpowder flasks on slings about their shoulders. The man with the musket wore a leather bandolier hung with paper cartridges.

And each man was tall. At least the same height as Dwayne. Some were taller. They wore their hair long, some in complex braids, and beards were the order of the day. They were blonds and redheads mostly with light-colored eyes. The man with the fine musket, a one-eyed pirate-looking guy with a patch made from a large silver coin, stepped to the old Indian. The greeting was cordial and the two men, the one towering over the other, shook hands before One-Eye stepped past him to have a good look at Dwayne.

One-Eye spoke directly to Dwayne. A more gruffly phrased version of the singsong the old man had tried on him. It was plainly a question.

"I'm not getting any of that. Sorry, bro," Dwayne said. The man took Dwayne's hand and tapped the silver bracelet on the Ranger's arm. He asked a question, lowering his head to study Dwayne's face for a reply.

"Yeah. It's mine. Maybe you know how it works. I haven't had much luck."

The other man's brow knitted, and his mouth turned down in a frown. He directed another question at Dwayne, eyes narrowed to study the Ranger's face for recognition. It was a European language, for sure. Dwayne tried German.

"*Es tut uns leid. Ich verstehe das nichts, Bruder.*" His grasp of the language got him through well enough to order meals, drinks, and pick up women back when he was posted at Ramstein. One-Eye cocked his head and clucked a bit.

One-Eye flexed his fingers, bidding Dwayne to say more. "*Schau Freund, entweder füttere mich, fick mich oder kämp-fe gegen mich. Ich bin müde. Ich bin einen langen Weg gegangen. Und deine Scheiße langweilt mich,"* Dwayne said.

The first part of his response he'd learned from a specialist from the 82nd. "Either feed me, fuck me, or fight me." He thought it was worth trying out on the musketeer. He eye-balled One-Eye in the man's remaining orb.

One-Eye's brows shot up. Yellow teeth showed through his beard.

"Allamani. Südländer," he said.

"Yeah. *Ja.* German. *Deutsche,"* Dwayne said. The Roenbachs came from the Fatherland way back.

One-Eye gripped Dwayne by the arm and turned to the other armored men.

"Südländer. Tyskmann," he said and pointed at the Ranger. The others nodded.

One-Eye turned back to the old Indian. They entered into a back and forth discussion with lots of gesturing. Dwayne knew he was the main topic from their glances and gestures. They came to an agreement. Hands were clasped again with much nodding and reassurances. One-Eye dipped a hand into a leather pouch on his belt and dropped a pile of silver coins into the old Indian's cupped hands.

One consolation to being sold into slavery for the second time. Dwayne's price was going up.

SNIPE HUNT

"First thing we need to know," Lee Hammond said. "Are these widgets weaponized?"

"Not in a directly destructive way," Morris Tauber said. "What the hell's that mean, Doc?" Jimbo said.

Morris looked up from the worktable where he'd further disassembled what was left of the mini-drone intruder caught in a hail of buckshot. He had the guts of the thing laid out under a magnifying light. Wiring, diodes, transistors, and a solid fuel power source as well as battery back-up.

"It's a surveillance device. The threat it represents is in the data it streamed back through this transmitter. Our temporal address. It's got scanners of all kinds on board. The two remaining widgets were more than enough to send back everything they wanted to know about us. That's my best guess anyway." Morris idly tapped the tabletop with a screwdriver handle.

"We need better than guesses," Lee said.

"Well, that's all I have to offer right now," Morris said. "There's a lot of tech I don't recognize. Some of it, like this here, is adapted from the transmitter I came up with. It's intertemporal capable. It was sending back data through the field until it was disabled."

"What kind of data?" Jimbo said.

"Beyond our exact location? Number of crewmembers. Radiation levels. Presence of fissionable material. The dimensions of the ship. And *when* we are. As I said, I'm guessing here. This tech is sophisticated beyond the current state of the science. Some of it is theoretical. This fuel they used for the jets is frankly unknown to me. The battery is one I've never seen before. Its energy capacity is way beyond what something this size should be able to hold. And the level of miniaturization alone brings me to some very uncomfortable suppositions."

"And?" Lee said.

Morris poked through the tangle of components with needle-nose pliers and came up with a gray ovoid the size of a Tylenol tablet. He held it up for the Rangers to see.

"This is a combined hard drive and processor. That's its function. But that's clearly impossible. This little pill has two hundred gigs of RAM and holds thirty terabytes of data."

"That's a lot?" Chaz said.

"Not if it's in a much larger box. In a package this size, it's currently not doable. It requires quantum computing and storage, and that's only theoretical at this point. Government and tech companies are in a race to make quantum processing a reality. It's the next leap in computing and AI. No one's had much luck. DARPA built a model program that fails catastrophically half the time after spending billions on the project."

"It's from the future," Jimbo said.

"Okay. We're *in* the future. Could these theories be realities in that time?" Lee said.

"It is from a future but not *our* future," Morris said.

"You see anything yet, Bruce?" Boats said into the walkie.

A squawk and hiss came back as his only answer.

"You press the button to talk and release it to listen." The SEAL shouted up into the vent opening over his head.

"Nothing. I see nothing." Byrus' voice sounded strained and far away.

And no wonder. He was wedged into the vent cowling, squirming his way forward inch-by-inch. One hand before him to aim a penlight down the long, aluminum tunnel running along the underside of the crew decks. His other hand was jammed against his side, the handheld radio in his palm. The Macedonian was volunteered for the job because of his small stature. Even Bat Jaffe was taller. After years spent as a slave in Roman mines, Byrus had a total lack of claustrophobia. He was already black with grease from the years of built-up grime on the vent's walls. The edges of unfinished joins and the points of sheet screws gouged bleeding tears on his arms and legs. He came across a number of rat carcasses as well, desiccated hair-bags of tiny bones.

Somewhere in the dark before him, he could hear the metallic whirring noise that was not a fan or pump noise. It was a whining sound, rising and falling in timber and tone. The channel he was squeezed into came to a T-intersection thirty feet ahead. The mechanical noise grew louder as he neared the inter-section.

At the end of the channel, he used his free hand to pull himself forward until he could see down the crossing section. The sound came from the vent shaft to the right. Byrus twisted and squirmed until he was on his side. He was then able to aim the penlight toward the source of the whirring sound.

The beam of light found the mini-drone hovering in the shaft where the vent ended twenty feet to starboard.

"I found one of them," Byrus shouted. His fingers pressed the button on the walkie held against his thigh.

"Say again, Bruce." Boats' voice echoed in the shaft behind him.

"I found one! One of the metal birds! What am I to do, Boots?"

"Kick your feet! Let us hear where you are!"

"I am kicking!"

Mimicking a brisk walking pace, Byrus banged his bare feet on the top and bottom of the shaft creating a kettle drum boom. As he trotted in place, he kept the penlight beam on the drone, ready to wriggle back if it should approach.

"We hear you! Keep it up!" The SEAL's voice from the radio reached him over the sound of his kicking.

He placed the penlight in his mouth and pressed his hand against the far wall of the intersecting vent for better purchase. His feet drummed the sides of the main vent now in a rapid staccato. In the bobbing pool of light, he saw the mini-drone's tiny jet engines go cold. The little craft dropped to the floor of the vent and came to rest.

The Macedonian wondered if the steel bird was dead or if it was ever alive. His new friends aboard the *Raj* assured him that machines were soulless creations made to serve men. They were not animals. Not alive. And yet these men cursed and praised the instruments they insisted were devoid of any divine spark. Sometimes they even named them. Maybe no one knew the truth.

A single red light came to life on the mechanism. To Byrus, it looked like a malevolent eye, blinking at him from the dark. The pace of its flashes picked up until it was throwing off a strobing glare that turned the steel cave surrounding it crimson.

Byrus didn't care for this sudden change. He stopped kicking and started squeezing himself back the way he came when the blast shook the walls around him, making them crinkle and pop with the sudden concussive force.

Though he did not lose consciousness, the vent went dark.

It was silent also. Like a tomb.

"It was an EMP," Morris said. "The second one went off at the same time. The detonator must have been damaged when Chaz shot that first one."

"You're welcome," Chaz said.

"Other than Bruce, what damage was done?" Lee said. They stood in a passageway outside the ship's infirmary. Boats and Jimbo were inside with the Macedonian.

"Minimal. The bridge and most of the telemetrics on board are shielded from pulses already. We made most of the areas with electronics into Faraday boxes. Geteye says there's some circuit breakers and fuses that need replacing. But we got off light."

"The objective was obvious," Bat said.

"Only after they confirmed our chronal location," Morris said.

Jimbo swung the infirmary door open to join them. "How's your boy?" Chaz said.

"He'll have ringing in his ears and God's own migraine for a while. Mild concussion, maybe," the Pima said. "But he's one tough little monkey."

"Mo says it was an EMP," Lee said. "Whoever sent those birds knows when and where we are and expects to find us dead in the water."

"Then maybe we shouldn't disappoint them," Jimbo said.

THE REFUGE

D wayne was beckoned to follow the bearded men into the fortress.

"You want me to walk with you?" he said.

"*Ja. Gå med meg,*" One-Eye said, waving him forward. Inside the walls of upright timbers, the place was obviously a military camp. Raised firing platforms ran the length of the walls all around. There were cannons with ornately decorated brass barrels set in earthen embrasures. A pair of neat rows of log huts roofed with canvas tent tops led to a two-story lodge house with a stone first floor and timber upper. The roof was wood shakes. A more permanent, older structure that the newer fortifications were constructed to defend. The largest building inside the walls was a long stable of rough wood planks. A crew of shirtless men was digging muck from the stalls. Hefty steel-shod war horses stood in a row on a hitch line. Bays and dappled grays with grooms running curry combs over them.

Only One-Eye and his entourage were in full armored getup. Probably to present a martial presence in their meeting with the locals. The men in the fort were mostly dressed in belted tunics and leggings. All wore bladed weapons or pistols. There were neat stacks of muskets at hand everywhere. It all reminded Dwayne of a forward operating base, ready for a fight but no imminent threat on the radar. On a war footing but still away from the fighting.

Dwayne followed One-Eye and his men up the steps onto a broad deck that ran around the lodge house on three sides. They expected him to accompany them inside. Whatever his new status was with these guys, he wasn't a slave.

The inside of the lodge house was dark and smoky. Beams of sunlight sliced down through the gloom from vent holes in the roof. The floorboards creaked under the heavy tread of the armed men as they strode deeper into the vaulted great room.

Once his eyes adjusted, Dwayne could see that the rafters were hung with painted shields. Strictly decorative, as the firearms would have made them obsolete as protection. Some were round in shape and some teardrop. Iron rimmed and leather-covered, painted, or embossed in fading colors with ornate images of dragons, bears, wolves, and eagles.

A smoldering fire pit lay under an open area in the roof. What remained of a pig carcass hung from a steel spit over the embers. Long tables set about the pit were still littered with clay jars and mugs from a revel the night before. The smell of stale hops and scorched pork hung thick in the air. Dwayne thought the place could use a woman's touch. There were no women in sight, only men of military age.

On the other side of the fire pit, a man in a brocaded robe leaned on a table sorting through piles of maps. One-Eye approached him, speaking in low tones. Whoever the guy in the robe was, the tough cyclopean bastard was deferring to him. This guy was an officer or lord or chief or something else. The man in charge.

They spoke in the singsong lingo. Dwayne strained to hear but still needed sub-titles. He knew he'd heard this spoken before, some version of it.

The man in the robe turned to regard the Ranger with eyes the color of a summer pond in a clean-shaven face. Dwayne looked from his face to the man's wrist. A silver bracelet showed there beneath the sleeve of the robe, a bracelet matching the one Dwayne wore. The man smiled and stepped from the table with a hand extended.

"You're a long way from home," Samuel Renzi said.

YO HO

The drone confirmed what the sonar was picking up.

Eighteen miles north of the *Ocean Raj's* position three fast craft were on a direct course for them. The drone showed them as a growing cloud of mist blooming from nothing at the relative location of the Taan installation seventy million years away in The Now.

"Three RHIBs loaded with personnel," Jimbo said, eyes on the monitor up on the bridge of the *Raj*.

He adjusted the controls to zoom in on the black shapes bounding over the waves in a loose arrow formation. Twenty-eight-foot rigid-hull inflatables. Armed and armored men sat in the crash seats. A man balanced at the bow of each gripped the shoulder rests of 20mm guns mounted on pintels. The crew was military without any insignia. Hired guns. Mercenaries.

"This is Harnesh, has to be," Lee said.

"That's right. Taan's people only recreated the framework I asked for. Whoever's behind this is using Tube tech to open their own manifestation field," Morris said.

"That's over thirty heavily-armed gun hands heading for us," Chaz said.

"And those cannons could sink us. Punch holes below the waterline from a hundred yards off," Boats said.

"Harnesh wants his baby back. He didn't come all this way to send the *Raj* to the bottom," Lee said. "They'll offer us a deal first then try to board us."

"Either option, they're going to need to get close. They think our comms are out after that EMP. They'll come alongside to hail us," Jimbo said.

"Close is good. I like close," Boats said.

The cargo ship came in sight of the lead RHIB as evening fell. There were no lights on board, and no wake or bow wave. The ship was not under power and adrift in the prevailing southward current, drawing it further from the Panama coast and into open water.

Maurice Franck gripped the armrests of his jump seat with eyes locked on the growing wedge visible against the orange sky. He was a Taan hire but had requested to join this op organized by a man who introduced himself only as Bohrs.

Bohrs, a South African from his accent, was the hire of an outside interest brought in by the board of Taan Enterprises to deal with Jason Taan's abduction. That stung. The decision to take the recovery operation out of the hands of Maurice and his security unit was a humiliation for the Belgian. It took a great deal of insistence on his part to be allowed on this mission. For him, it was payback. These rogue Americans made him look a fool when they vanished in thin air, taking his boss with them. Maurice used the level of personal trust that Jason Taan had for him to secure himself a place on one of the RHIBs.

The rest of the mercs on board with him looked less than impressed with their surroundings. Maurice wondered where they came from. The world of private security and military contractors was a small one, yet he'd never encountered even one of the thirty-two men in this unit. They were a disparate bunch and obviously hardened professionals. Every attempt to engage any of them in conversation was either ignored or quelled with terse, vague replies.

He couldn't tamp down his excitement at their current location. Though it looked like any other seascape, he knew, knew in his bones, that this was an alien place. The air itself smelled different, strangely sweeter than any other tropical clime he'd ever been deployed in. And the punishing heat following their trip through the arctic cloud. Nearly unbearable. His clothes were plastered to him under his body armor.

The sensation of traveling through the field from the floating steel cage off Isla Jicarita was unpleasant in the extreme. A sense of disassociation, of delirious vertigo that had him retching over the gunwale of the raft. The other men with him seemed discomfited but not to the degree he was suffering. They had been through this experience before. That was apparent. What kind of men were these that a trip across millions of years of time was just another day on the job?

In the end, Maurice knew he would get no answers to these questions. It was best to focus on the mission at hand, to make a good show of himself. And, Priority One, see his employer safely out of the hands of these American pirates. There were also men from his own security team on board the cargo ship. He wasn't sure how many of them were captive. Or even if any of them were alive.

He had severe doubts that the others on the op shared that priority, at least not as the prime objective. They carried weaponry and explosives enough to sink a vessel the size of the one they targeted. Clearly, this was not to be a salvage operation. They were ready and willing to lose the *Ocean Raj* in order to keep it, and whatever was aboard, from the hands of its crew.

Bohrs commanded the raft he was on. The South African

ordered the pilot to slow them. The three big outboards at the aft died from a growl to a purr. He gestured to the other craft, a hand slashed across his throat, and they decelerated as well. He waved them away either side. The rafts drifted closer, slowed to under five knots, spreading out in a row to cover the length of the starboard hull.

There was no one visible at the rail above. No sign of life or movement aboard. Had they abandoned ship? The horizon was empty of any craft of any kind. They might have been able to get out of sight over the horizon in the time it took the RHIBs to reach the *Raj*, but Maurice doubted it. Marooned tens of millions of years in the past with no hope of return? More likely, the Americans and their crew were concealing themselves on board with a plan to repel any boarders.

"Attention, *Ocean Raj*," Bohrs said into a loudhailer held to his mouth. "You know where we are from and why we are here. You will let down ladders and allow us to come on board."

Silence from above.

"Delays will buy you nothing, *Ocean Raj*. My orders authorize me to use all force necessary to take control of your vessel. That includes everything from lethal force to the destruction of this boat of yours. Do not be foolish. Lower ladders now."

The ship looming silently above rocked unanchored in the current, rising and falling on a mild sea.

Bohrs barked an order Maurice Franck could not understand. The pilot throttled up and turned them to run along the hull toward the aft section. They swung about, and the RHIB moved close to the flat hull section, the legend OCEAN RAJ, ALEXAN-DRIA in faded paint on the rust-streaked steel plate high above.

The men stood now on the shifting deck. The other two rafts drifted behind, coming about to lend support fire if needed. Maurice rose and leaned on the gunwale. The gentle chop lapping against the rafts' buoyant nacelles was lime-green with vegetation that blossomed all along the big ship's hull. A smell of jungle rot rose from the stew that made Maurice's stomach clench like a fist. He swallowed bile.

With silent professionalism, the men on board raised twelve-foot steel ladders with hooks on the ends. They balanced on the deck, shifting to respond to the swells and drops, angling the top of the ladder over a railing above.

A voice shouted from the deck above, the caller invisible. An order of some kind. With a groan of a motor and a metallic shriek, the end of a crane swung out overhead. Suspended on a length of steel cable beneath the end of the crane was a fifty-gallon steel drum.

Bohrs ordered the raft to back away from under the drum. Ladders were lowered, and guns were up. Eyes searched the railings above. Nothing moved. No sounds. The barrel swung on squeaking chains.

A burst of automatic fire broke the silence. The men on the rafts responded in kind. Suppression fire raked the hull and upper structure of the *Raj* despite the lack of any visible targets. Sparks flew from metalwork.

None of the rounds fired from above came anywhere near the rafts. Instead, the long burst had drilled holes in the drum swinging overhead. Streams of viscous fluid sprayed from holes punched through the steel to trickle down into the green sea. It was a stinking soup that filled the mercenaries' noses and eyes with the sharp stink of putrefaction. An oily skim spread atop the water.

A second volley of fire turned the trickle to a shower. The men on the nearest raft were bathed in the spray of nauseating effluvia. The raft deck below their feet was a puddle of chunky broth. A man on one of the other rafts brayed a sudden laugh, and others made remarks in a babel of languages. Bohrs cut them a murderous glare, driving them to silence.

The men, splashed with the stinking filth, were more determined than ever to raise the ladders and get aboard. The RHIB sidled near enough to bump against the hull. They swung the ladders close, straining to get them secured.

Maurice stood ready to follow them upward, and his weapon charged and ready in his combat harness. He looked back at the other rafts where men stood swaying with weapons trained upward, ready to supply support fire. A movement in the water behind the other RHIBs caught Maurice's eye. A protuberance above the surface behind a curl of creaming foam.

A dorsal fin. The first of many. On a direct bearing for the scent of blood and flesh.

WRONG WORLD

"How is my father?" Samuel asked.

"He was okay the last time I saw him. Still on the mend but cranky as ever," Dwayne said.

"Tell me the circumstances under which you left them."

Dwayne told him about their interrupted vacation on the Baja. The run-in with a killer team, the flight into the desert. He and N'itha encountering an armed unit that manifested out of thin air to retrieve them and take them somewhere or somewhen. He told a truncated version of his adventures since he'd arrived in this parallel plane.

"So, I can't tell you what happened after I bugged out. If anyone could make it back to your dad and Caroline, it's N'itha. I can only hope and pray that they made it away."

"We need to reunite you with them as soon as we can," Samuel said. He turned to look at One-Eye and his entourage in conversation at a table across the great room. They were drinking something poured from a barrel into clay jars. A plate of cold meat, pepper, and scallions was shared by the group.

"Guess you don't have a spare one of these?" Dwayne said. He waggled his arm. The silver bracelet caught the light coming from the ceiling.

"Only the one I have on. And I use that sparingly. It sends off a signal with each use, allows Harnesh and his followers to lock onto me. I lost them here."

"And why are you here?"

"To find you, Dwayne."

"And how the hell does that work? A whole planet and all of time to look in, and you show up right here. A month or so late, but you find me. The odds of that happening are fucking ridiculous."

"Caroline sent me after you."

"How? When did you see her?"

The corner of Samuel's mouth turned up for a heartbeat in the closest the man ever got to a smile. Dwayne's eyes had adjusted to the gloom. He could see the lines around the other man's eyes, the graying of the hair at his temples. Samuel had been a few years younger than Dwayne the last time they'd met. The man before him was a good twenty years older than him now.

"Yeah. Right. Dumb question," Dwayne said.

"Not 'dumb.' Irrelevant. Let me see." Samuel gestured for the bracelet. Dwayne undid the concealed catch and handed it over. Samuel examined it.

"Looks like a power source problem. I can repair it, send you back. Send you anywher. But it must be carefully done. There are systems installed that would send out a signal if activated. It would draw our enemies to us."

"But you can fix it?"

"Given time." Another flash of a smile.

"Okay. So, what do we do in the meantime? I mean, what's your deal here? Shit, what's the deal *with* here?"

"This is one of Guhathakurta's model worlds." Samuel used Neal Harnesh's birth name, the name he had when he was a humble state telephone lineman in India. "This plane of reality has diverged from the one you are familiar with in many significant and sinister ways. There is no Buddha. No Jesus. No Muhammed. Without the presence of the Christians, the Jews are an obscure cult, few in number and without a home."

"Is this the past or the present or..." Dwayne shrugged. "Yeah. Irrelevant, right?"

"It is the past. You are seeing, living, the history of a world I am familiar with."

"A fucked-up place to be, right?"

"It is a fate I hope the human race has avoided. You made that possible by the actions of you and your men in Roman Judea. You averted the course of history. That reality will never be realized."

"Hold on. If we accomplished our goals in Judea, then why is all this still here? I thought it would just go up in smoke or whatever. This place is over a thousand years past the first century AD, right? Firearms for one thing." Dwayne thought back to the days they'd spent in the highlands above Nazareth in a running fight with a Roman legion. He still couldn't get his head around the fact that they might have played a part in saving the life of a young Jesus Christ. Every time he tried, he felt like he was pushing at the limits of his own sanity. How could any of this be real?

"It doesn't work that way. Though the main current of reality corrected itself, returned to its natural course, because of your actions, this plane remains as a remnant, going forward to a future with a stark end, centuries from now. All you see here will simply go black one day, as though it never was."

"Like a deleted scene in a movie."

"If that helps you understand it," Samuel said.

He knew the guy wasn't trying to make him feel stupid, but Dwayne still felt like he was always being schooled.

"These guys, One-Eye and his crew, they're like Vikings, right?" Dwayne nodded toward the drinking men. They were now playing a game of some kind involving dice or bones, getting louder with drink and play. Coins clinked, and fists pounded the tabletop.

"Yes, as you know them. Northmen. They are the rulers of Europe from the Atlantic Ocean to the steppes. They control much of the Mediterranean region as well. The rest of the world, Asia and the eastern coast of Africa is in the hands of the Mughal khans, the descendants of the Mongols, based out of India."

"Mongols. Like Genghis Khan?"

"The same. They have been at war with an alliance of European kingdoms under Norse rule for two hundred years. This is a place where religion is primitive, pantheistic. The Danes and Franks and Allemani with their gods of weather, death, and war. The Mughals have a bastardized system of beliefs, a combination of their own animistic theology combined with the pantheon of the Hindu Vedas. Both faiths are populated by capricious gods whom they believe have little interest or relation to the lives of men. And so, the societies here are not guided by spiritual laws, and they do not recognize any kind of divinity in man. They are ruled by the laws of men only. And that can only lead to either anarchy or tyranny. I've seen the final result of all this, and it is ugly."

"Hell. Why would Harnesh want to make a place like this?"

"To make a world in his image, perhaps. Madness? I don't know or care. I only know that he has to be stopped."

"Again, and again."

"Yes."

"And what's going on here? This feels like a war zone. These guys are gearing up for a fight."

"This hemisphere is called *Ylfsland* by the Northmen after the tribe who first came here. To the Mughals, it is *Pedonkibhoomah*, meaning 'land of trees' in a mangled form of Hindi. They have been fighting for possession of it for eighty or more years. The struggle has been at a standstill for decades. A static front exists along what you would know as the Mississippi River. They fight for a gain of meters. Offensive and counter-offensive with neither side gaining an advantage."

"What are we doing here, Samuel? What part are we expected to play here while you figure out how to fix that device?"

"I have been earning my keep here teaching their gunsmiths the advantages of a rifled barrel. I am seen as something of a seer, touched by the gods."

"Crazy, you mean."

"Yes. But this culture values madness. You'll be under my protection. Your familiarity with firearms will be helpful."

"Jesus. Jimbo would love all this. Wish he was here instead of me."

"There is a battle coming. We are to sail under the next new moon. We will be expected to take part if I can't get your manifestation unit in functioning order by then."

"Soldiering. Can I explain I'm retired?"

Samuel said nothing in reply. His attention was focused on the bracelet he'd taken from Dwayne.

"Sam, what if you can't get that thing working?"

The other man looked up then, the answer in his light green eyes.

BUTCHER'S TIDE

The engines of the *Ocean Raj* came to life, the screws revving, white water roiling in its wake as the big ship pulled away from the feeding frenzy.

Once out of effective weapons range, the passengers and crew lined the sternward rails to witness the carnage.

"Those poor bastards," Jimbo said. He had scopes to his eyes and trained on the RHIBs growing smaller in their wake. He offered the binoculars to Bat who waved them away.

"Fuck 'em," Lee said. He watched through Zeiss binoculars. The three inflatables turned about, looking for an escape from the gathering of sharks churning the water to white foam all around them. Measured against the twenty-eight-foot length of the RHIBs, some of these animals were almost twice the size of the inflatables. The rest weren't much smaller. They were prehistoric great whites, no different from their cousins in The Now but for size and appetite.

The rafts were spun around in the chop raised by the swarm of killers just beneath the surface. Dozens of fins were visible, with many more gliding unseen below. A raft was knocked sideways by a rising body, the underside exposed. By some miracle, the crew righted it before it was capsized or swamped. The mercenaries on board fired weapons into the massed bodies, creating crimson suds of blood and matter. The water turned into a consommé of excreta and tissue that only served to madden the mass of predators to greater fury.

A red mouth bristling with triangular razors rose from the wash to clamp down on the bow of a raft. The beast used its massive weight to try and drag the nose into the water. The deck canted, and men tumbled forward. His shoulders braced in the rests, one of the mercs fired the big 20mm point-blank into the wedge of the big shark's skull. Geysers of blood exploded upward to come down in a stinking rain.

The big fish was dead, but its grip on the prow of the raft remained locked. Other sharks turned on the carcass, striking left and right to take bites and worry at the fresh meat. The raft spun about on the axis of feeding sharks. The aft end left the water, the three outboards screaming as the props whirled in empty air. A thirty-footer broached underneath to tip the RHIB higher. Men spilled over the gunwales as the long raft flipped over. The men appeared, fighting to stay afloat for a few precious seconds. Their mouths opened in soundless screams before being dragged under in a welter of frothing water and flashing teeth.

The other two rafts fared no better. One was flooded to the gunwales after a monster shark leaped from the water to slide athwart it amidships. The beast crashed back into the water, a merc struggling between its jaws. The full weight of the shark ruptured the port pod. Air escaped above and below the water-line. The results were catastrophic, the crew battling to bail the sinking craft as more bodies buffeted it from all sides. The men were up to their knees in rising water, the deck beneath them descended further. They gave up bailing to defend themselves from the converging throng of glistening bodies. With oars and firearms, they made a desperate show of defiance before vanishing under the swirling eddy of hungering mouths.

The surviving raft turned left and right, seeking a way out of the feeding zone. Bow up, it engaged all three outboards. Up at the bow, a gunner worked the cannon to cut a lane before them. An arc of glowing tracers carved a furrow in the infested water. Crimson gouts rose in a shower forty feet ahead of the raft's nose. The RHIB, prow raised, broke from the ring of carnivores at top speed on a course toward open water.

The sea swelled before the racing raft. An island of living flesh breached the surface, a bladed tail slashing the water. One of the sea's largest predators had been drawn to the killing pool. The mosasaur turned its snout toward the closing craft. The gate-mouth yawned open and rows of ivory colored knives lined the crimson maw.

The raft jinked hard to starboard. It heeled over in a sudden correction to carry itself around the monster lying in its path. The mosasaur swerved to remain in the RHIB's way. Too late, the pilot turned the bow to port. The raft skimmed alongside the body of the great beast, flat hull sliding the length of the slippery hide. It re-entered the water bow first at the end of a lazy spin. The impact hurled men into the water. The craft slewed sideways, all forward momentum gone. The rotors found purchase once more as the mosasaur plunged out of sight.

Leaving men treading water behind, the RHIB motored away only to explode from the water, driven skyward off the snout of the sixty-foot saurian returning to the surface. Men dropped into the foaming green. The raft landed, upended, the motors dying as they flooded.

Lee Hammond lowered his scopes. It was over. The rest had stopped watching long before him. It was hard to witness. These men had come to kill them. But for all that, this fate felt extreme. This world, this time, stripped everything down to kill or be killed, eat or be eaten. A realization that was as raw as it was cold. And all the more resonant for their own narrow escape in the crocodilian swamp. It brought the Rangers no satisfaction to see their enemies die this way.

Byrus leaned on the railing, watching the scene of horror now distant in their wake.

"Tartarii," he said in a whisper.

"Better them than us," Lee said.

"I've seen enough. This isn't fun anymore," Jimbo said. "So, how do we get home?" Chaz said.

Henning Bohrs sank into the bottle-green water. It was as warm as a drawn bath.

He shed his vest and weaponry and stroked for the surface. Below him, he could see dark shapes drifting past. Enormous shapes.

Bohrs broke the surface, hands reaching for a bit of detritus floating there. He clawed for purchase, feet kicking. It was the body of a man he knew as Torst. Or part of his body, a torso snapped in half at the waistline, ropes of guts trailing in the chop. He kicked away, frantic to get away from the man-turned-bait.

Other voices could be heard. Men crying out in rage or terror or agony. Hoarse voices coming from sources out of sight over the top of green swells. One man could be heard cursing God in Serbian.

A broad fin cut the surface, and Bohrs rose on the swell it created. A long, shiny body coursed close by, a reddish eye turning to lock on him. A tail raised a wavelet as the beast changed tack to bring its jaws to bear on this new temptation. The merc dropped under the water, turning toward the mosasaur now coming about to aim its long snout his way. His fingers found the silver bracelet on his wrist. He tore his eyes, stinging with salt, from the advancing monster to tab the controls on the device.

Bohrs would die one day. But not here. Not now.

The saurian powered forward to snap its jaws closed on empty water where there had been a wriggling morsel a half-second before. Its prey was gone, leaving only an icy spray of bubbles behind. The lost morsel forgotten, the great beast turned toward other shapes still paddling above.

33

A PLAN COMES TOGETHER

"These were not my men. These were not my orders." Jason Taan sat at the end of the chart table, regarding the men standing before him. He was defiant, his lips pressed white with contained anger.

"Did you have some sort of security protocol set-up in advance? A fail-safe?" Lee Hammond asked.

"There were contingencies, of course. I am a man of some value. Attacks and abduction are always a danger."

"Maybe he snuck something by us. Found a way to reach out to his people," Boats said.

"You reviewed the video I made before sending it off. Did I blink my eyes to send a message in code? Perhaps I used mental telepathy."

"You don't exactly fill us with trust, Taan," Lee said.

"I could just as easily have been killed as you. Why would I wish for a direct confrontation? And have you asked yourself how these men traveled to this time and to this place? If I had that capability, I would not have needed to contract you." Taan's grip on his ire was slipping. He spat the last words.

Morris Tauber said, "Contracted? Nice. That's what you call it when you drugged me and smuggled me to Shanghai?" He took a step toward Taan.

"Slow down, Doc. He's right about one thing. His outfit can't travel through time."

"It's Harnesh," Taan said.

"What's your connection to him?" Lee said.

"Harnesh? Neil Harnesh? The Indian billionaire?"

"That's the one."

"He's a rival. A competitor. Dr. Tauber can tell you, I only learned about your damned device when security officers of mine bought a stolen database from a hacker. I was looking for a leg up in oil transshipment. Instead, we found records of this mad experiment."

"And we're all here because of your hobby," Lee said.

"Yes. Treasure hunting. Antiquities. Should have taken up something safer, I suppose," Taan said.

"Like porno," Boats put in.

Lee took a seat at the table across from Taan. He poured them both a mug of coffee from a carafe. He tilted a flask into his and offered Taan the same. The billionaire waved him away, taking up the mug and sipping.

"So, Harnesh played his hand. It won't be the last time. You understand that he wants all of us dead now, right?" Lee said.

Taan nodded.

"Whatever's going on back in The Now, he's taken over your operations. He's filled the void you left. Could that happen? Would Beijing allow that?"

"A hostile takeover. A *lethal* takeover. I have made a study of Sir Neal. Knowing the man is knowing his next move. He would take over my holdings through an intermediary. The loyalty of my subordinates has a price. Especially with me absent. Through threats or greed, it would be a simple enough thing for a man like Harnesh to run my interests through a puppet. The Central Committee could be kept in the dark. Or bought."

"Harnesh isn't going to sit still. He'll keep sending more teams against us. Next time it might be a gunship," Lee said.

"Or a helo or three. We'd have no defense against an air strike," Boats said.

"We have no exit path, guys," Morris said. "Harnesh holds the gate, our only way back."

"That can change," Jimbo spoke for the first time. "We find a way or make one."

"Who said that?" Lee said.

"Hannibal."

"Cool. Love *The A-Team*," Boats said.

Being a former SEAL with ten years in the Navy, Boats was the natural choice to lead the op.

"We have to be a ways over the horizon when we drop," he told the Rangers. "The last thing we need is more of those drones fucking up our day. We raft in close, go the rest of the way underwater. That means strong swimmers only. Geteye's going as my number two. He's never been a SEAL, but I can vouch that the man's half-fish. Since I've never rolled out with any of you guys, I'm gonna need your word on how good you are in the water."

"I used to lifeguard. Two summers," Lee said. "At the YMCA or open ocean?" Boats said.

"Cotton Bayou on the Shoals."

"You swim for real or just chase pussy?"

"Top of my class at five hundred yard three-style."

"Ever dive?"

"Scuba-dived a few times. Antigua. Trinidad. Barrier Reefs. I can hack. I wouldn't bullshit you, sailor."

"I'll take Hammond, then. Anyone else? No heroes. I know you can fight, but I need swimmers," Boats said.

"Raised in a desert," Jimbo said.

"I don't float so good," Chaz said.

"I won a swimming medal at summer camp," Bat said.

"When was this?" Boats said.

"I was ten."

"Mazel tov. No girls this trip. Anyone else?"

Shan raised a hand.

"You swim, buddy?" Boats said.

"Special Naval Operations, PLAN."

"Ever been on a diving op, Shan?"

"Gulf of Aden. 2010."

"Killed a few pirates, huh?"

"They do not take Chinese ships anymore."

Boats laughed. Shan allowed himself a fleeting smile.

"Welcome along. That's my team," the SEAL said.

34

TO THE GULF

"We are marching."

Samuel woke Dwayne shortly after dawn. He sat up from the cot assigned him in one of the log bunkhouses. He held his fingers to his temples, his skull feeling too small for his brain. The world was tinged in red. Every pulse beat was like twin hammers in his ears.

All around, men were gathering weapons and pulling on boots. Dwayne marveled at their constitutions. These guys partied hard until late into the night. They drained barrels of the skunkiest ale Dwayne had ever smelled or tasted before switching to a stronger drink that was like vodka but not clear. There were oaths taken and prayers to the gods and more than one fistfight. The last thing he recalled was stumbling over bodies on the longhouse floor to reach his cot.

"Marching?" he said.

"The portents are good. The seers found promising omens in the entrails of this morning's sacrifice," Samuel said.

"Please tell me it wasn't a human sacrifice."

"A goat. That smell is it roasting for breakfast."

Dwayne's stomach clenched at the greasy odor that permeated the bunkhouse. He shoved Samuel aside and made it outside where he knelt in the dirt to heave his guts up. The ale was skunkier coming up. Some men leaned on muskets and snorted at him.

Samuel joined him, carrying Dwayne's sneakers.

"We're going with them," he said. "Now?"

"Njarl says that you are lucky for him."

"Nuh-jarl? Is that the guy with one eye?"

"Njarl Hadradi. He claims your arrival is an omen. A good one. These men prize luck above everything else. They want you by their side."

"What the hell did I do to impress this crowd?"

"You sang a song to them."

"Shit. No."

"I think it was ABBA."

"Shit. That movie. Caroline's watched it like a hundred times."

"You got very drunk."

"No shit."

One-Eye's, Njarl's, voice boomed as he approached along the muddy lane between the cabins and tents. He was in a chainmail shirt and leather choker. A bandolier of paper cartridges across his chest. A brace of pistols in his sash. A helmet with a snarling face mask under his arm. A two-handed sword slung on his back.

"Mamma Mia!" he roared and clapped the Ranger on the back. Dwayne staggered under the blow. He couldn't believe that he'd stepped over this man's snoring body only a few hours before. Njarl looked hale and hardy and ready to slay a dragon.

"Yeah. *Ja*. Thanks for the invitation." Dwayne tried to work up some enthusiasm. The best he could do was a weak smile.

Njarl spoke some more to Samuel and him. Dwayne couldn't follow any of it. The big bastard strode off, shouting to some men loading goods into a two-wheeled cart.

"We go to lay siege to Nadikakahaana," Samuel said. "It's a

Mughal fortress at the mouth of the Mississippi. Roughly where you'd think of as New Orleans."

"I'm guessing we're not walking there," Dwayne said.

"We'll be joining the fleet to sail across the Gulf."

"That's just great. A boat ride too," Dwayne said before puking again.

———

A half-day's march brought them to the coastline and a sheltered harbor. Dwayne was allowed to ride at the head of the column with Njarl and his housecarls. They rode ponies ahead of a thousand troops on foot followed by a baggage train of ox-drawn carts, mules, and camels. Along with the Norsemen marched near-naked locals carrying bundles of spears.

Cooler air blew in off the sea under a cloudless sky. Dwayne's head was clearing. The sun felt good on his skin. He was surprised to find that he was getting hungry. He found himself enjoying the bizarre experience of joining an army that never was in a war that could never be. Riding a horse to a battle with men in armor carrying antiquated weapons. The smell of leather and sweat and the calls of warriors in foreign voices. It wasn't his cause or his battle, but he began to feel the familiar thrill of anticipation.

He had to remind himself again that he didn't belong here.

No dog in this hunt.

"We don't really have a choice in this, right?" Dwayne said. He was riding alongside Samuel on a painted pony. He turned against the high cantle to look back at the dense cloud of dust rising behind them from the van.

"Remember that I'm not the only one who will be looking for you here, Dwayne," Samuel said.

"Safety in numbers?"

"Something like that. Were we to desert, Njarl would take it as a slight. Or a betrayal."

"And we don't need more enemies. You think Harnesh's guys will find us here?"

"This campaign is reaching something of a chokepoint," Samuel said. "The Northmen and their allies are all joining in this siege. Armies are on the march from all over the Yucatan. More will join us at sea from ports in what you know as Cuba and Florida. This is a historical turning point here."

"The guys looking for me will be drawn here too."

"They could already be among us."

They arrived at a bay set back in the protection of a curved peninsula. Dwayne guessed it was Vera Cruz.

Along the sandy beaches and across the dunes was spread a city of colorful tents surrounded by earthworks lined with spikes. Embrasures were dug in the sand for long-barreled cannons pointed at the sea. Banners flew from poles. Horns sounded at their approach.

Ships were at anchor on the dappled gray water. There were sleek shallow-draft vessels lined with oars that resembled Viking longboats except for the lateen-rigged sails hung from triple masts. Hundreds of barges lay moored with huge, bell-shaped brass mortars housed inside and protected by high iron-plated hulls. Dominating the armada were five dreadnaughts with three gun decks each and hundreds of cannon behind ports on either side. These ships had broad decks and square-rigged sails with raised quarterdecks trimmed in brass. They resembled English ships of the line from the age of sail with the addition of decorative shields down either flank, and high prows carved in the shapes of roaring dragons. The other difference was long sweeps drawn inward to an oar deck just above the waterline.

It was an invasion fleet. It would carry tens of thousands of men and mounts across the Gulf to the shoals of Louisiana. According to Samuel, this was a major push to take the Mississippi Delta from the Mughals. That would allow the Northmen to own the seaward access of what they called *Sturslaange Elv,* Big Serpent River. From there, they could deny the Mughal forts of supplies as well as sending their shallow-draft creek ships upriver on raids that would break the decades-long stalemate.

An eerily similar strategy to the one employed by the Union army during the War Between the States. Dwayne had gone through a phase of reading books about the Civil War. Played right, Grant's grand strategy could be just as successful for the Vikings.

"Do they succeed?" Dwayne said. "What do you mean?" Samuel said.

"This army. Do they win the day? Take the city?"

"It is a long siege. In the end, they win. It takes the next fifty years, but the Northmen will dominate the continent from sea to sea."

"Good to know we're on the winning side."

"This is not your fight. Nor mine."

"Just wanted to know how the movie ends," Dwayne said.

They rode down the sandy slope into the bowl of the harbor at a gallop, horns blaring and men shouting a welcome.

35

HOSTILE WATER

After three tries and the tweaking of multiple algorithms, Morris Tauber opened a mission-optimal field into The Now, A post-midnight arrival in the Gulf of Chiriqui thirty miles to the north of Isla de Coiba off the Pacific coast of Panama. Boats ran the Zodiac's Evinrudes at half speed to reduce noise. The lights of cargo craft dotted the horizon far to the west, the shipping lane of heavy carriers coming to and from the Canal Zone. To the east, the coastline was invisible under the haze of torrential rain that washed away the stars. The glow of anvil lightning pulsed at the heart of a vast front of dark clouds.

By the time the raft came to a stop, a hammering rain was falling. The chop whipped up to high white caps under a punishing wind. A tropical storm was building to its full fury.

"This is good!" Boats shouted to be heard over the thunder rolling above them. "Good luck for us!"

Gripping a side of the bobbing Zodiac, Lee wondered what bad luck looked like. But he understood. The storm would provide cover for their approach. Despite the howling winds and rain, he was running with sweat under the neoprene wetsuit. He'd be happier when they got into the cooler water. Boats held a waterproof pad out to him. Isla Jicarita was five miles south of their position. The floating platform they sought was a mile or so west of the islet's southern tip. Or so they hoped. A drone recon was risky and probably impossible in this weather.

"What now? We go?" Lee called out.

"We go. Gear up." Boats undid bungees and handed tanks to the others. They strapped up, put on flippers, swim gloves, and buoyancy compensation vests before slipping on their masks. Then the tanks went on. Waterproof weapons packs were buckled on last. Boats moved from one man to the other, pulling straps snug and making sure the seal around the face-masks was tight, and mouthpieces and lines were firmly in place and untangled. Last minute checks of regulators and gauges before Geteye was the first to drop over the side.

Lee and Shan managed to lift a tubular sea scooter from the shifting deck and slide it over the nacelle to Geteye floating alongside. Gripping the control handles, the Ethiopian was lying atop the diver propulsion vehicle like a surfer awaiting the next curler. Shan was next, and Boats and Lee levered his DPV into the water to him. Lee slipped into the water, dragging his scooter after him with the SEAL's help.

The other three rode the surface, rising and falling on the swells, watching Boats undo the cocks on the Zodiac. The raft began taking on water in a rush and was soon down, flooded and pulled under the chop by the weight of the outboards. The SEAL kicked clear as the raft sank, propelling his DPV under his own power to join the others. The prow of the raft slid under the water at the bottom of a trough. They kicked toward one another, keeping each other in sight on the heaving sea. The storm current was strong and trying hard to separate them.

"That's my last Zodiac!" he called to the others.

"We'll go shopping! Whatever you want is on me!" Lee shouted back.

"Check hoses. Check levels." The SEAL was all business now.

Thumbs up all around. Each man broke a light stick dangling on a lanyard around their necks.

"On me!" Boats shouted before placing his mouthpiece in his teeth. He adjusted ballast on his DPV and sank out of sight. The others followed.

The pull of the currents grew weaker as they sank through the dark water and down into a silent world. At a depth of thirty feet, they powered up their DPVs. Each snapped on his headlamp, the beams turning the black sea to dingy emerald. Boats pointed at the GPS pad secured to his wrist and stabbed a finger south. The powerful Sea Jets pulled them forward in the wake of the SEAL leading them deeper into the murk.

36

DARLA

To the south and east, the enormous, metal-clad box that was Dex-Tan 11 bobbed on an angry sea buffeted by winds gusting to gale force.

In the three years since its construction, the huge floating rig had acquired a patina of orange rust on the exposed surfaces of steel sheeting that covered three sides of the super-structure. There was no roof. The cage of carbon steel alloy was left exposed to the elements from the top and the open end at one side. Basically, the Taan-financed rig served as a floating boathouse built exclusively to house the *Ocean Raj,* a vessel no one aboard the rig had ever seen. Jason Taan and his engineers were unaware until it was too late that the garage was actually an up-sized version of the Tauber Tube. It allowed for the vanishing act that took the *Raj,* and its crew, and passengers to the world as it was seventy million years prior. And took the boss along with it.

Now the huge barn of a platform sat in the roiling sea, waiting for the *Raj* to return. Year after year of patient vigil. Many aboard the rig had no idea what precisely they were waiting for. But they were well-paid and well-employed to watch sonar and video monitors set to scan the seas around them. This included an array of sensors that monitored local variations in temperature. In particular, they watched for the sudden drops in temps that would mean that their guest was returning. It was a waiting game. The regular crewmembers were becoming proficient in Spanish from listening to pop music stations out of Panama City. *¿Qué sopá, pelao?*

The crew shack at the aft end was manned by a skeleton crew on two-week rotations. Their only job, most days, was to wait for further orders. They ate and slept on board the rig. For entertainment, there was Wi-Fi and a library of BluRays. For exercise, there was a gym room with a treadmill, stationary bike, and weight machine. During good weather, they could also run laps on the gangway that spanned three sides of the rig atop the massive ballast tanks that kept them afloat. When off-duty, they were helicoptered to Panama City for a two-week respite at the Dex-Tan compound situated in the extensive dry-dock and storage facility owned by the company. The compound was on Margarita Island, and one of many Chinese-owned port complexes at the Pacific mouth of the canal. Dex-Tan was the holding company owned by Jason Taan and the entity to which the rig was registered.

The tedium was broken that night by the approaching tropical depression. It was upgraded to an early-season tropical storm and given the name "Darla." According to protocol, the weather conditions required them to move the rig into port. They radioed for a tug out of the maritime center at Embajada de China in P.C. The tug was on its way, a few hours out.

In the meantime, Jiao-Long Ho, effectively the skipper of this massive, powerless raft, was busying himself with the preparations for their upcoming move. He only had four men with any real nautical experience. The other five men aboard were security, gunmen. But in the current situation, Ho could issue them orders, and they were obligated to follow. He drilled them on the procedures for hauling up the four enormous anchors that held the rig in place. They would need to be raised ahead of the arrival of the tug. Each man was given tasks such as securing gear and making sure hatches were sealed tight. There was much to do before the gargantuan floating boathouse could be taken to safe portage in the lee of one of the barrier islands.

Ho was an experienced hand, proud of this assignment and determined to do his best to secure his charge. At forty-two, he was well past the age when he would ever be given the captaincy of an actual, ocean-going vessel. After many tests and examinations, the closest he ever came to a commander's stripes was second mate on the *Xiānggǎng lánhuā*, at eight-hundred feet in length it was just under Panama dimensions and small by Dex-Tan standards.

This motorless rig, a sea-going garage for all purposes, was the nearest he would ever come to having the helm. He meant to see his duty through, and the rig safely moored to weather the worst Darla had to offer.

The satellite weather updates showed the system moving west off the landmass after ravaging the Gulf all the way down from the Yucatan. Rather than losing power traveling over the isthmus, the storm was building. It would be a Cat One hurricane by the time it reached the rig's mooring. Possibly Cat Two. A mild storm, but one that still posed an existential threat to the structure with its steep flat planes and high center of gravity.

The reports on his screens and the printouts from Navimeteo nautical weather services assured Captain Ho that the tug would beat the worst of the storm to the rig. They'd have the cushion of three hours or more to get the tug in place and be underway. Even so, the effects of Darla could already be felt. The deck under his feet, in the room he insisted on calling "the bridge," shifted up and down in an irregular rhythm. A coffee mug and pencils slid off the chart table along with a pile of maps and stack of meteorological reports. He secured them in a bin.

The radio crackled, and a voice hailed him first in English and then in Mandarin.

"Xia Gang Tuo Three-One to Dex-Tan Ten-One."

"This is D-T Ten-One. Jiao-Long Ho, captain. Respond," Ho said into the hand mike.

"We can see your lights, Ten-One. We are approaching from south-southeast of your position. Is everything prepared?"

"Can you give me an estimated time of arrival?"

"Inside of thirty minutes. We have a following sea at ten knots. It is making maneuvering a bit challenging. We will require directions."

"I will guide you in myself," Ho said. He could see the blip on the sonar on the bearing the Three-One transmitted.

Switching to the onboard tannoy system, Ho depressed the send button on a mike mounted on the control console and ordered the crew to hoist anchor. He could picture them moving to the gas-powered capstan winches that would draw the weights and the heavy chains off the seafloor. Voices returned to him over the console speakers. Each of the four capstan stations called in. They were freeing the rig in preparation of the tug's arrival.

Though a challenge even for experienced pilots on a placid sea, a rig floating free presented less of a danger than if it were chained. The tug skipper and his crew could better anticipate the movement of the huge floating platform as it surrendered to the same sea conditions as the smaller vessel. Chained down, the rig could act as a massive flail, rocking one way only to be whipped back by the weight of the anchors. Free to roll, the tug could match its attitude and bring its prow into the docking notch at the aft section designed for this purpose. Still, a daunting piece of seamanship by all aboard the vessels. Rather than being designed for being hauled, the rig was set up to be pushed across the open sea by a tug craft like the *Xia Gang Tuo,* a powerful 4000 class maneuvering vessel. The skipper would expertly pilot the prow of his tug into a V-shaped inverted wedge of forged steel set at the platform's aft section. The big four-thousand kilo-watt engines would power up and move the rig, slow but steady, to an anchorage in a deep-water cove on the east shore of Isla de Coiba.

"D-T Ten-One to *Xia Gang Tuo.* Join me on channel two," Ho said.

"Roger that. Channel two."

Ho slipped on a rain slicker and secured the hood over his head. He removed a handheld radio from a battery stand and exited the shed. The driving rain did little to cut the sauna heat on the exposed weather deck. Inside the slicker, Ho was instantly greased with sweat. He scanned the horizon to the south, searching for the running lights of the tug. The line between sea and sky was a blur with the effects of the storm and low cloud cover. The lights atop the rig would be visible from the tug's bridge long before the opposite was true. The smaller tug was still invisible over the curve of the planet even from the height of the deck Ho stood on.

The deck rolled under his feet, the rig floating free now, turning to port in a motion so slow it was almost imperceptible. The anchors would be aboard by now. Ho held a hand across his brow to shield his eyes from the downpour. The heavy rain created a haze he couldn't see through. The man at the forward port capstan was out there in the dark but concealed from his view. His eye did catch movement just below him. A dark shape was moving up a ladder on the outside of the port float tanks. No one, not crew or security, had any business on that ladder at this time. Ho felt an anger rise in him, a burning fist in his gut. This was his time to show his masters what a capable officer he could be. And here was someone playing about like a monkey on a sea ladder.

He leaned well out over the railing to shout at the figure below. A streak of lightning tore the sky in half, turning midnight to high noon for a fraction of second. The sudden glare showed not one but two figures climbing the ladder, men in slick black suits coming from the sea like ghosts.

THE WAITING SEA

The Norse started everything with a party. And, with the gathering of the armies, there was reason to celebrate. The makeshift settlement along the Gulf shore was home to families as well as soldiers. Wives and children were encamped there.

Fires were built and lit. Kegs were tapped. Mountains of salted fish were set on long tables under the starry sky. In their own camps, the native troops roasted wild pigs trapped during an afternoon hunt in the brush-choked dunes.

Lord Magnussen, a housecarl of the imperial family and cousin to Emperor Gustav back in København, was the highest-ranking official present and de facto supreme commander for the armada and the invasion. A big bastard in a long bear-skin cloak worn over a shining cuirass and striped breeches. His silver hair was worn in long braids banded with gold. He climbed atop a stage of planks and barrels and addressed the thousands gathered on the beach. He shouted words of war and promises of victory that were echoed by criers set among the crowd. He raised a sword that flared in the firelight, and all swords were raised in a forest of blades as the men shared in a shouted oath.

Then the drinking started and, though he'd sworn "never again," Dwayne joined in if only to be drunk enough to answer the pleas to sing more ABBA songs to his hosts. He thought again of Caroline. She was never far from his thoughts. The desire to tell her about teaching Swedish pop songs to a bunch of Vikings made him even more anxious to get back to her.

They ate, and they drank, and they sang. And Dwayne recalled little of it except a brief bare-knuckle fight over a chubby little blonde. He wanted to think the fight was over his refusal to go into a tent with the girl. Some mile-wide fucker with three teeth called him a name, and Dwayne knew his manhood had been called into question. His sucker punch landed with little effect, and they rolled on the sand awhile until Samuel broke it up by dashing a bucket to splinters over the skull of the larger man. Following that, the evening was a fire-lit blur.

And Dwayne could only remember that much because of the reminder of a raised weal under one eye where a fist or elbow had landed. At least it drew some attention away from his new hangover. He woke on the sand with the sun hanging over the surf, trying to pry his lids open. Samuel was seated by him and offered him a mango from a bowl by his side. Dwayne shook his head and regretted it. The simple motion made his vision swim.

"What was that fight about?" Dwayne asked.

"Bjarn's sister wanted to have sex with you, and you refused," Samuel said.

"And he called me a name."

"I don't know how you know that. But, yes, he did."

"And I hit him. And he hit me. What did you say to break it up?"

"I told them that your mate was lost to you and that you took an oath not to enjoy another woman until your sword had tasted blood in battle."

"Bet they loved that," Dwayne said.

"I saw a few of them weeping," Samuel said and tossed the empty bowl aside.

"They don't happen to have coffee here, do they?" Dwayne massaged his temples and managed only to move the pain from his eyes to the crown of his head.

"As a matter of fact, they do." Samuel stood and reached out a hand to help Dwayne up.

"I'll take a grande black. Lead the way."

———

The boats were stocked and manned in a remarkably short time. Goodbyes were said, and the boats launched into the surf. Supplies were hauled aboard, and men clambered up ladders and nets to take their places aboard the longboats and men-of-war.

Horses, cows, and other mounts and livestock were being loaded by crane into the bellies of fat cargo ships. Crates of live chickens and turkeys along with pallets of salted pork barrels and great wheels of cheese. Kegs of ale and spirits as well were hauled aboard each ship. It was all performed with machine-like efficiency under the watch of bosuns roaring orders to the sweating men.

Dwayne and Samuel joined Njarl and his closest guard in a longboat that was rowed out to the armada, swaying in the anchor chains well beyond the lazy surf. Njarl stood at the prow, anxious to be aboard his dreadnaught. The angry visage of a dragon with splayed claws and spread wings glowered down from the prow as they approached. The ship was the height of a four-story building from the waterline to the gunwales. The long oars were drawn inboard, and boarding nets dropped down the hull to allow the passengers of approaching boats to climb to the main deck.

"What part of the year is this?" Dwayne said. He nodded toward dark clouds low on the horizon over the gulf.

"It is maybe a month before the winter solstice," Samuel said.

"So, after hurricane season."

"The seers chose their goat wisely."

After the long climb aboard, Dwayne and Samuel toured the ship. Below the main deck were the three gun decks with black-barreled cannons tied down tight, and trunnions chocked. Every spare inch of deck space was piled with cannon balls and canister shot secured to the decking under stout nets to prevent rolling. The walls were white-washed, and decks were smooth from a recent sanding. Njarl kept a tight ship. Beneath the gun levels were the ranks of oars and benches for the rowers. They sat now, stripped to their waists in the muggy closeness, and drank watered vinegar and ate slabs of cheese and salted bread. They bore no chains. These men were not slaves but skilled laborers, well-trained and prized for their experience at the sweeps. In a pitched battle at sea, a captain couldn't rely on inexperienced oarsmen pulling against their will and self-interest.

Dwayne knew this from his own experience aboard a Phoenician warship. These old wooden ships took great skill to pilot and maneuver. Every hand at every oar had to be adept.

Crew quarters were spread through the ship wherever there was room. And there was little room available with a full complement of crew aboard as well as several hundred soldiers and passengers for the next several days' travel. And they might be anchored for weeks off the delta. No one could predict how long the siege of shoal fortresses would take.

Back in the sunlight of the open deck, Samuel learned that they would be quartered under the shelter of sections of sailcloth strung above the main deck as protection against the weather. They would lie on the deck wherever there was space for them. Samuel had arranged for sheepskin covers and some woven blankets as well as other supplies they might need. That included a rifle and a pistol for each of them as well as a sword and dagger apiece. Dwayne's outfit, borrowed an age ago from the hunter he rode to this parallel existence, was in sorry shape. He traded it for a woolen jerkin, leather belt, and breeches. He kept his sneakers, still the most serviceable footwear available to him. Common footwear was not made for comfort in this time and place. His New Balance cross-trainers were wrapped in fresh rawhide strips and drew little attention other than derision from his hosts.

Dwayne watched the armada get underway from a forward port rail. Orders were called. Men worked to turn the capstans and draw anchors on board, heavy chains rumbling and clanking. Pulley wheels squealed as sails were dropped and dogged. Curiously, the ships of the Northmen used a tiller to move the rudder rather than a wheel. To steer a vessel of this size took three hugely muscled men responding to the barks of a sailing master relaying the orders of the captain, Njarl, who paced the high quarter-deck, gesturing this way and that, giving orders that were called out along the decks in sing-song rhythm.

Out on the placid Gulf waters, the longboats dropped oars and pulled to bring their prows about to the harbor opening. Each pulled its own long string of mortar barges connected by yards of tarred ropes thick as a man's wrist and chains of rusted steel. The longboats were the first to make for the open sea, making way for the men-of-war to come about. The oars were slid outward on greased locks with a tremor that shook the timbers beneath Dwayne's feet. Fully sixty feet in length and adzed and planed from a single length of timber, the giant oars took a crew of four men each to pull them through the water. From the lower decks, the beat of a drum started up, punctuated by shouted orders from a powerful set of lungs. First port oars worked then starboard and, slow as a minute hand around a clock face, the big ship's bow swung toward the open sea.

The big sails caught a seaward wind blowing off the shoreline and filled with a crack and boom. With sails taut and the oars turning steady, the ship made its way to the gulf, bow down, and leaving a milky furrow in its wake. The rest of the armada followed suit, falling into a loose arrowhead formation behind Njarl's ship. The one-eyed housecarl was up in the rigging now, shouting at the ships aft of him. He laughed and shook a fist.

"It's a race, right?" Dwayne said to Samuel, who had joined him at the rail.

"It is. Njarl wagered with Dalgaard that he would be first from the port and into open sea. The rest place bets as well," Samuel said.

Dwayne moved sternward along the rail for a better view of the competition. The other ships were closing to narrow the distance as well as block the way of the others. Their sails were belled, and sweeps out and working. Great gouts of foam exploded up the faces of the fearsome prows. Two ships drew too close to one another. Oars struck one another in a tangle and then shattered like matchsticks as the vessels ground along each other's hull with a terrible sound. Dwayne thought he saw a man spill from aloft into the churning water at the bottom of the momentary gap formed between the towering sides before they slammed together again.

Two more ships struck at an angle, the rigging from their top spars snarling together until one ship leaned hard starboard taking a cross-tie and a jumble of line with it. The result for the damaged ship was a long tear to a mainsail that luffed useless, hanging from its spar like so much laundry.

Through all this, Njarl howled and brayed and shrieked brazen insults to the amusement of his crew who roared with laughter.

"Hope the emperor's cousin has a sense of humor, the way Njarl's fucking with him," Dwayne said.

"These men live by the moment. By the day," Samuel said.

"Not that they have a lot of choice living in a world unloved by God."

"And where they know that death waits for them over the horizon."

Njarl's ship was first to sea and swung about to follow the longboats and barges north to the unfriendly shore and war.

38

BODY COUNT

S han was first up the ladder with Lee Hammond climbing behind. He looked up through the driving rain to see movement against the lights from the crew shack.

A man was standing at the railing, watching from the deck above them. The hooded figure moved down the rail for a better look. Rather than draw his weapon, Shan waved to the man. The man leaned out farther, calling something lost on the wind. Shan mimed calling back a reply as he climbed toward the man.

The ascent up the ladder was a challenge. The rungs were slippery wet under their bare feet, and the whole platform swung back and forth like a cork. The ladder was sometimes at a ten percent inverted incline, requiring the climbers to hook an arm through the rungs just to maintain their purchase. Shan climbed close enough to hear the shouting man's voice if not his words. He reached the top and slipped over the rail to see a chubby-faced Chinese in a slicker.

"Are you from Dex-Tan?" the man shouted in Mandarin. Shan saw a handheld radio in the man's fist. His other hand gripped the rail for support on the heaving deck.

"They thought you might need help in this storm," Shan shouted back.

The man's smile faded as his eyes traveled over the plastic-encased rifle strapped to the stranger's chest. His eyes grew wider at the sight of the bearded white man swinging a leg over the rail. He turned to run. Shan caught a handful of the slicker's hood and yanked the man back into a chokehold. The radio tumbled to the deck and skimmed along the decking into the sea.

Lee covered them with his rifle as Shan dragged the now-unconscious crewman toward the lights of the metal shed. They killed the lights once they were inside. The wind was rattling the sheet-steel walls as the rain hammered the glass. There was a desk with a comm console that crackled with calls for the man who now lay in a puddle on the floor. A pair of open laptops lit the room with animated weather maps on their screens.

"*Xia Gang Tuo* Three-One to Dex-Tan Ten-One. Come in D-T ten-one."

Shan picked up the mike and keyed it. "This is Ten-One. Go ahead."

"Who is this? Is this Ho?"

"Ho is busy elsewhere."

"Who am I speaking to?"

Shan turned to Lee, who didn't speak Mandarin. All he understood were the numbers.

"This is Leong. I am the comm officer."

"Are you ready for us? Anchors free and lines secure?"

"Yes. Slow speed and come ahead."

The shed door slammed open. Lee and Shan turned to see a drenched man stumble in on a spray of rain. He wore military boots and a Molle vest with ammo pouches stuffed with magazines. He regarded the two strangers in wet suits, his hands going for the stubby bullpup rifle that hung on a sling under this arm.

Lee dropped him with a double-tap high to the chest. The

man flopped to the deck, boot soles squeaking on the tiles. Lee finished him with a headshot.

The glass of the shed imploded. Lee and Shan dropped low, both sending fire through the steel sheeting in the general direction they determined the fire had come from.

"Can't stay here," Lee called over the wind whistling through the fresh bullet holes. He was lying on his back, slapping a new magazine in place.

"We cannot leave them the radio," Shan said. The mike was swinging free on its cord. The speakers squawked with calls from the tug, unintelligible in the rising noise of the storm.

More fire from outside. This time drilling down through the roof of the shed. Lee kicked himself across the wet tile, loosing a long burst up through the ceiling. Shan got to a knee and took out the radio and computer array with a half mag. Sparks and plastic shards went flying.

They rolled out a door on the opposite end to a rain-swept deck. Automatic fire sprayed down in their wake. Lee swung his weapon left and right hunting for movement above. A shadow passed between struts. He gave the shadow some lead and fired controlled bursts. The movement stopped, the shooter now concealed or hit. He turned to follow Shan, moving toward the aft section at a run.

A pair of men in yellow Dex-Tan slickers climbed toward them from a lower deck. No weapons in view. Shan met them halfway down the steps, weapon raised. He barked orders at them. They raised splayed hands, eyes crazed with fright. Shan barked again, and they shouted back replies, speaking over one another.

Lee crouched at the head of the stairs, weapon up and scanning the superstructure above.

"What're they saying?" he called.

"They are crewmen. They were raising the anchors," Shan shouted back.

"How much security?"

"Five guards."

One dead. Maybe another dead or wounded. That left three gunmen on board a vessel the length of two football fields.

"We can hunt, or we can hide," Lee said. He glanced back to Shan, holding a weapon on the two frightened crewmen kneeling on the rolling deck.

Sparks sprayed them, struck off the metal piping above them.

"You hide! I hunt!" Lee shouted. He rolled across the deck to the shelter of a bulkhead. Shan shoved the two crewmen away sternward.

Lee belly crawled backward, elbows and knees, to a hatchway and rolled inside. A narrow catwalk followed the interior wall of the boathouse around three sides. Above them, the carbon steel arches of the massive Tauber Tube were black against the lowering clouds. Staying pressed to the wall and moving from shadow to shadow, he swiveled his head up and down and side to side in search of movement, eyes sighting over the top of the rifle in his fists.

The guy he'd waxed back in the shed was armed but not in body armor. No NODs gear either. Chances were these guys, no matter what kind of high-priced talent Harnesh hired, had their edge blunted after months of tedious guard duty. All this time at sea, stationary and waiting for a threat that might never come, might have made them complacent. It was something. But Lee knew better than to count on these guys not being as sharp as him. And they knew this floating shithouse better than he did. He had to at least even the odds before the tug got here.

39

HAMMER AND ANVIL

The broad delta of the Mississippi was protected by a series of fortified islands dotted around the great river's mouth. These were situated to discourage approach by enemy ships. The angled walls housed batteries of long-range cannons set to create a deadly storm of enfilading fire that could shred any vessel that sailed within range.

The walled Mughal city of Nadikakahaana sat far north of the estuary lakes Pontchartrain and Maurepas, called Padapaanee and Thodapaanee in this time and place. This was more securely situated than New Orleans as well as higher above sea level. And all along the river route were fortresses and earthworks bristling with guns.

The bold plan of the Northmen's armada was to hammer away at a pair of large forts set on Grand Isle and Mendicant Island. Once those were reduced, they'd be assaulted by ground troops landing in smaller boats. When the forts were taken, the longboats would make their way into Barataria Bay and through the marshy inlets to arrive at the river above the island forts. From there, they would choke off the Mughal's path to the sea and the forts. The guns along the ramparts would be turned to the sea, leaving the landward walls unprotected. In this way, the forts could be brought down one by one.

That was the plan anyway. And, like most plans, it would not survive the first encounter.

Dwayne was welcomed up onto the command deck of Njarl's ship. From there, he could see the mortar barges anchored in a half-moon pattern a few miles offshore of the fort at the eastern tip of Grand Isle. Night and day, the huge brass mortars belched five-hundred-pound iron balls and round-shaped stones in long arcs to land in and around the sloped faces of the stone fort. Often the shot was heated in furnaces and soared like comets trailing white smoke. These were launched to ignite fires within the fort's walls. Four days of shelling and there was still no sign of a blaze in the Mughal position.

And that was when they could see the coastline at all. A thick pall of smoke from the Mughal's return fire enclosed it most of the time. The Viking barges were at the extreme range of the fort's long guns. Most shots fell far short, raising gouts of water within the half-circle. Their second night in place, a heated mortar round fired from the fort struck a barge abeam, igniting the powder stores. The flat-bottomed vessel erupted in a flare that lit the sea like sunrise. The concussive impact was felt by all watching from the main fleet at anchor miles away on the open water. Encouraged, the defenders picked up the pace of their fire. But after a week of exchanges, they had no further success, their charges falling useless into the sea. All the while, the balls from the mortar barges fell with predictable accuracy to weaken the stone walls of the fort.

Through a telescope, when the wind had cleared the shore of smoke, Dwayne could see that the seaward walls of the fortress were marred by craters. A tower at a corner of the walls was partially collapsed. He thought he could see a wisp of black smoke rising from the fort's interior. Maybe a heated round found something combustible. Maybe the Mughals and their conscripts were, even now, inside fighting a fire to keep it from spreading.

As epic as the fire and counterfire of the siege were, the most furious fighting was going on across the water inside the ring of fire. Three longboats sailed back and forth within range of the land-based cannon as a screen against Mughal vessels that set out from the shore on sallies against the mortar barges. These long-boats were packed with musketeers, and each had a small-bore cannonade mounted in the prow.

Lateen-rigged catches and barks made their way from the sally port of the fortress. They sailed across the water toward the anchored barges. Each small craft bristled with small-caliber cannon, the decks crowded with men bearing muskets and bangalores, intent on breaking the chain that was strangling the island fort.

With suicidal zeal, the longboats rowed to intercept these attacks. Scopes were at a premium and, in the early days, Dwayne had to share with others eager to watch the action. The Norsemen were like a Super Bowl crowd, drinking and cheering and shouting oaths. This was party-time, Viking style. Dwayne saw men grip the handles of their swords or daggers, eyes locked on the far-off action, wishing they were in the bloody mix.

Dwayne watched as a longboat rammed a bark amidships, shattering the oars to flinders all down the port side. Ramps were dropped, and armed men rushed over the boards to leap into the belly of the enemy vessel. All under the cover of withering musket fire from both vessels. It was a dumb show as seen through the lenses, the battle too far away for the sounds to reach him other than the remote pops of muskets. A creamy fog of gun smoke engulfed the entangled boats now turning in the grip of the current, locked on a shared course that carried them closer to the shore. Eventually, they were well within accurate range of the fort's cannon.

A ball dropped close to the embattled boats. A second still

closer raised a drenching tower of water that spilled over the fight and dispelled the pall of smoke. For a few seconds, Dwayne could see the furious melee clearly. Sunlight flashed off spear-points and sword blades. Men were packed close on the deck of the smaller bark, raising and lowering weapons. Pointblank fire from muskets and pistols raised a new cloud of yellow smoke that rose up the masts of both boats to conceal them from view.

He raised his eye from the telescope in time to see the jumbled vessels take a direct hit from a round fired from the fort. It dropped somewhere in the packed mass of skirmishers and raised a dome of animate and inanimate debris. The main mast of the longboat collapsed, falling into the water and creating an anchor about which the stricken vessels spun. A second ball dropped directly into the mess and ignited something aboard one or the other of the boats.

The Mughals sacrificed their own crew in an inferno that, in a fiery instant, shredded the longboat and bark to matchwood. All that remained was a mist drifting over broken sections of hull and decking floating atop the foam. The lives of two hundred or more men gone in a heartbeat.

Dwayne looked about him to the grim faces of the Norsemen lining the rails of the quarterdeck, mouths turned down, and eyes ablaze.

Njarl drew his sword and held it over his head, roaring an oath at the sky. The other men joined him, holding blades and rifles aloft and chanting along with their chief. More voices, calling in kind, echoed over the water that separated the other men of war, tenders, and longboats anchored in a ragged line miles in length.

Samuel joined Dwayne at the railing.

"They died well," Samuel said. "That's what they're chanting."

"Figured it was something like that," Dwayne said.

Njarl roared for silence, and all aboard quieted down to listen up. He sheathed his sword and spoke loudly enough to be heard over the distant boom of man-made thunder. His words were relayed all along the lower deck so that every man could understand. The big man thumped his chest, and everyone nodded along with his words. Their enthusiasm grew as Njarl pointed off the starboard rail at the fortress enshrouded in smoke. His voice grew louder, more insistent, and the men broke into an answering rumble that rose to a shout.

Caught up in the moment, Dwayne raised a fist in the air with a "Fuck, yeah! Hooah!" Some of the men near him grinned broadly and joined him. He had a band about him pumping fists and mimicking his war cry.

"Hooah! Hooah! Hooah!"

Njarl stood beaming at them, his one remaining eye glassy with tears of joy and pride. He lifted a hand in a broad gesture, and barrels were rolled across the deck to the cheers of all. Taps were hammered in, and mugs appeared from nowhere. The whole crew from oar decks to the topmasts started in on a kick-ass, monumental drunk.

"Why am I getting that feeling that we've all just volunteered for something insane?" Dwayne said.

"Because we did. Njarl has told his crew that he is sending a message to Admiral Dalgaard on the flagship. This crew will be the first ashore to assault the fort," Samuel said.

"And that includes us," Dwayne said.

As if for confirmation, Njarl crossed the deck to clap a hand on Dwayne's shoulder. All smiles, he spoke words of encouragement and handed Dwayne a mug brimming with foam.

"You are his good fortune," Samuel translated. "The day will belong to them because of you."

"Yeah. That's fucking great," Dwayne said, returning Njarl's feral grin. "But where the hell's *my* lucky charm?"

40

HEAVY CHOP

The skipper of the *Xia Gang Tuo* had his work cut out for him.

He stood in the dimly lit bridge squinting through the windscreen as the wipers slapped side to side to clear the glass. Behind him, his second stood at the controls. The powerful tug craft plowed through the high chop sending sprays of water flying over the bow walls. The sea pounded the tempered glass of the bridge house at firehose pressure.

Before them, the enormous shape of the Dex-Tan platform towered, yawing back and forth on ten-foot rollers. The aft section was lit like a stage with powerful lamps. The convex "V" of the docking port swayed to port on the current.

"Three degrees port. Engines slow," he said.

His second called back the order for confirmation.

"Anything from the Dee-Tee?" the skipper asked the man standing braced at the radio.

"Nothing after their last reply."

"Damn them. This is no time to go silent. Two more degrees, port." The big box was swinging away from them with the open bow-end as an axis.

A door from the weather deck banged open, and a wet mist blew across the bridge, fogging the windscreens and covering every surface with fine beads of salt spray.

The skipper whirled to roar at the crewman stupid enough to enter the bridge from outside during a squall. Two men had entered and moved toward his radioman and second. An enormous man with red hair. The man was smiling, his lips pulled back to reveal white teeth in his soaked beard. The other was a black man with a long face and narrowed eyes. Both wore wet suits slick with rain and both raised rifles at him and his crew.

The larger man yanked the crewman away from the radio and forced him down on the deck. The African moved up behind the second, who was standing rigid, awaiting orders at the levers, a rictus grimace on his face.

"Anyone speak English here?" the mad redhead said.

"We all do," the skipper said.

"Great. You just keep doing what you were doing, Cap'n. But anyone goes near that radio or hits a claxon, and I'll have to do things neither of us will like."

"I understand," the skipper said.

"That's all I need to know. Proceed." The redhead dropped into the captain's chair, his weapon across his lap. He pulled a radio in a plastic sheath from a pouch on his belt.

"The tug is ours." Boats' voice over the radio.

"We have not secured the platform," Shan replied.

"Put the Coors on ice. We're coming in anyway. Boats out." The radio went dead.

Shan knelt on the deck by a toolshed in which he'd locked the two crewmen they'd found and one other man he'd met on the way aft. That and the man back in the comm shed accounted for all the crew. Looking aft through the railings, he watched the tug closing in through the glare of the powerful lamps mounted high on the superstructure. In the brilliant light, the waves looked like drifts of white snow heaving up and down. The drops of rain were black in the glare. Lights atop the swaying yards of the tug added to the noontime brilliance.

The free-floating platform tilted suddenly, making Shan brace himself to keep from sliding. The rear dropped into a deep trough, a chasm of water opening up behind it with dizzying speed. The tug rose higher and higher on a massive crest before pointing its prow down the green wall of water to line up for its approach. For a few seconds, it looked as though both vessels would meet in a catastrophic collision at the floor of the trench. Then the deck of the platform leveled as the tug vanished behind the artificial horizon of the building swell. The bow lights appeared over the rolling foam again like twin suns. The *Xia Gang Tuo* rose into view behind an exploding prow wave.

Shan decided to join the hunt for the rest of Harnesh's guards. The SEAL could bring the vessels in line without help from him. He made his way along the deck toward Lee's last position, blinking through the rain over his sights.

They were the worst combat conditions Lee Hammond had ever experienced, worse than Helmand in a sandstorm, worse than Fallujah during Ramadan.

Visibility was shit. The noise of the storm covered every sound.

The deck under his feet moved like a theme park ride.

All he could do was move and shoot, shoot and move. He dropped a guy standing twenty feet from him when a lightning flash lit the interior of the boathouse like a sound stage. That was two down with the guy in the crew shack. Maybe three if he'd clipped the guy who'd fired down on them from the catwalk earlier.

Lee moved low and slow along the catwalk away from the lights at the stern. Before him, rain lashed the sea in front of the open end of the huge cyclopean box. Rollers lapped the walls in gouts of spray as they roared into the channel between the high walls. The noise rose to deafening levels with the wind shear and surge effect. If it was shit conditions for him, then it was shit conditions for them. But then, they could just hole up and make him come for them. One of those assholes left to roam could fuck up the whole op, ruin everybody's day. He swung his sights to the right and down to cover the walk on the opposite wall and the broader deck below. He leaned out, hand gripping a curved ladder rail, to train the rifle down at a pile of containers that had spilled over in turbulence. A few containers floated in the open water below, banging against the edge of the dock and one another in the swirling current. They made a discordant drumbeat as they slammed into the cowling. A fucked up soundtrack for a fucked up situation.

A shift in the shadows. A change in the play of light somewhere off in the corner of his vision. He turned, dropping into a crouch, to bring his weapon around. A shape was moving from the dark between two upright supports. He'd missed the fucker, walked right past him. The guy was raising a pistol toward him, face ghostly white in a sudden shimmer of sheet lightning.

A series of flashes threw the gunman into silhouette. The guy crashed to the deck, handgun bouncing over the plating. From the dark behind him, Shan advanced, rifle up and trailing smoke.

"Are you all right?" Shan shouted. He'd reached the fallen man, aiming a kick, two kicks at the ribs.

Lee stepped closer and fired two rounds into the back of the fallen man's head.

"I am now," he said, leaning close for Shan to hear.

They stood back-to-back, weapons traversing the dark.

"How many left now?" Shan said.

"Two at the most. Maybe only one. Hear from Boats?"

"He's bringing the tug in now."

"Well, that's his end covered anyway," Lee said.

Together, they continued down the catwalk, the barrels of their rifles arcing back and forth to cover the night.

41

SONG FOR THE SLAIN

The Mughal fortress had fallen silent under a pall of black smoke that spilled over its walls to cover the water in swirling fog. There were fires within the fort. The sharp tang of wood smoke could be smelled miles away. The waters under the walls turned gray with ash.

Sailing into the smoke, Njarl's ship came as close to the fortress as the depth of the waters would allow. The big man-of-war turned its port side toward the walls and let loose a series of rolling fusillades that punched craters in the face of the stronghold.

Only desultory fire from jezails and rockets answered from the besieged fortress. Missiles fizzed out of the haze to land in the water far beyond the ship's position. Musket balls, fired blind, peppered the sail canvas. The ship replied with twenty-pound balls, hammering away until the return fire died away to random potshots.

Njarl roared commands, and the oars were drawn in and boats were lowered to the water. Nets were dropped for men to clamber down for the direct assault on the Mughal redoubt. From the top spars, sharpshooters kept up a withering suppression fire on defenders at the top of the fortress walls. A wind off the water stirred the barrier of smoke, clearing it enough to make visible a tower collapsed into the water, leaving a broad gap in the defenses.

Dwayne trained a scope on the gap and could see men working to pile baskets filled with earth and rubble across the break. Dark men. Some naked but for loincloths. Many of them fell to rifle fire and charges of grapeshot from the ship's top and gun decks, causing the rest to retreat. But the dark men were soon back to work, pulling and straining to build a makeshift defense. More of them dropped to the punishing fire and others stepped in to take their places. Dwayne suspected there were unseen men with whips urging the slaves on, safely out of the line of fire, of course.

Musketoons, large-bore mini-cannons, were brought to the port face and fixed in place along the gunwales. Men loaded them with canister shot under the barks of a bald man, his blond beard and face black with powder. The fire from these guns was trained on the work party piling gabions before the break in the wall. The slaves vanished in a red mist as the golf ball-sized shot shredded flesh and bone as well as collapsing a long section of baskets.

The Ranger took his eyes from the lens when he felt a presence come close by him at the rail.

"We are in the next wave," Samuel said.

"Lucky us," Dwayne said.

They watched Njarl climb down into a waiting boat. The silver bosses on his leather chest armor flashed in the light of the guns going off above. His mouth was open in a continuous stream of profanity or orders or encouragement. Dwayne had no idea which, as the big man could not be heard over the constant exchange of fire between the ship and fort. Njarl dropped down into the boat and waved them toward the surf. The boat was pushed from the hull, packed to capacity with armed men all joining their chief in a chant or song or prayer. Longboats skimmed past fore and aft of the ship on their way shoreward where they drove up on the sandy beach in the shadow of the walls. Men vaulted the gunwales, calling oaths or shrieking wordless cries of berserker rage from the throats of Viking and Allemani troops. Heard among these calls were the keening whoops of Mayan and Xi-uian mercenaries, near-naked, bodies painted and carrying long spears and quivers loaded with barbed arrows.

The narrow beach before the walls was quickly crowded with groups of men milling over the sand. Explosions erupted at the foot of the walls. Bombs of some kind dropped from above. Stones rained down as well.

The chaos ashore began to take on some order as men moved toward the slope of rubble that led to the wall of gabions that blocked the break in a forlorn attempt to keep the Northmen out. Dwayne watched the boats returning to the ship to take more men to battle. He and Samuel would soon be in the midst of the hell on land, and the slaughter that would happen within the walls. He'd been here before, witnessed a scene much like this when he'd joined an Imperial Chinese army as they invested a stronghold of the Tai Peng rebels. This was warfare at its worst, men unleashed upon each other without mercy. Two enemies that hated one another. One was on its knees but fought on. The other was gaining the upper hand and would make the defenders pay, and the price would be torture, death, and for the fortunate survivors, a lifetime of slavery.

"What's our mission goal here, Sammy?" Dwayne said.

"Stay alive," he answered.

"That means we fight."

"I see no other way."

A hoarse cry from above turned their eyes to where a rifleman sat athwart a spar with a long-barreled gun across his knees. He was calling out and pointing off the starboard side toward the open gulf.

Lateen rigged sails showed on the horizon. They were on course for the remainder of the Northman fleet waiting at anchor to join the assault. The men-of-war sat alone without a screen of gunboats. The shallow draft skirmishing craft had all joined the amphibious assault.

The triangular sails loomed closer and grew in number as they closed on the fleet. Towers of white water rose in the sea between as the two fleets came within range of each other. For now, the shots fell short. Soon they'd be in killing distance, and the Viking fleet would be outnumbered.

A man named Ivar, Njarl's second-in-command, shouted orders to a man stationed at the tiller. The man put his lips to a long oxen horn mounted there and blew three long calls. Even over the din of the battle ashore a series of replies reached them. Horns bleated in answer through the haze of smoke. Njarl now alerted, a series of pennant flags were run up a line where they flapped high against the topsails.

Ivar leaned on the quarter-deck rail, an ear cocked landward. A series of horn blasts caused him to pound a fist on the rail post. He took in a lungful of air with a hiss and bellowed orders that had the crew racing to their posts. Oars were run out. Within seconds, the blades of the sweeps were churning the water in answer to the beat of drums. The big ship turned about, its prow aimed for a return to the threatened fleet and enough seaway to bring its guns to bear.

"They're leaving their chief behind?" Dwayne said.

"No choice. If the fleet is sunk or taken, they're all trapped anyway," Samuel said.

All around them, men were in movement, independent but unified. Men raced belowdecks to their guns. The remaining assault troops were handed repelling weapons, long pikes, hooks, halberds, and axes. The musketoons were unshipped and carried forward where they were mounted to the rails along the bow. Fighting nets were strung over the main deck to catch debris— the tackle, spars, and, bodies—that would fall from above in the coming duel of cannons.

A growling man in a bristling white beard shoved a thick barreled musket into Dwayne's hands. It weighed a good thirty pounds. The barrel ended in a curved ax head on one side and a spade-shaped dagger on the other. White Beard snapped and spat, and the words needed no translation. "Get your ass into the fight!" The guy would have been right at home bawling out wannabes at Ranger school. Dwayne once had a jump instructor who laughed like a mental patient as he shoved mewling greenies out of the hatch at ten thousand feet. That guy and White Beard could have partied.

Bow down, the big ship hove for the open sea with spritsails spread and angled to catch the easterly wind. The deck was tilted forward. A loose cannonball tumbled along the deck in front of Dwayne and Samuel as they joined the men at the prow.

Two or so miles before them, the fighting between the two fleets was joining. Strikes were landing closer and amid the Norse fleet raising tall gouts of water that sprayed the decks. In return, balls landed in the collection of Mughal ships that were approaching in a loose arrow formation for the heart of the enemy. There were no tactics on display here as far as Dwayne could see. This was blunt force fueled by centuries-old rage. These armadas would join at ramming speed, the crews of each anxious to get at the throats of the other.

The Mughal vessels looked like theme park attractions more than warships. A forest of angled sails rose above the decks, all painted in garish Hindi symbols against stripes and madras prints that had to be silk. A hundred oars cut the water from two rowing decks staggered atop one another. The hulls were high, and the decks broad. They looked clumsy and unwieldy, much broader across the beam than the sleeker Norse boats. And the tall sides were painted in bright colors of yellow and red and trimmed in what looked like real gold plate. Every surface that wasn't festooned with the mouths of brass cannons was carved in figures from the Hindu pantheon. The lead ship's prow featured a preposterously detailed and painted sculpture of Kali, the hands at the end of the many arms holding daggers, a goblet, a scroll, an arrow, and the severed head of what was unmistakably a Norseman dangling from a topknot of blond hair.

Close behind Kali was a second, larger ship with the bow fashioned in the visage of Ganesh, the elephant god, dressed in crimson robes trimmed in gold. Like the rest of the ships that Dwayne could see, the Mughal craft were loaded with guns rising from the waterline in four rows of ports. He counted fifty or more guns down one side of the Kali. Near twice that on the Ganesh. And, high up on the masts, were fighting platforms packed with figures already firing muskets though hopelessly out of range. They left contrails of smoke behind them as the ships glided closer.

From both vessels came the steady pulse of drums carried across the water by the wind. Atop that rhythm came the joined voices of men calling out in time.

"They are preparing for what comes ahead. Swearing loyalty to their chosen god. Promising vengeance for the khans in this life or the next," Samuel said.

In contrast to the chorus raised from the advancing armada, the usually raucous Northmen were muttering to themselves. Rather than prayers or oaths or curses, each man sounded as if he were reciting a list. Samuel caught Dwayne's curious gaze.

"They are saying the names of those who have passed before, telling the dead to ready their place in Valhalla."

42

TARGETED

The he monster tug was rising and falling, first, bow down then stern. It bucked wildly, buffeted to starboard then to port in the crossfire currents. The bow lumbered thirty degrees in either direction with each new assault.

Boats took the rudder and throttle levers while Geteye held his rifle on the skipper and his two crewmen. The SEAL cursed through clenched teeth as he fought to keep the bow true, in line with the heaving docking bay barely visible through the blinding spray. Getting the big boat into the padded "V" of the push bay was going to be like threading a needle blind. Or near blind.

As the tug hove closer, it came under the shelter of the looming edifice of the floating dock. That cut down on the wind shear. The torrential downpour died away a bit. The SEAL leaned the tug hard to the right. The bow dipped to bury its nose deep in a green wall that rose and broke over the front deck and crested against the bridge with a booming crash. The angle was steep enough to raise the tug's screws up out of the water long enough for Boats to lose thrust.

They settled down hard into the water once again, sending charts, coffee mugs, pens, and a laptop sliding to the deck. Boats gunned the engine and swung to port, aiming for one of the long, padded arms hung with water-filled nacelles that would serve as buffers. He throttled back to dead slow, ratcheting the wheel hard to starboard. The port bow struck the arm on that side with enough impact to collapse three of the nacelles. They burst like two-hundred-gallon water balloons. The skipper winced at the high squealing sound of metal on metal as his boat slid in along the steel arm. He made an involuntary move to help. Geteye made a gesture with his rifle barrel. The skipper stepped back, returning to join his two mates.

Boats drove the wheel half a turn to port and let out a long whistle as the tug slowed, slowed and came to a halt with a shuddering thump against the reinforced crotch of the "V." The two craft were joined now and rose and fell in unison atop the rolling seas.

"And that's how you park a car, ladies." Boats turned to the others with a grin.

"What do we do now, skipper?" Geteye said.

"You need to lash on, or the current will drag us apart again," the captain said.

"Order your men to do that. Remind them that we'll kill their captain at the first whiff of bullshit," Boats said.

"Do you understand?" the captain said to his two crewmen. Both nodded in unison.

His second posed a question in Cantonese.

"English only, assholes!" Boats said.

"He asks if we will live through this night."

"You all do as we say, and everyone goes home to their families. *Nee lee-ow-jee wo ma?*" Boats said, finishing in tortured Cantonese.

The second and radioman nodded once more and stepped through the hatch onto the weather deck and were gone into the night.

Lee and Shan continued their search for the remaining gunhands, one or two, still on the loose aboard the floating platform. They felt rather than heard the tug sliding into place against the aft dock. The powerful bow lights mounted in the front of the boat beamed into the shed interior throwing shadows everywhere.

They stuck together, covering each other's backs and their surroundings in a three-sixty arc. Both men were aware that they were very probably under the eyes of hostiles. Scattered debris along the interior decks offered enough cover for a platoon. The catwalks and superstructure that crossed high above made for perfect roosts for a sniper or snipers.

"I wish I knew how many fuckers we're looking for," Lee said. He had to shout to be heard over the growing gale howling through the platform.

"A straight foot is not afraid of a crooked shoe," Shan said.

"Is that some ancient Chinese wisdom?"

"Something that my mother used to say. I do not know why I think of it now."

"What's it mean?"

"I never dared asked her. My mother was not a woman to be questioned."

"That's great, Shan."

"Did your mother offer you any wisdom?"

"Yeah. She told me never to get involved with a woman who didn't like dogs."

Gang Zhou, soaked to the skin through his BDUs, belly-crawled along the narrow shelf that ran just under the flat sheet awning that covered the top of Dex-Tan 11's port wall.

He was deaf from the pelting rain hammering the steel inches above his head. He kept eyes on the pair of men, Americans probably, walking the deck far below.

They could wait.

The more important target was the boat approaching the stern section on course for the docking bay. It only followed that these soldiers had taken control of the tug as well as the platform. If they had not, they would soon attempt to do so. Their objective was obviously to move the D-T 11 to another location, to steal it. Why, Gang did not know. He only knew that he had to stop them. It was more than a question of loyalty. It was also a matter of survival. The men below had killed his brother guards. They would not allow him to live.

He would live. He was ex-special forces. A wolf warrior. An army of one. At twenty-eight years old he was in his prime, a natural killer of men. He only joined this private army for the promise of action. In the PLA, he was a warrior without a war. And Gang dreamed of combat.

Moving with stealth, he lowered himself from the shelf to a catwalk that ran athwart the shed building. He took care not to strike any of the support structure with the barrel of the rifle slung from his back. The catwalk was exposed to the sky and slick with running rainfall. Gang waited until the two soldiers had moved past below him before moving low along the catwalk to where it crossed a central joist that ran from the open end of the shed back to where the glare of the tug's spotlights was turning night into day.

With his rifle cradled in the crooks of his elbows, he crawled on his knees along the broad steel beam toward the source of the light. He came to rest short of a gap in the stern wall where the top of the wall came to a stop six feet from the peak of the awning that ran along the wall's top. He was concealed in shadows with a clear field of fire at the tug's front deck and superstructure.

Gang sighted over the top of the scope mounted atop his rifle. He swept the front deck where he could see two crewmen securing bulky lines that led to cleats set on the D-T 11's dock. They were unarmed in jeans and work shirts plastered to their bodies by the downfall. They were not targets. He swept the front sight upward.

The lights inside of the tug's bridge illuminated the interior. Even through the wavering haze of rainfall, he could see figures moving in the cabin. Three men. Two were large men.

He popped the lens caps from the scope and held his eye close to the cup to look through the lenses.

The bridge loomed in his view. The distance made the image flat. The three figures moved as if on the stage of a puppet show. A big man with a beard stood at the wheel. He wore body armor over a diving suit. A rifle rested atop a console within reach. A soldier. Gang moved the scope view to his left and was surprised to see a negro, also in body armor and armed with a black rifle. The third figure was a Chinese. That man looked out through the rain-streaked glass gloomily. Probably the captain.

The sailors on the front deck finished their task of fastening the two vessels together. They hobbled along the canting deck back toward the bridge. Gang needed to act before they returned indoors and into his killing zone.

He settled into a prone position, the rifle steadied by his left arm. He chose his target, lining up on the negro first. He held the reticle firm on the pane of glass at the front of the bridge. The target rose and fell slightly, the black man rising into view then dropping beneath the crosshairs before rising again. Gang timed the rhythm, anticipating when the man would surge up again into his lens for a center mass shot.

Down he went. Up he came. Gang rested his finger on the trigger and drew in a lungful of air. Down. Up.

He let out the air slowly through pursed lips, eye locked on the target. Lungs empty and nerves rock steady, he waited.

Down. Up. The negro climbed into view, the crosshairs fixed, for a half second, on his chest.

Gang squeezed the trigger home. The rifle bucked into his shoulder. He brought the rifle back down on target. As he did so, a frisson of tension swarmed up his body. This was not the adrenaline rush of impending combat, the thrill of the hunt. His hair stood on end. There was a crackling in the air as blue fingers of light danced up the beams of the shed from the water. They wriggled across the ceiling above him in a coruscating field of azure. The beam under him began to tingle with static energy that pricked at his skin through his clothing.

With the field of energy came a drop in temperature carried by a chill mist. Gang watched as frost formed on the beam beneath him. The rain droplets falling through the mist turned to ice.

Crawling backward, Gang moved to return to the cross catwalk behind him. The blue field turned white about him until it built to a harsh, blinding glare. His hand slipped on the slick surface under him. He was disoriented. A leg slid from the beam into the open air. The rifle fell from his hands to drop to the water six stories below. He lost his balance, his chin striking the beam surface with a crack. And then he was falling into the billowing clouds that rose about him.

Gang prepared himself for the plunge into the water.

Instead, sooner than he anticipated, he landed on a hard, ridged surface. He lost consciousness as his skull split in a topline fracture. The sudden impact snapped his spine. He was dead in seconds.

The crew of the *Ocean Raj* would not find his body for days. Not until they were drawn to investigate by the gaggle of gulls worrying at his corpse atop the stack of containers piled on the foredeck.

43

GAUNTLET

The ocean quaked under peal after peal of cannon fire as the two armadas closed with one another and let loose cannonades across the narrow gullies of water that separated them. Round and canister shot tore sails to flying tatters as well as sweeping decks clean of life, leaving only a crimson wash behind. Hot loads blasted through firing decks, creating storms of flying wood shards that turned men to bloody rags. Somewhere in the melee, a ship was burning. It spilled a dense cloud of smoke atop the waves. Dwayne couldn't see through the pall to know whether the vessel afire was Mughal or Norse.

Under orders shrieked by their acting captain Ivar, the dragon-helmed dreadnaught veered hard aport on its way toward the fight. Their new course sent them toward the rear of the Mughal armada. They slipped in through a miles-long gap where the vanguard had drawn ahead of slower moving transport following in a train of broad-beamed vessels stretched to the horizon.

The stern guns of the rearward ships of the main body clawed for them as Ivar ordered the tillermen to bring them about to cross the Mughals' wake. The fat stern of an enormous gunship lay off their starboard less than a hundred yards distant. They moved well within the arc of fire, the Mughal stern gun unable to adjust their angle of fire to hit the dragon-prowed vessel now thwart their ass-end. Balls and shot sailed over the Norse tops to land harmlessly in the sea beyond, to the amusement of the crew.

Ivar bellowed, and his order was relayed down to the gundecks. Almost as one, the guns along the starboard side discharged with a fury that canted the deck to port causing unwary men to tumble against the thwarts. One poor bastard, who'd failed to get a firm grip above, fell screaming from an upper spar, shaken loose by the sudden and violent yaw of the keel. The world vanished in black fug that reeked of the rotten egg stink of burnt sulfur.

Their continued forward motion drew them clear of their own gun smoke cloud, and Dwayne could see the terrible damage the full broadside had created. The big Mughal ship was adrift now, the towering stern face unrecognizable now. The ports and windows were punched in as if by a gargantuan fist. The high command deck had collapsed, and somewhere amidships a mast had been struck, the bole of it swinging in a tangle of cording and lines and rent sails. The weight of it finally snapped it off above the deck, and it fell with a crash, the top striking the water, creating a sea anchor that caused the ship to veer farther port at an angle that was all wrong. In the crippled vessel's wake floated a trail of broken timbers and broken men.

Dwayne could only imagine the damage he couldn't see. The combined fusillade had torn through the rear end of the big boat and would have killed anyone in its path. All those men, fusiliers, and oarsmen, trapped together in the close quarters of the fighting decks. It was a damned ugly way to die, Dwayne thought.

Not done with his prey, Ivar ordered his crew to turn the ship about to bring his starboard guns to bear once again, this time along the side of the Mughal vessel. Guns were reloaded and run out once more for a rolling broadside that swept along the decks and hull in a merciless hail.

Through it all, to Dwayne's amazement, the enemy ship kept up a fight with jezails and musketoons firing away from within the floating wreck. Arrows rained down from the sky, fired by archers perched high on the forward mast. One landed near the toe of his boot, the steel head burying itself in the decking, the shaft thrumming with the impact.

The men on the main deck called to Ivar, raising weapons in their fists and howling like wolves. Ivar leaned on the quarter-deck rail and shouted at them, face red with anger. One man started to climb the steps to the high deck. Ivar met him at the head of the steps and planted a boot in the man's chest, sending him crashing to the boards.

"What's that about?" Dwayne said.

"Some of the men want to board the ship and take it as a prize," Samuel said. "He accused them of being low dogs when the day calls for wolves. They're backing down for now." It was true. Some of the men were even laughing at the guy who took a tumble down the steps. He was hobbling over the deck, favoring a leg that was clearly broken. Ivar wasn't making any friends here, but he had the respect of the wild gang of blood-mad savages. They'd follow him to Hell.

A call from above was joined by other voices. All eyes followed their pointing fingers toward the van of the Mughal fleet. A vessel had pulled in front of the slower transport ships. It was low and squat and without sails. Oars worked in relentless time on either thwart. The bow raised a high cone of spray as it plowed the water on a course for the Norse ship. Ivar called an order. The guns that could be brought to bear, along the port side, fired at will, raising sprays of water before and aft of the mystery ship.

"It's a bomb ketch," Samuel said.

Dwayne gave him a squint.

"It's packed with black powder and manned by either zealots or slaves out of their minds on bhat," Samuel said.

"Suicide bombers."

"Yes. Unless the guns can either cripple the boat or ignite the explosives before it comes in range."

Dwayne leaned well out to study the ketch. He saw a round shot strike it squarely amidships. The ball caromed away to land with a splash in the boat's wake. The rowing deck was covered over with rows of plate giving the boat the appearance of an iron turtle. More fire fell on and around it, but the oars continued turning, drawing the boat closer with every second.

Ivar had allowed his sails to luff when he made the turn to rake the Mughal dreadnaught a second time. He slid down the ladder to the main deck and called through the open hatch to the oarsmen to come about. Slowly, slowly, the big ship turned on its axis, propelled by some impressive teamwork from the rowers three decks below. The plan was clear, to present as small a target as possible to the bomb ketch and bring the sails back to an angle where the easterly wind could fill them once more.

Every man not engaged in the work of pulling an oar, loading or firing or clewing a line was at the port rails with eyes locked on the humpbacked little boat streaming toward them. The massive effort of the oarsmen under that iron shell was causing the boat to rock fore and aft. The motion raised the point of a ram above the bow wave. It was mounted at the prow just below the waterline, a barbed stinger meant to drive its way home into the timbers of its target and remain there until the powder in its belly was ignited.

The larger battle going on a few miles east of them was forgotten in their own private struggle to survive the next few moments.

The ship came about, the deck canted. With a boom, the sails began to fill, the strain of the fabric making lines crack like whips as all remaining slack came out of them. Men worked hard, sailors and warriors alike, to haul lines in place where they could be secured about cleats to consume every breath of force the wind could bring to bear.

It was all too late. From Dwayne's vantage point along the port rail, he saw the little ketch vanish behind the swaying section of the quarterdeck on a direct bearing for the dread-naught's unprotected stern.

They'd torn the Mughal giant a new asshole, and now they'd share the same fate. The decking shuddered under their feet as the ram slammed home, driven through the planking with the force of a ten-ton hammer blow. The men at the tiller howled with fury or fear but kept their hands to the bar. One man moved to flee the quarterdeck. Ivar slammed him to the boards with a single blow.

"Figures that bitch Karma would be on their side," Dwayne said.

The horizon tilted at a crazy angle. The deck came crashing upward, driven by a clap of thunder that tore the world to pieces.

THE DEVIL HIS DUE

D wayne awoke to a world of silence. Hands had hold of him and lifted him bodily from the tilted deck.

He opened his eyes to find Samuel shouting at him without making a sound. There was nothing to hear but a warbling whine in both ears. The other man's face was caked with dried blood from a gash along his hairline. Samuel shoved him against a thwart, and Dwayne found his legs again. He braced himself on a railing and shook his hearing clear. The whine faded, replaced by a muffled roar punctuated by the beating of his heart.

Samuel pulled him across the sloping main deck through a crowd of rushing men. Dead and wounded littered the deck. Men and pieces of men lay everywhere in a wash of crimson water sloshing back and forth as the deck lifted and yawed at the mercy of the sea. Dwayne turned his head to look sternward. The quarterdeck was simply gone. In its place, a scorched tangle of broken timbers. The tiller, rudder, captain's cabin, and the captain himself had vanished in the blast from the bomb ketch. By some miracle, the ship was still afloat. But not for long.

The two men made their way through the chaos to the starboard deck. Dwayne leaned over to see the oars working in time to propel them into a coordinated turn to port. Without a rudder, the attitude of the ship was determined by the strong backs, arms, and legs of the men pulling below.

The maneuver was happening at a crawl, the prow swinging by degrees and by inches. The four rows of sweeps toward the aft section lay idle in their locks, shattered to kindling by the explosion that tore the rear out of the vessel.

Dwayne felt Samuel's fingers grip his arm. He turned to see the other man speaking sternly. Dwayne could only shake his head. Samuel pointed out over the water. Closing on them was a pair of the lumbering troop transports that had been following in the wake of the Mughal warships. The fat ships were coming bow down at speed. The sails were belled out and with sweeps rising and falling. The tops were crowded with figures. Men lined either side of the high prow watching eagerly as they neared their prey.

The Northmen's' ship was foundering, its sails blown to strips, and the number of oars reduced. It was turning to flee the boats running down on it, but making little headway with the wind and current against it.

Men joined them at the rail, shouting and waving weapons aloft. Puffs of smoke appeared before the lead Mughal boat, bow chasers. A ball passed overhead, snapping dangling lines and tackle on its way to land in the water far off the port side. A second ball struck the timbers toward the bow, raising a geyser of splinters.

Dwayne felt a tremor through the deck boards as the guns below him were run out. Muted thunder and a curtain of white smoke rose up and was torn away on the breeze. Canister peppered the water either side of the lead Mughal vessel. A mainsail went limp as a ball sailed through the silk. But the boat came on, the blades all along the gunwales glittering in the glare of the sun off the wave tops turned copper in the late afternoon sun.

Cannonade followed cannonade as the two ships clawed at

one another. The Viking ship, set as it was abaft of the approaching vessels, took most of the punishment. Broad abeam as it was, the Mughal ship was presenting itself by the bow, the more difficult target by far.

They drew into the range of small arms, and the Northmen lined the gunwales to send a blizzard of musket balls out across the narrowing gap. The Mughals and their conscripts answered in kind with fire of their own. Volleys of arrows fell from above as well. They came in hundreds, wave after wave loosed from the platforms set on the main masts like branches on an evil tree. Men in white pantaloons, shimmering iron breastplates, and high red turbans pulled back on reflex bows to send forth the storms of three-foot shafts tipped with barbed heads of steel.

A man by Dwayne took an arrow straight through the crown of his head. The point exploded from the back of his neck before he slumped kicking to the deck. Another man fell from above, a pair of arrows in him. He landed in the fighting nets, spraying blood on those below. Other arrows found homes in flesh, causing many of the men to pull the decorative shields from their hangers along the ports and hold them overhead. From under this makeshift shell, the sharpshooters continued their fusillade, firing in volleys now. Men dropped from the gunwales of the Mughal boat, their bodies lost in the water churned to foam by the bite of the oars.

The tall bow of the transport was drawing closer, close enough to see the individual features of the men tense and fierce and keen to board the vessel of their hated enemy. Faces mustached and bearded, eyes glaring beneath glittering helmets and colorful striped turbans. There were darker men there as well, naked but for loincloths, heads crowned with thick manes of matted hair. They waved curved swords and axes above their heads and leveled blunderbusses and pistols. Every face was a mask of fury and bloodlust. For certain, the majority of them found courage in hashish or some other drug.

For their own part, the Norsemen were getting their drink on as well. Hogsheads of ale and harder stuff sat on the deck with the tops knocked off. The men dipped mugs, helmets, and even hands into the open kegs to take in their fill even as shot and shafts flew past them. One guy bent to dip his head into a barrel like he was ducking for apples. An arrow took him in the ass up to the fletching, the point jutting from the flesh above his navel. He rolled on the deck yowling while his buddies laughed themselves sick at the sight.

Dwayne felt Samuel take his wrist in a vice-like grip. He turned to see Samuel trying to fix a silver bracelet onto his wrist. Samuel's arm was bare, a tan line where his bracelet had been. He was trying to send Dwayne off with his own device. With a shove and jerk, Dwayne pulled from Samuel's grasp. He backed away, Samuel following him across the deck, speaking with an earnest expression. Dwayne could guess what the other man was saying, but he wasn't buying it. He'd never leave a man behind, and he'd damn sure never run from a fight. He continued away from Samuel, breaking through a clutch of men rolling a squat barreled mortar across the deck. He got to the other side of them and lost himself in the throng of warriors and sailors waiting for the fight to come.

Dwayne plucked a pair of pistols from the body of a man lying against a thwart. The man was missing a head and one arm. Dwayne's eyes were for the pistols. Both big-bore jobs with twin barrels. He made sure that each was loaded and primed before they went into his sash. His own sword was gone, lost when the blast tossed him. He found another, a broad-bladed claymore with a screaming falcon head atop the pommel. This he kept in his fist. There was a rising and falling susurration in his ears now. His hearing was returning. It was the voices of men calling in rhythm. The Norsemen were singing as the shadow of the enemy vessel hove closer.

The lead Mughal boat struck the Norse vessel hard abeam at

an oblique angle. The impact sent a quake through the timbers, the deck tilting upward before falling once again and causing all to stumble. The force of it tore a long section of spar loose to swing across the main deck like a pendulum. A few men were caught in its deadly arc and fell with skulls cracked and ribs crushed.

Carried by its momentum, the enemy ship caromed along the starboard side, the iron-studded bow snapping oars off at the rowlocks. It shuddered to a stop, a section of its higher deck locked tight against the hull of the Norse ship.

A dense cloud of cream-colored smoke blossomed as each side spent one last volley before the killing began in earnest. Iron grapples were flung on loops of heavy rope, the blades biting into woodwork and decking faster than the pull ropes could be chopped away. The smoke cleared to show the side of the Mughal vessel covered in a torrent of men scaling down from the gunwales, dropping from lines or simply leaping the distance, shrieking like madmen.

The Vikings stood their ground, shoulder to shoulder, creating a wedge and firing weapons over the tops of the once-decorative shields. Any enemy who made it through that withering fire was brought down by spear points and ax heads while freshly loaded weapons were brought forward.

Emboldened rather than cowed by the carnage, the Mughal swordsmen and musketeers fell in greater number over the rails of their ship. They were being covered by archers lining the hull to fire at will with lethal accuracy. These were Tartars, with powerful reflex bows of sinew and horn. The shield wall bristled with broken shafts. Norsemen fell impaled on arrows that smashed through the shields or streaked over the tops of the moving defense.

A large knot of Mughal troops gathered for a rush as the wall of shields parted just enough to allow the mouth of that big-bellied mortar through.

It went off with a crack and a belch of black smoke. Driven by the kick of the discharge, it rolled away on its trunnions, men leaping aside to avoid being pulped under the wheels of the two-ton bulk of the beast.

The contents of the barrel, hundreds of balls of canister shot packed with wadding, turned the deck before it into an abattoir. A wide swath of rent flesh and blood covered the boards, unrecognizable as the gang of living men who were rushing forward a second before. The balls also took out a broad section of the starboard rail in its killing swath.

From the roar of the mortar or, more likely, the sudden change in air pressure, some of Dwayne's hearing returned with a pop. He was dizzy for a moment and spit a thick wad of bloody phlegm to the deck. But he could distinguish individual sounds now. Rising above all was the hoarse roar of a Norseman shouting to the others, a musketoon with a burning fuse cradled in his arms. He was a stout fucker with arms thick as thighs. A fresh cut across his nose was sending blood into his mouth, and when he spoke, it was with a crimson spray. His eyes were wild with an exultant rage, the whites showing all around like a mad dog. The others responded with roars of their own.

The stout guy turned to a fresh shower of near-naked Mughals descending from the other ship. From the hip, he cut loose with the musketoon. A fine spray of shot spilled screaming men to the deck with missing limbs, trailing ropey bundles of guts from rent bellies. The stout guy tossed the smoking musketoon aside and jerked his sword from the scabbard on his back.

With a defiant wail, the mass of Norsemen rushed the gap in the railing and began climbing the hull of the Mughal ship. They hauled themselves up lines, leaped from rigging, and climbed hand and footholds punched in the hull of the enemy ship by the point-blank mortar load. The sons of bitches were going on the attack. Dwayne stared in open-mouth admiration at the balls on these guys.

Swept up by the sheer insanity of it all, Dwayne charged with them for the face of the enemy hull. The others were calling out dire threats, the names of their gods or swearing oaths of courage.

"Hoo-ah! Rangers go forward!" Dwayne bellowed as he grabbed a swinging line and hauled himself aloft, his scabbarded sword in its bandolier slapping on his back.

45

TAIL OF THE LEVIATHAN

The crew of the *Ocean Raj* worked in a race with the weather. Darla had built to a Cat Four and was bearing down on them. The ten-foot seas and sixty-kilometer winds were just the outer bands of a monstrous bitch of a storm on a westerly course. Eskinder led the crew to secure the big barn of a floating platform as securely as possible to the *Raj* for a long tow. There was no time for welding. Chains, cables, and even rope lines were the best they could do. The tow would be a tricky one, with the platform acting as a natural sail in the hurricane winds.

Jimbo, Bat, and Morris Tauber scoured the bridge, living quarters and guard shack for any kind of device that might be used to trace their position. Transponders, cell phones, radios, dishes, and any other electronics with radio, wi-fi, or satellite access were torn free and tossed overboard. They even unshipped the sonar and radar arrays and pitched them into the roiling water.

Lee and Shan continued the search for the phantom sniper but found nothing. Byrus clambered up in into the platform's superstructure in winds that threatened to tear him away to the Colombia coast. He found no evidence of the man they sought.

Down in the wildly swaying hold, Parviz and Quebat took turns puking. Persians were not traditionally very able seamen.

Jason Taan and his former bodyguards sat securely locked in the improvised brig of a Conex container.

Aboard the tug vessel, Geteye glanced now and then at the starred depression in the glass of the windscreen that was level with his eyes. Someone came close to taking his head off if not for the heavy tempered panes meant to protect the bridge from the impact of gale winds and tons of water.

"Too close," he said.

"Good as a miss," Boats said.

"Too many close misses, skipper. I am using up all of my luck."

The tug captain and his two crewmen looked from one man to another. They'd been joined by the other four crewmen of the tug. All were seated cross-legged on the deck in a forward corner of the bridge away from any hatches. They barely understood this exchange between the two Americans. They did have a sense that this was over. Though what that meant for them, none of them knew.

"Listen, captain," the red-bearded giant said. "We're almost done here. We'll be leaving you. I suggest that you have two choices. You can try to get back to port into the teeth of that."

Boats nodded toward the crying wind and the thrashing rain outside the bridge.

"With no radio?" the captain said.

"Exactly. Glad you agree. Best thing for you is to run ahead of the storm," the SEAL said. "I'd suggest south-sou'west. Head for deep water."

"You let us live?"

"We got what we came for," Boats said. His face split in a broad grin.

The smile was returned by all as the American's words were translated for the others.

The next twelve hours were a grueling slog that felt like as many days.

The cargo freighter fought its way up the face of rolling waves, towing the Dex-Tan rig behind them. The dead weight acted as a sea anchor as well as a rogue sail. Sometimes it threatened to be a bludgeon as it rose high behind the stern on its towlines, looking as though it could come crashing down on the aft deck of the *Raj* with the next wave.

In the bridge, Boats and Geteye worked at the unforgiving grind of navigating through a tropical depression. Mile after mile of humping green hills and black valleys marched to the horizon. Eyes locked on the sea ahead, they worked throttle and wheel to keep the bow up, and the course as true as the weather would allow. They were making their way east/ northeast at best speed possible which was turtle slow. Still, they were a few knots an hour over the following storm's best speed.

It wasn't until the following evening that they saw stars in the sky. The *Raj* was clear of all but the outer effects of the storm. Darla had veered south to follow the coast of the isthmus bound for the Guianas.

Boats returned to his bunk with a bottle for a well-deserved crash. Geteye retired as well after assigning mates to a rotation of short watches so they could rest in spells. They continued the *Raj's* course into the Pacific and far from any of the commonly frequented shipping lanes.

Down in the chartroom, the way ahead was being planned over eggs, bacon, and generously laced Irish coffee. The ship was quiet after days of evil weather and frantic activity. Most everyone but the Rangers and Morris Tauber was racked out on bunks somewhere.

"This will work, right?" Jimbo said.

"Theoretically," Morris said.

"Shit," Bat said.

"Fuck me," Lee said.

"No. There's no reason I can see that this isn't perfectly feasible," Morris said.

"Even though I really need some sleep."

"I don't like leaving that big ugly box where anyone can find it," Chaz said.

"Boats assures me that even an object the size of that floating platform will be nearly impossible to find on the open sea. Especially when they won't know exactly what course we took," Morris said.

"How 'nearly impossible,' Mo?'" Lee said.

"In his words, 'the Pacific Ocean is just stupidly, fucking big' and finding the platform will be like 'finding a virgin in Iceland.'"

"And how hard is that?" Jimbo asked. He was honestly curious.

"Well, according to Boats, in Iceland, there's a virgin behind every tree."

"Fucking sailor," Lee said.

"Still don't like it," Chaz said.

"We'll only need to leave it anchored for a few days," Morris said.

"But you said that it might take weeks to get what we need," Lee said.

"I know you're bushed, bro. Try to keep up," Jimbo said.

Lee sighed then growled as he rubbed the heel of his hand into an eye.

"Yeah. Yeah. Time machine. Fuck."

"So, you told us where we're going. But *when* are we going?" Chaz said.

"1976 should work," Morris said.

The rest were too tired to make even the feeblest joke about disco.

46

TOMORROW'S DOORWAY

The sea was on fire.

Jarl Dalgaard's massive dreadnaught was engulfed in flames and burning down to the waterline. Members of its crew who made it to the water either drowned outright or were executed by arrow and shot by Mughals using them for sport. Another Norse ship careened about, leaving a thick haze of black smoke in its wake, sails ablaze.

The rest of the men-of-war were either overwhelmed by boarders or shot to lifeless hulks under brutal broadsides from Mughal ships passing in columns down either hull unopposed. Longboats lay capsized or demolished to smears of flotsam carried away on the current. Mortar barges, left behind by their towing vessels and abandoned by their crews, drifted without course, tangled together in their towlines.

On shore, Njarl's forces lay in the jaws of a vice, their assault stalled by the fierce resistance of the fort's defenders. Emboldened by the approach of friendly banners, the Mughals within the walls fought all the harder. Skiffs were let down from troopships and disembarked a fresh horde of howling warriors, all under the cover of punishing suppression fire from shallow- draft gunboats pulled close to shore.

To a man, Njarl's company fell on the blood-soaked sand under blade, shot, and shaft. Njarl Hadradi died gargling curses, his back to the outer wall of the fortress, an arrow through his neck, and the blade of a Mughal tulwar sunk deep in his guts.

Miles from the clash of armadas, three ships lay locked on their own private war.

Bound by grapple and line, the Mughal and Norse ships spun at the mercy of the wind while their crews battled for survival on the blood-slick decks. Vikings drove off the first wave of boarders and clambered over their own starboard rails to climb aboard their attacker.

A second Mughal vessel, another fat-bellied transport, made its way around the floating melee to tie up to the bow end. It moved to close for a direct assault on the man-of-war from the port side.

Mughal archers fired down from the gunwales and tops of the boat bound in a death struggle with its enemy. Shafts struck deep in the mass of Northmen climbing the hull to engage. Men tumbled back to the deck of the Viking man-of-war or dropped into the gap to be mashed to pulp between the grinding keels. Even the deadly shower of arrows was not enough to slow the momentum of berserker rage.

Musket fire from the tops of the Norse ship poured down on the Tartar archers causing them to retreat. The momentary lull was all the Vikings needed to clamber over the gunwales, swinging axes and swords. They fired pistols and blunderbusses into the packed bowmen, sending them back against their own foremast. More howling men swung over on lines to drop to the deck. The knot of boarders in the fo'castle grew in number and advanced at a run at the startled Mughals. Dwayne charged with them. He fired a double charge from a pistol, turning a man's face to bloody mush. The other pistol loads drove a massive swordsman to the deck boards, slipping in his own guts. Gripping the discharged pistols by the barrels, he flailed away into the first rank of archers. The iron-capped butt ends acted as blunt weapons. The Mughal archers had abandoned their bows and raised short swords in defense. They were joined by pikemen, who made a hedge of spear points. Behind them shrieked war whoops could be heard from above through the cacophony. Among the company of defenders were red Indians paid in silver to fight in the army of the Khans. Hurons and Creek in fearsome war paint under iron helms. They wielded muskets held like clubs, the stock ends capped in studded brass to add a killing heft. They threw tomahawks with fatal skill, sending them spinning into the ranks of the Vikings.

Without hesitation or fear, the Northmen battered spear shafts aside and rammed hard into the line of defenders to create a gap that split the mob at the foremast in two. Into this breach poured more bearded Northmen until they gained the main deck. The Mughal defenders were driven back to their own quarterdeck, those who were not shoved against the gunwales and slain outright. Shot and arrows still rained down from above but were paid no heed by the attackers high on bloodlust. Northmen fell to the fire, and their brothers stepped over them to press the attack.

Painted with the blood of other men, Dwayne raised his sword arm again and again, at the head of the merciless phalanx grinding through the Mughal crew. This was the work of battle. A strong arm and a determined mind. The first adrenaline rush of battle was waning. Now he had to draw on the same reserves of will that saw him through so many other days that seemed lost. The last brutal leg of a survival course back at Benning. An ambush in Tikrit. A pitched battle with an army of cannibals. Standing outnumbered against a Roman century. Now it was about stamina, training, and grit. No glory, no brotherhood. Just the strenuous labor of murder.

The boards were slick with gore, blood running from the scuppers to leave a wake of pink foam. The tide aboard the deck of the Mughal carrack was turning. The Northmen could sense it in the air, see it in the eyes of their opponents. Dwayne joined them in the rush that carried them up the ladders to the raised deck and the ship's masters. A Mughal chief in bright silks and a helmet crested in gold stood with his back against the ship's wheel and called orders. A mixed band of painted savages and broad-shouldered swordsmen, his immortals, formed a ring around him for what both sides knew would be the final onslaught.

Dwayne rushed forward to take his place in the fight only to feel an arm strike him across the chest. Samuel was there in front of him, blocking him as others rushed roaring past. Those strange green eyes bored into his as he was pressed back. Samuel pushed him to the taffrail, hands to Dwayne's shoulders.

"You have to live!" Samuel shouted to be heard over the din.

"We're winning this! I can't back down now!" Dwayne tried to shake out of the other man's grip. No go. Samuel held him firmly against the rail.

"This crew is doomed." Samuel nodded back toward the bow. From their vantage point, they could see the second Mughal vessel was joined hull to hull to the Norse ship, and a mob of warriors was coming over the gunwale in a wave.

Dwayne looked at the fight around the wheel. All he saw was slaughter. Men locked in a death struggle and neither side clearly winning. Samuel was right. This last melee was a forlorn effort. With the arrival of the second ship, they were outnumbered. Their ship was no longer sea-worthy. Even if, by some miracle and the grace of the gods, the Northmen came out on top, they could never escape. The guns of the Mughal armada would blast them to pieces long before they made open water.

He felt Samuel's grip release him.

"You have to go," the other man said. Samuel slid his own bracelet over Dwayne's hand, and it snapped it closed.

"I can't leave you here to die," Dwayne said.

"We'll meet again. Remember?" One of Samuel's rare smiles.

"Remember? You can't know that for sure."

"I do know. For sure. As sure as I know that you can't be allowed to die here, Dwayne Roenbach." Samuel pressed on the bracelet and was gone.

All was gone. The smoke and fury of combat. The shrieks of dying men. The thunder of guns.

And Dwayne was falling. Above him was a black sky sprayed with stars. Below him were the dark waters of the Mississippi Delta.

47

FIESTA

Anchoring off Puerto Vallarta cost them every pre-1976 piece of currency they had along with some other loot from the *Raj's* stores. Mo balked at them handing over some cases of canned goods marked with expiration dates four decades in the future. He was overridden by the Rangers. The bribes were paid at 1976 prices, so it was a bargain.

The Mexican customs officials might have been curious at the unusual ship, and its even stranger crew of *gabachos* and Africans. If they were, they kept it to themselves. They certainly didn't bother to find out that the *Ocean Raj* was on no country's registry and would not be for another twelve years. Their supply of any kind of light craft was exhausted, so they had to rely on hiring a launch to take them to shore. And they had business ashore.

Boats leaned on the starboard rail, watching a thirty-foot tender motoring toward them from the rows of cruise ships docked along the shoreline. The alabaster towers of hotels rose to the south where the broad white sugar beaches stretched for miles. The hills above were dotted with white buildings and red rooftops. Morris stood by him, enjoying the warm sun and the view.

"You know what's out there?" Boats asked. He nodded ashore.

"All I see is Puerto Vallarta."

"Nineteen *seventies* Puerto Vallarta, Mo."

"Yeah. The Bicentennial. Jimmy Carter. And *Star Wars* won't be out till next year."

Boats turned to him in astonishment.

"You're a hopeless pogue, bro. That's Partytown south of the border. Pre-AIDs pussy as far as the eye can see. If it's Spring Break, I may *never* come back."

Morris turned red as a radish.

"Remember, we have business. We have to get back to the platform."

"And all the time in the world to do it." The SEAL slapped Morris on the shoulder, teeth showing through his ginger bush.

It was a week before the materials they needed were delivered from a foundry near Mexico City. Stacks of carbon steel sheeting cut to specific lengths and widths and drilled through to allow them to be bolted to a framework. Wooden cases of large gauge bolts made from the same steel arrived as well. In addition, the *Raj* was resupplied with food, fresh water, diesel, and all the other supplies the company of men needed for a trip back to sea.

To pay for it all required exchanging some of their onboard gold stores for pesos. The rates were pure robbery everywhere they went, but the prices, except for the diesel, were low in comparison to what they were used to.

The Rangers and crew took some leave as well, enjoying the anonymity that being out of place in time offered. Even Morris had a good time though he wouldn't answer any questions about the LSU coed named Linda he hooked up with no matter how much he was teased. His only reply was a shy smile that never failed to give the Rangers a charge.

Even Taan and his guards were allowed ashore. There was nowhere for them to run in a world where they hadn't been born yet. And none of them were anxious to get back to a China still run by the Gang of Four. Every one of them returned aboard the freighter when promised.

On their last day in port, a search party had to go ashore to find the Iranians. The first cab driver they asked knew just where the three *maricon* bars were in town. They managed to tear Parviz and Quebat away from a cantina packed with *nuestros amigos* with the promise that they could come back "sometime."

The *Raj* set out on the evening tide, stores full and decks stacked with the new steel plating.

The shed was waiting right where they'd anchored it, broadcasting an encrypted location signal via satellite four times a day.

"Is this one of those 'so crazy it'll work' ideas?" Jimbo said. The *Raj* was moving easily through the open end of the Dex-Tan 11 on a glass surface sea.

"There's no reason I can see that it won't." Morris looked up at the rectangle of sky visible above them, framed by the high sheet walls.

"Sounds like one of those Russian dolls to me," Jimbo said. "The Tube inside the Raj, the Raj inside the box, the box inside another box."

"You have to think outside the box. Literally," Morris said. "It's really about the field. We produce more of a jolt than we actually need each time we open the Tube field. There's no reason we can't double or even triple the encompassing field area. The new sheeting of alloy will allow that."

"Enough to include this whole dock?"

"Yes."

"And the whole damned thing just goes 'whoosh,' and we're gone?"

"Without a trace."

"Yes. No sign we've ever been there."

"So, we never have to return to where we've been before. There's no chokepoint. No re-entry point where an ambush or some other nasty surprise will be waiting for us."

"That is the plan, Jimbo. Total portability. Go where and when we like and far from the reach of Sir Neal Harnesh."

"When do we leave?" A broad grin creased the Pima's face.

48

BAYOU SPECIAL

The night sky was limned in a coral glow as William James Crory drove east on State One along Grand Isle Beach. He was always the first one in to work, well before dawn. It made sense since the place, Billy-Jim's, was named for him, well, his dad, actually. Him being Billy Jim Junior.

He had to get there to meet the food truck that came each morning. He'd check the order while his cousin Mark, if he was on time and sober, put the cold goods in the meat locker. Then they'd both work to get breakfast ready. Billy Jim getting the grits started and Mark peeling and chopping potatoes for home fries. Half the island showed up to start the day at Billy-Jim's, a shack of a place that served the best breakfast platter in the delta. That's what the faded metal sign that hung out front claimed, anyway. The place was a madhouse during fishing season and a shabby little goldmine.

As he hooked the Silverado into a left off empty and dark Highway One onto Englebach, Billy Jim could see a figure seated on the sidewalk under the awning by the front door stoop. Looked like a big man. Looking for strong coffee to sober up, most likely.

He pulled onto the gravel behind the clapboard building that sat sagging on pilings off a lot big enough for maybe ten cars to park. The reefer truck from Bayshore Foods was waiting, the driver seated in the cab with the AC on full and playing with a phone. Mark was waiting in his usual place, seated on the edge of the narrow back porch with a Kool smoldering in one hand and a mug of black coffee steaming in the other. "Let's get to it," Billy Jim said, banging the flat of his hand of the cab door of the reefer as he'd done every morning for the last sixteen years.

They checked, unloaded, and stowed the order of eggs, bacon, ham steaks, andouille sausages, onions, tomatoes, potatoes, milk, cream, orange juice, lard, and bread. Billy paid the driver in cash for the order, and the day got started for real.

Grits started, biscuit dough going, the grill fired up and seasoned, three huge urns of coffee brewing. Mark chopped onions and taters. Eggs, sausage, bacon, and steaks were loaded into the cooler drawer by the grill. The drawer would be refilled three or more times before breakfast ended at eleven. A horn beeped, and Billy Jim wiped his hands on his apron to go out and greet the bakery truck. Trays of crullers, donuts, and bear claws were handed in for Mark to slide into a display case behind the counter that ran the length of the ten-table dining area.

"Some guy's out front," Mark said upon returning to the kitchen.

"Saw him when I's pullin' in," Billy Jim said as he punched biscuits from a layer of dough spread on a floured tabletop.

"Looks kind of strange."

"Yeah?"

"Like he's wearing a costume."

"Well, he's late for Mardi Gras and a hundred miles lost." Billy Jim checked the man out for himself when he unlocked the front door and stepped into the dawn light to set out the hand-painted sandwich sign that announced BREAKFAST 7 'TIL 11 on both sides to traffic moving past on Gulfview.

The guy did indeed look strange. Bearded and hair longish. He wore leather breeches and some kind of woolen tunic belted at the waist with a broad tooled belt. His feet were bare, and he was soaking wet. Big man, like Billy Jim noticed earlier. Broad shoulders and the hands of someone who worked for a living. The featureless silver band about his wrist seemed incongruous with the rest of his clothes.

The man was standing when Billy Jim came back from setting out the sign.

"That bacon I smell?" he said. The man's eyelids were swollen. He had a fresh scar on his forehead that had scabbed over.

"And ham steaks and sausage."

"You interested in a trade?"

"What'choo got?" Everything about this guy's appearance should have set off alarm bells in Billy Jim's head. But something about his bearing, something in his eyes, told Billy Jim the guy was all right despite his weird outfit.

The guy unhooked a dagger from his belt and held it out to Billy Jim. A pretty thing with a real bone scabbard trimmed in bronze. An Arkansas toothpick with a spade-shaped blade over eight inches long. It was engraved with some kind of runic symbols. The handle, inlaid and capped with silver, felt like real ivory under his fingers.

"That worth a full breakfast and the use of your phone?" the big man said.

"Sure. Done deal."

"The call will be long distance."

"Still a good deal." Billy Jim was already thinking of where to put it on one of the walls of the dining room where he hung vintage fishing gear and framed photos of celebrities who'd stopped by for breakfast. The dagger would look just fine next to his autographed picture of Don Johnson.

"I appreciate it."

"That bracelet's nice, too."

"Trust me. You don't want this bracelet."

"Cursed?"

"Something like that."

"Good enough. You need to get out of those clothes. You mind wearing kitchen whites? Had a fella 'bout your size used to work for me."

"You might just be my new best friend," the big man said.

"Call me Billy Jim." Billy Jim stuck out his hand and the other man took it.

"Russ Baumeister," Dwayne Roenbach lied.

49

BIGGEST LITTLE CITY IN THE WORLD

They had a back-up, fail-safe, drop-dead plan they put in place in another time and place.

It was in the form of a collection of off-the-rack flip phones with an account paid five years in advance. This latest burner was installed in a safe deposit box in Reno under the name Mrs. Bonita Chamberlain. The only way it could fail was if the carrier went out of business.

Caroline retrieved the phone from the poky little branch office of Nevada Trust and checked into the Dunes Motor Lodge under the name Cynthia Petrie. Her son was introduced as "Charlie," which always made the little boy giggle for some reason. She paid a week ahead and spent her days watching the boy in the kiddie pool and reading a thick paperback novel she never seemed to make much progress in. She turned away the clumsy pick-up attempts from male guests by saying that she was "waiting for a call." She would nod to the practically antique burner resting on the chaise by her.

She stepped from the shower to an unfamiliar buzzing sound. Exiting the bathroom, she found Stephen still asleep in the middle of their shared double bed. Pre-dawn light peeped through a narrow gap in the drapes.

The buzz was from the flip phone. She'd never heard it ring before. With trembling hands, she picked it up, opened it, and tabbed the answer key.

"Hello?"

"Caroline?"

"Oh, baby. Where the hell have you been?"

The End

ABOUT THE AUTHOR

Chuck Dixon is the prolific author of thousands of comic book scripts for *Batman and Robin, the Punisher, Nightwing, Conan the Barbarian, Airboy, the Simpsons, Alien Legion,* and countless other titles.

Together with Graham Nolan, Chuck created the now iconic Batman villain Bane. He also wrote the international bestselling graphic novel adaptation of J.R.R Tolkien's *The Hobbit.*

His first foray into prose, the *SEAL Team 6* novels from Dynamite Entertainment, have become an ebook sensation. He currently scripts *GI Joe Special Missions* for IDW publishing as well as the *Pellucidar* weekly comic strip for ERB Inc.

He calls Florida home these days.

You can connect with Chuck here:

Facebook:
https://www.facebook.com/chuck.dixon.779

Website
http://dixonverse.blogspot.com/

Amazon
https://www.amazon.com/Chuck-Dixon/e/B001HOL26O